THE CRITICAL INCIDENT SERIES, EPISODES 1 - 3: SUPERCELL, FREE FALL, LOST ART

DOUGLAS DOROW

MTSPress

SUPERCELL - A NOVELLA

Critical Incident #1

SuperCell

Critical Incident #1

A novella
by Douglas Dorow

Copyright © 2016 by Douglas Dorow

All rights reserved.

ABOUT SUPERCELL - CRITICAL INCIDENT #1

The FBI's Hostage Rescue Team is called to the plains of Nebraska when a supercell storm sweeps across the state and hits the Nebraska State Penitentiary, a maximum security prison.

Chaos strikes the prison and two inmates escape.

Special Agent Ross Fruen is on his first assignment with the HRT after transferring into the team.

SuperCell is a spin-off novella from The Ninth District - FBI thriller #1.

For updates on new releases, exclusive promotions and other information, sign up for Douglas Dorow's Thriller Reader list at www.douglasdorow.com and get four FREE short stories.

R oss Fruen walked through the dormitory looking for his room. His footsteps echoed down the hall. He had a pack across his back and a duffel bag grasped in his right hand. The air-conditioning was helping, but it couldn't quite match the heat and humidity of the afternoon. Sweat dribbled down his back between his shoulder blades and formed on his forehead.

He'd forgotten about the constant popping noise from the gun range. Or had just grown so used to it when he was here before that he didn't notice it.

Quantico hadn't changed much since he completed his training as an FBI special agent.

His assignment papers said he was sharing a room with two agents; Stevens and Rupert. He squeezed past a couple of agents in training wearing matching blue t-shirts. "Room 115?" he asked.

"Keep going. Down on your left, Sir," one of them answered.

Sir? Some things didn't change; the new agents in training

always helpful, always polite, thinking they're always being evaluated.

ROSS FOUND the room and stood outside the open door. So, these were the quarters for the FBI's Hostage Rescue Team. He took a deep breath. OK, ready. He stepped into the room. There were two beds, one on either side, just like he remembered, built in desks, dressers and closets, linoleum tiled floor, an overhead fluorescent light.

An oscillating fan slowly turned back and forth blowing air across the room. Yep, things hadn't changed much. On the bed to his right, there was a guy lying on his back, napping. On the bed to his left, there was a dog curled up, napping. Now, *that's* different, he thought. There weren't dogs in the rooms before. The dog's ear twitched and he opened one eye to look at Ross.

Ross cleared his throat and set his bags down on the floor. The guy opened his eyes. "Hey," Ross said. "My papers say I'm assigned here, with agents Stevens and Rupert."

The man swung his legs out of bed. Feet on the floor, he yawned and rubbed the sleep from his eyes. He looked Ross over and stood. He wore shorts and a white tank top. He was about Ross' height, six foot one inch, maybe a little taller, and broader in the shoulders. One shoulder bore a tattoo, his dark hair was cut short, his head was tanned. He crossed the room and stuck out his hand. "I'm Stevens." He pointed at the dog. "And this is Rupert."

Ross shook hands and looked Stevens in the eye. He had a firm grip, dark eyes, and a mixture of seriousness and fun in his stare.

"Ross Fruen. Wasn't expecting one of my roommates was a dog." Rupert hopped off the bed and walked over to sniff Ross' pants.

"Go ahead, kneel down and get to know him, you're part of the team, part of the pack where the dogs are concerned," urged Stevens.

Ross hung his arm down and let Rupert sniff the back of his hand. "I'm not real good with dogs."

"Rupert will change your mind, once you get to know him." Stevens reached down and grabbed one of Ross' bags and placed the bag on the bed. "Now he knows that's your bed. He'll leave it alone now." Stevens lay back down on his own bed and flicked his hand. Rupert found his dog bed at the foot of Stevens' and curled into a ball to nap again.

"He reads your mind?" Ross asked.

Stevens smiled. "Sometimes it seems like it. We've been partners for a long time."

Ross started emptying his bags onto his bed, sorting items into the appropriate piles before he placed them in the right drawer or shelf in the closet and dresser next to his bed. "I didn't know HRT had dogs."

"They didn't. We're the first handler, dog team."

"Not FBI?" Ross asked.

"We weren't. We are now. I was Army, finishing up my duty in Afghanistan working with Rupert. We had a couple of HRT guys in our unit looking for terrorists. Somebody in the FBI asked what I was going to do next and talked me into joining the FBI after they negotiated with the military to let Rupert come with me. We're an experiment. Just finished our training and got our initial assignment. What's your story?"

Ross moved a couple of things to make room and sat on his bed. "Another new guy, another experiment. I'm an agent, but they let me into HRT before I completed the mandatory two years as a field agent. I was in Minneapolis on my first assignment after graduating from the academy. Helped solve a big case and they gave me my choice of next assignments. I heard HRT was staffing up, so I asked to be placed here. Just got assigned to Palmer's team here after completing my HRT training."

"Well, welcome to the team." Stevens stood and grabbed a tennis ball. Rupert stood at attention. "Time for us to go play. We'll leave you to get settled. Our team's up tonight in the shoot house at nineteen hundred hours. See you there."

THE PLAINS OF NEBRASKA

The lights flickered and the cell block went dark. The emergency siren repeated its warning, blaring again and again. Back-up lights illuminated the halls and the exits casting shadows along the walls. Inmates yelled, whistled, screamed and laughed. Joe Kelly stood at the door of his cell, palms placed against the solid metal door, head cocked to one side, listening, taking it all in.

"What's going on, Joe?" Tommy Martinelli yelled from across the hall. Tommy was new to the maximum security prison sitting on the plains of Nebraska, a wind-break pelted by sand in the summer and snow in the winter as winds blew from Colorado to Iowa. He'd played junior college football, defensive tackle, where his size and temper made him lethal. He was also lethal off the field and that's why he was here. He killed an old farmer and his wife when they caught him trying to steal some of their cattle to support his drug habit.

"Just a storm, Tommy!" Joe yelled back. "Nothing to worry about. The Corn Crib isn't going anywhere." Joe Kelly had called the Nebraska State Penitentiary - maximum security prison, commonly referred to as The Crib, home for five years. It was his second prison home. He had been in a prison in Missouri serving his second year of a twenty-year sentence for a murder during a jewelry store robbery, when he was transferred here. He was transferred after he killed a fellow inmate and critically injured a prison guard. In his five years in The Crib, he'd seen everything Mother Nature had to throw at the place.

"I feel trapped, Joe! I want to be able to see outside!"

Joe yelled back during the silence between the blaring alarm signal. "Just sit down...and relax. ... They'll turn the horns off...soon enough."

HUGH HANCOCK STOOD in front of the green screen in his white shirt, sleeves rolled up to his elbows, his tie hanging loosely around his neck. He shifted from foot to foot and bounced on the balls of his feet. Meteorologists lived for this moment. The camera light turned on signaling he was live.

"At four-thirty this afternoon, the National Weather Service issued a tornado warning for Baxter and Henry Counties in central Nebraska. Everyone in the path of this storm should seek immediate shelter." Off camera, he watched the monitor to see the picture of the weather front behind him. The clicker to toggle the image was in the palm of his right hand. Stepping to the side, he swept his arms to show how the two storm cells were merging.

"Doppler radar indicates we have two massive supercells meeting southwest of Thompson. There are reports of multiple funnel clouds, so please seek shelter at this time. Get to your basements and cellars and tune into us on your radios for continued weather updates."

He shifted to the other side, turned to look at the screen and changed the image. "There are reports of hail along the leading edge of this storm. Temperatures are dropping rapidly." He put his hand up to his ear to better hear through his earpiece. "We have a report of a funnel on the ground near the intersection of County Roads I and Twenty-One and it's moving to the northeast towards Thompson. I repeat, if you are in the path of this storm, anywhere near Thompson you should seek immediate shelter."

FBI ACADEMY - QUANTICO, VIRGINIA

"New guy, Agent Fruen, you're up."

Ross tensed after the team leader called his name. His gut twinged like he'd made the plunge on an amusement park roller coaster and the temperature in the room felt like it jumped twenty degrees. He wiped the sweat from his forehead and moved to the front of the group. Time to prove he was ready. His job to lead them on their first run of the night through the maze of rubber-coated walls of the shooting house, configured to represent the floor plan of a house. As the first one through the doors, he was the eyes for those behind him. He was also the one most at risk of getting shot if they encountered any bad guys along the way.

Even though this was only a drill, everything seemed real. Dressed for combat, weapons loaded with live ammo, the team took up positions behind him. They were like a football team lined up at the line of scrimmage waiting for the snap of the ball to unleash their power. A soundtrack played over speakers with the creaks and groans of a building and the sounds of traffic and barking dogs outside a house.

Concentration zoomed into the task at hand. Ross started forward deliberately, heel-toe across the floor to the closed door, his MP5 pointed ahead of him, ready to shoot any unfriendlies in his path. The team moved behind him as one.

At the door, he stepped to the side and the agent behind him applied a strip of explosive charges around the side edges of the door by the hinges and the door knob. Everyone turned away from the door and the agent counted down with his fingers, three, two, one. A small explosion and Ross immediately turned and pushed the door into the room, where it fell flat to the floor. He followed it in and swept his eyes and his gun to the right, assessing the room in a blink of an eye. An enemy target stood in the corner. He shot it with two quick shots, center mass. An agent was right behind him, covering the room to the left, a third took the center. He knew they were there without looking because that's where they were supposed to be. They quickly regrouped to move on to the next room. There was no time to assess or evaluate. They needed to keep moving.

An open doorway in the far, left corner appeared to lead down a hallway. Ross peeked around the corner. The hallway was clear. He signaled and led the way, again in a slight crouch, light footsteps, his entire focus ahead of him. He knew his teammates were behind him checking the rear and one over each shoulder maximizing the firepower and vision ahead of them while making as small of a target as possible.

Ten feet ahead another hallway ran perpendicular to the one they were in. When they reached the corner, the agent on the left used his left hand to toss a flashbang grenade around the corner and down the next hallway. The bang and concussion was the signal to proceed. Anyone in the hallway would be temporarily stunned.

Ross moved to enter the hallway. Someone grabbed the

neck of his protective vest, yanked him back and pushed him into the wall.

"What're you doing?"

Ross stayed silent, sensing it wasn't a question he was supposed to answer.

"Look, then enter. Just 'cuz we flashbanged the hall doesn't mean they can't shoot. They might just start firing blindly down the hall and catch you with a bullet as you round the corner." The patch over the agent's heart read "Palmer". "You did OK, up to here, for an effin' new guy. But always look before you leap. We can't afford to carry you out and I don't want the extra paperwork. "

Palmer, the lead, watched Ross, evaluating him, coaching him. They didn't know each other yet and this was Ross' first drill with the team. Ross knew he had to prove himself to Palmer and the rest of the team. He nodded and moved to get to the "ready" position back at the corner to the hallway.

Palmer stood behind him and tapped him on the shoulder. "OK, Agent Fruen, let's try it again. This time let's send the dog down the hallway first."

Ross glanced behind him and found Stevens. His partner, Rupert, part shepherd, part lab and part Cujo crazy, stood alert at his side, dressed for battle in a ballistic vest and head gear. Ross signaled them up. Rupert was ready to go, in a slight squat, his haunches like springs ready for action. "We need to send in the dog and see what's up ahead around that corner," Ross explained to Stevens.

"We've got it, roomie." Stevens checked the video output from the camera strapped to Rupert's head to make sure they'd have a visual. He sent the dog on his way with a few hand signals and a command, "Rupert, Vooruit."

Ross glanced at Stevens and then Rupert, not sure what Stevens had said.

Rupert crept down the hallway, hugging the wall until he got to the corner. Ross covered him with his weapon. Stevens monitored the video feed, whispered updates into his microphone and Rupert heard his commands in the small speaker stuck into his ear.

NEBRASKA

"Tornado sighting, tornado sighting, this is not a drill!" The warning sounded over the loudspeakers and echoed down the prison hallways.

Joe Kelly forced a yawn to equalize the pressure in his ears. The weather front moving past outside must be severe if he could feel the pressure change like this. He moved to the corner of his cell and squatted, preparing for the worst.

"Joooooe!" Tommy yelled from across the hall.

Kelly stayed in his spot against the wall. The Crib was heavily fortified, but that didn't mean he'd be foolish and stand at the door. Better to be safe, than sorry. Back against the wall. Heels pulled into his butt. He cleared his ears again, bent his head and put his face into his thighs and covered the back of his head with his hands. Around him it sounded like a freight train was approaching and passing on the other side of the wall. He felt the wall vibrating against his back, like the building itself was afraid of the oncoming storm. He closed his eyes and took a deep breath.

～

AN EXPLOSION ROCKED THE CRIB. Kelly held his tucked position and felt sand and dust raining down on the backs of his hands. Then he felt something wet hit. He put his hand in front of his face and looked at it. Something liquid hit his head. He looked up and saw a three-foot gash in the ceiling. Rain was coming through the hole into his cell.

"Jooooe! You OK?" Tommy yelled from across the hall.

Kelly stood and looked up at the hole while he walked to the door. "Tommy, there's a hole in the roof in here. You OK?"

"Yeah, what the hell happened?" Tommy yelled back.

"I think that tornado made a direct hit on us." Joe looked back up at the hole. "Is your cell OK?"

"Mine's good!"

Kelly heard a lot of yelling out in the hallway. "Hey, Tommy, hang on! Sounds like something's going on out there!" Then he heard the familiar sound of the automatic cell doors unlocking. Next, as if by magic, his door slid open and he watched across the hall as Tommy's opened too.

Tommy stepped into the hallway, looked one way, then the other. "Come on, Joe, let's go." He stood in the hallway, holding his arms out, enjoying the freedom.

Joe took a step into the hallway. Sirens started blaring. Not the weather sirens, but the prison's emergency sirens they heard when officers were needed to respond to some sort of prisoner conflict. A shotgun blast echoed from the walls down to his left. Followed by another. He grabbed Tommy's shirt and tugged him back into his own cell.

"What're you doing? This may be our chance to get out of here."

"Or get shot, trying," Joe answered. Then the cell door automatically started to slide shut.

Tommy jumped to the door and tried to slow its closure.

He grabbed the edge of the door, but it didn't slow and continued closing until it was sealed and locked. He turned and looked at Kelly. "Now we're fucked."

HUGH HANCOCK LOOKED into the camera. "We have witnesses who are reporting a tornado has touched down and damaged the Nebraska maximum security prison. No reports of injuries at this time, but we are waiting to hear. Word is that the prison is secure."

JOE LOOKED up at the hole in the ceiling. He couldn't reach it alone, it was too high. But together they might be able to reach it. "You ready to get out of here?" he asked. "If we're going to do it, we have to do it now while everything is still crazy."

"Let's do it. We'll never get another chance like this," Tommy answered.

Joe grabbed the blanket from his bed and stood in the corner below the hole. "Give me a boost up. Once I'm through I'll tie off the blanket up there and you can use it to climb up while I pull you up."

"GOOD THING I'm in the cell across the hall from you and not Chip." Tommy said. "That tub of lard would've never squeezed his fat ass through that hole."

"Well, you almost didn't make it through. For a minute there, I thought I was going to have to leave you behind.

That's why I stay lean and mean. You're never too skinny to fit through something," Joe said.

They were on the roof of the prison. It looked like a bomb had exploded. The tornado had carried a lot of debris with it and when it hit the prison some of the debris, including cars and trucks, had slammed into the wall. Joe didn't understand the science of it, but something had opened up a crack where his ceiling met the walls. On the roof of the prison, huge air-conditioning units were torn from their mounts and lay in a heap along with car bodies, wood, trees and other garbage.

"Must've been one hell of a tornado," Joe said.

"Never thought I'd say this, but I'm glad we were inside," Tommy said.

They cautiously walked to the edge of the building, stepping over the debris while they looked around to make sure nobody saw them. It was dark out and lights still lit up the ground below, except where they had been torn out by the storm. Joe pointed to the strip of dark ground. "That's our only chance. Going out while it's still dark, through there. They'll all be focused on the inside with all of the mayhem going on."

"Then, what?" Tommy asked.

"One step at a time. It's not like we have a plan. We'll need to improvise while we go. But we have to go now, or not at all."

They ripped the blanket into four strips, tied the pieces together and secured one end to the carcass of a rooftop air-conditioning unit and dropped the other end over the side of the building. "I'll go first," Joe said. "I'm going to hit the ground and walk straight out into the dark. I'll go a ways out and wait for you. Don't run. We'll attract less attention just walking. Give me about a ten second head start. That way you'll know if I'm seen or not."

Tommy stuck out his hand. "Good luck." They shook hands. "I'll be right behind you."

Joe slipped over the side and held onto the blanket, kind of sliding and lowering himself hand over hand towards the ground. Three sections of the makeshift rope hung over the side of the building leaving a five or six foot drop to the ground. As he reached the last section and all of his weight was supported by it, he felt it start to move. The knot was slipping. He let go, not quite sure how far he had to fall. He bent his knees to absorb the impact, hit the ground, let his legs collapse and rolled onto his back, then over onto his stomach. A quick check of his arms and legs, everything seemed OK. He quickly looked around. He didn't see anyone, so he pushed himself up to his feet and walked away from the prison into the dark.

When he reached the count of eight he looked back to see how Tommy was doing. He saw that the makeshift rope was going to stand out against the side of the building. He wished they had thought of a way to remove it so it wasn't visible for the guards to see how they'd escaped right away. Tommy started down from the roof. Joe watched as Tommy lowered himself towards the ground. "Come on, Tommy," he whispered. When he reached the last section of the blanket Joe reflexively crossed his fingers, hoping the knot would hold until Tommy got to the end and had a shorter distance to drop. "Shit," he said, when he saw the knot slip and Tommy fall to the ground.

Tommy let out a muffled scream when he hit the ground. His legs hit cockeyed and one buckled. Joe crouched and waited to see if he was OK or if anyone heard him. He prepared to run if he had to.

. . .

TOMMY ROLLED onto his stomach and pushed himself up onto one leg, the good one. He tried walking towards Joe, but he was limping heavily. He stopped and looked out into the dark. Joe considered leaving him, but he didn't want to leave any sign of his escape behind. The blanket that was hanging down the wall from the roof had rebounded back onto the roof when the knot slipped, the tension slinging it up and the wind helping to push it back onto the roof. On the ground, by the wall was the bottom section of the blanket and Tommy. Joe eased up and quickly walked back to the wall. He grabbed the blanket off the ground and walked back to Tommy. "Put your arm over my shoulder, let's go."

"Thanks for coming back for me, Joe. Think I sprained my fucking ankle."

"Yeah. Let's get out of here and find a place to stop and check out your leg."

JOE AND TOMMY walked away from the prison quickly, like a couple of kids in a three-legged race. Tommy limped every other step while Joe supported him. Ahead of them about two hundred yards, a red, Ford pick-up truck stood in the road. "Hey, look what somebody left for us," Joe said.

The cab was a little crushed, looking like it had rolled across the road a few times. "Think it's driveable?" Tommy asked.

"Shh, listen." They stopped walking. "Sounds like it's still running. Let's go." Joe led them up to the truck. "Still has all four wheels. Anything is better than walking, especially with your ankle the way it is."

A man hung out of the open driver's door. The cab over the driver's seat was pushed about halfway down. Over the passenger seat, the cab was even with the bed of the pickup. "Is he dead?" Tommy asked.

Joe nudged the man and then pulled him out of the truck. "He must've been trying to ride out the storm in the truck. The truck's in Park. Whoever he is, he doesn't need a truck now." Joe checked the man's pockets and pulled out a wallet and a mobile phone. He looked at Tommy and then inside the cab. "We can't both fit in there. Let's get you in back. You can lay in the bed. I'll drive."

"Should we leave him or take him with us?"

Joe thought for a moment and then answered, "Let's throw him in back. We can get rid of him later." He dragged the body over to the side of the truck, lifted it up and dumped it in the back.

Tommy limped over to the truck and lifted his bad leg off the ground as he gripped the edge of the bed. "Give me a hand and let's get out of here."

Joe helped push Tommy into the bed of the pickup and then climbed behind the wheel. He bent over so he could see out between the roof of the cab and the dash. Then he applied the brake and shifted into Drive. A couple of test turns of the steering wheel and he was ready to go.

"Where are we going, anyway?" Tommy asked.

"How's your Spanish?"

"Dos cervezas por favor."

Joe laughed. "You're ready. We're heading to Mexico, mi amigo" He stepped on the gas and they were on their way.

"THOSE OF YOU IN BAXTER, if you're in your basements, you'll be staying a while longer. If you aren't, you should get there quickly, if you can." Hugh looked into the camera in all seriousness. "The second wave is coming, so sit tight."

The picture behind him changed. "For those who can see

me, this picture behind me tells the story. But let me describe it in detail for those who can only hear me. "There's a large hook echo to the northeast and a second front is marching along the same path as the first. This second front may spout some additional tornadic activity."

FBI ACADEMY - QUANTICO, VIRGINIA

"That was a good session. You two are pretty amazing to watch together." Ross sat on his bed, tired physically and mentally.

"We're fitting in and Rupert's getting used to the drill and the team." Stevens scratched Rupert behind the ears and under his neck. "We're more used to operating outside, not so much close quarters indoors work. You did a good job of leading."

"I don't know," Ross answered. "I made a mistake and Palmer was all over me."

"That's his job. Don't sweat it."

Ross shook his head. "I can't afford to make mistakes. I'm here without the mandatory years of experience. I feel they're just looking for me to make a mistake."

"Snap out of it. They need you." Stevens grabbed Rupert's neck and scratched him behind the ears. "They need us. They're down on numbers so they're relaxing the requirements. You're in. Rupert and I are in. Just do the job and you'll be fine." Stevens laid back on his bed. "Think they'll let us sleep in after a night session?"

"I doubt it, so I'm going to see if I can get to sleep. Hopefully the adrenaline wears off and I crash hard."

"Sleep tight," Stevens said and then he signaled Rupert that it was downtime and the dog found his spot at the foot of the bed and curled up to rest. "I think we all need it."

Ross stared at the ceiling in the dark. "Let me ask you something."

"What?"

"When you sent Rupert down the hallway, you gave him some weird sounding verbal command."

Stevens answered in the dark. "All of his commands are in Dutch. That's how he was trained. It's how a lot of the military and police dogs are trained. There are some Czech, some Dutch. I had to learn the commands and how to say them close enough that he'd respond."

"So he wouldn't listen to me?"

"Not in English for sure, and probably not if you tried the Dutch commands. At least, not now. Maybe if we trained him together after a while he might." Stevens paused. "And it helps when the bad guys are trying to give him commands. Whether it's in English or Dutch, he ignores them."

"Good to know," Ross replied. "Is the dog going to snore tonight?"

Stevens laughed. "He was asking me the same thing about you."

LIGHTS FLASHED and an alarm repeated its signal. Ross pulled himself out of the dream he was having.

Rupert barked.

Over the intercom Ross heard "*Silver team deploy to the gymnasium. Silver team deploy to the gymnasium. This is not a drill.*"

"Is this a dream?" he asked Stevens. The clock showed they'd been asleep for a couple of hours.

"More like a nightmare."

They quickly got dressed. Ross knew that while they were getting ready there were other support members of HRT moving pre-packed cargo containers into trucks, planes or helicopters, depending on where they were going. They'd have everything needed when they got there, wherever there was. They'd find out soon enough. Ross and Stevens grabbed their GO bags. They were always packed and ready so they could deploy at a moment's notice.

"Let's go do some good," Ross said, and the three of them headed towards the gym.

EVERYONE RALLIED IN THE GYM. Looking around the group Ross could see that some of the team looked as groggy as he felt, while others looked rested and ready to go. There was a tension in the air and nervous joking. No one was talking about where they were going.

They were a core team of eleven, with Rupert a dozen. Stevens, Rupert and Ross were A Teamers, along with Ramirez. First ones through the doors. There were two snipers and floaters who either partnered with the snipers, taking notes, served as tacticians and logistics and communications for the team or joined the bangers. The other three were bangers and rappellers. They knocked down doors, overwhelmed, and restrained and contained as the team stormed through a location. The twelfth was Palmer - Control. The team's brain and decision maker once they got on location. He was on-site to talk with local police, coordinate resources and be the touch point back with the leaders at Quantico.

Palmer strode into the room and all talking ceased. "Gentlemen, we've got a mission. A tornado has touched down on the ground in Nebraska and damaged the maximum security prison there. Inmates have control of parts of the prison and have taken some of the guards hostage. They may get it under control, but we're heading out in case they don't. Briefing packets will be passed out en route. Any questions?" Palmer looked around the room, his stare drilling into each member of the team, one by one. He nodded and gave the order. "Saddle up."

THERE WAS a squadron of Blackhawks with pilots on standby at Quantico ready to ferry HRT teams around the globe to hotspots on a moment's notice. Just like everything else they drilled for, they'd drilled how to load into the Hawk. They didn't have time to waste. They'd loaded their gear and taken assigned seats in a matter of minutes. Ross got in last, the new member of the team. Johnson pointed to a seat and buckled in. The Blackhawk helicopter lifted into the air, hovered for a second, and they were on their way heading west running away from the sun. Briefing packets were passed out with instructions to digest and be ready in twenty minutes to talk through strategies and backup plans. The Omaha field office was closest to the scene and would have people on the ground providing updates while they were en-route.

Ross flipped through the briefing packet; eight hours with fuel stops. ETA 11:45 local time. They'd be there before lunch. There were overhead photos of the prison and layout drawings and schematics along with information on the prison population, the number of prisoners and guards on shift when the storm hit. When they landed they'd be up against a group of some of the most violent criminals in a contained environment that they knew well. The weather forecast was included too. The storm that had spawned the tornado had passed, but another was on its heels.

NEBRASKA

Tommy pounded on the crushed roof of the pickup. "Joe, we need to find someplace to hunker down."

Joe took his foot off the accelerator and the pickup slowed, shaking as it coasted to a stop. "What's up?" Joe yelled back through the broken window.

"See those clouds up ahead? The only time I've seen those is when a bad storm is coming. See the clouds? Puke green, all mixed up. That's not good."

"We already had a tornado."

"We could have another. If we're out here and it starts to hail, then you know you're fucked."

A couple of pea sized balls of ice bounced off the hood of the pickup "Hang on. There's a farmhouse about a half-mile up the road ahead of us." Joe gave the truck some gas.

THE PICKUP SKIDDED to a stop in the gravel drive of the farm. Hail pounded a drum solo on the truck. The farm yard was strewn with boards and tree limbs. A red barn lay in front of them. Its walls gone, the roof resting on the ground looking like the barn had lain down and gone to sleep. A brick silo stood sentry over them. Where the farm house stood was an old stone foundation covered with the remnants of what used to be there. Joe spied red storm cellar doors on the far side of the foundation. He weaved the truck through the yard to reach it.

Tommy swung down out of the pickup bed and stood next to the driver's window. "Let's go. I'm getting beat up here." He hopped over to the door on his good leg.

Joe climbed out the truck and put his arms over his head to protect it from the hail. At the storm cellar he pulled the door open. Its hinges squealed. A white light glowed from the cellar. Holding the door open, he helped Tommy as he stepped over a ledge onto the stone steps that led down. "Careful," he whispered. "Somebody's down there."

"HELLO?" Joe yelled down into the cellar. Tommy limped down the steps ahead of him. Joe lowered the steel doors and the drumming drowned out any sounds below. He stood still on the steps, waiting for his eyes to adjust. Tommy made it to the bottom without incident, he didn't fall and he didn't get shot, so things looked like they'd be OK. Objects started to come into focus in the dim light. Joe stepped down and stood behind Tommy. "Hello?" he said again and walked around Tommy into the main room. Sitting by a kerosene lamp was an old couple. "Hey, folks. Hope you don't mind if we join you."

"Sit on down," the farmer offered, "if the floor suits you. Sorry we don't have any chairs."

Joe laughed and then helped Tommy down to the floor, keeping them back in the shadows. "Thanks. My friend here, twisted his knee as we ran for the truck to get away from a funnel cloud we saw coming. We were driving by in our pickup and it started hailing again so we thought it best to get underground and saw your cellar doors."

"So, it's still pretty bad out there?" The farmer picked up his radio and turned it on. "We've been turning the radio on once in a while to listen. Trying to save the batteries since there's no power."

"There seems to be one storm front after another. We started driving after the first twister passed, but ran into another hailstorm. They say lightning doesn't strike twice, but I don't know if that applies to tornadoes."

The farmer nodded. "I stuck my head out and saw that everything's gone, so we decided to stay down here until we're sure it's safe to go out. We got what we need; some food and water for a while." The farmer's wife stayed silent and didn't make eye contact. She simply knitted, a bag at her feet with a string of yarn running up to her hands where she worked her knitting needles.

Joe looked around the cellar. The light from the kerosene lamp illuminating the walls which sparkled, the glass jars reflecting the light. His stomach rumbled. He took a step towards the shelves to inspect the jars. "Looks like you have some good stuff here; beets, corn, jam."

"The missus cans it. It's good."

Tommy's stomach growled and bubbled.

"Help yourself," the farmer said. "It sounds like you're hungry. I recommend the beets."

Joe plucked a jar off the shelf and tossed it to Tommy. He turned to the farmer to tell him he didn't like beets and saw him squint and study his clothes. Joe had stepped out of the shadows, his prison clothes visible in the light. They stared each other for a second, Joe tensed.

"Who are you boys?" the farmer asked. His wife looked up from her knitting, the clicking of the needles stopped.

"Everyone just stay calm," Joe said. He smiled at the

farmer. He could see he was tense, his right arm poised to reach from something behind the box to his right. "We're just looking for a place to wait out this storm and then we'll be on our way."

The farmer's wife looked over the top of her glasses at Tommy. "You look familiar. You're that boy who killed that couple near North Platte, aren't you?"

Before Tommy could reply the farmer reached behind him. Joe stepped forward, catching site of the double-barreled shotgun in the farmer's grasp. He punched the farmer in the head and grabbed his arm. "I said stay calm!"

"Watch it!" Tommy yelled.

Joe felt a sharp pain in the back of his left leg. "Damn!" The pain was intense. He couldn't let go of the farmer's arm and let him get at the gun. He looked over his left shoulder and saw the farmer's wife pulling the knitting needles back to stab him again.

A jar flew the air and hit the woman in the head. She fell back onto her seat. "Bullseye." Tommy hopped over. "Don't move, bitch."

Joe wrenched the gun from the farmer's grasp, stepped back and pointed the gun at the farmer. He motioned with the gun barrel from the farmer towards his wife. "Go sit with her. I can cover you both with this scatter gun." He popped the gun open to check that both barrels had shells in them and snapped it shut again. "Shit, she stabbed me." Joe felt his leg. He brought his hand back up and inspected it in the light. "Bleeding a little bit, but not too bad. But God that hurt." He limped back a couple of steps. "Take this," he handed the shotgun to Tommy. "Watch them. I'm going to go check outside." He took a step towards the stairs. "Just watch them."

"Sure," Tommy answered.

. . .

JOE PUSHED OPEN the storm cellar door and looked outside. The wind and rain made it impossible to see very far. He could make out the pickup, but that was about. It. He lowered the doors and went down the stairs into the cellar.

"Well?" Tommy asked.

"Looks like we'll be staying a while. Still storming out. We might as well get some rest and eat up before we hit the road." Joe grabbed a couple of jars from the shelves and handed one to Tommy. "Hand me the gun. I'll take the first shift watching these two. You get some sleep."

THE CORN CRIB

The Blackhawk banked and circled the prison. Out the window, Ross saw the scar the tornado left across the landscape, one black line drawn across the fields right up to the prison walls and then it continued past the walls towards the northeast. The sky in the south looked like it was ready to spawn another beast at any time.

"Teams one and two ready to deploy," the command from Palmer through Ross' headset. "Team one, first in the southeast corner. Secure a position and report. Team two, Northeast corner. We'll set up base in the southwest. The Hawk may need to leave, depending on conditions. Good luck."

The helicopter lowered, the wheels just contacting the dirt and team one deployed. The sniper was out first, his support followed and the helicopter moved on to the second spot and repeated the maneuver. Then, they touched down in the southwest corner and the rest of the team deployed. Stevens, with Rupert muzzled and on his leash, took up a point outside of the rotor wash and stood sentry. Palmer strode over to the group huddled by some vehicles; prison staff, FBI field agents and the local sheriff. The rest of the team unloaded the Blackhawk. Supply lockers were color coded and stored separate from each other, ensuring that the team knew what was where, supporting their need for speed and efficiency.

Each team member checked their gear and stood in small groups, focused on the prison, talking through scenarios and assignments. Palmer rejoined the team. "Gentlemen, gather round." He keyed his mic. "Ground teams hear me?" He nodded and continued. "The storms have been constant here, just letting up an hour or so ago. One wing is back under the control of the prison. Two wings still need to be secured. There are prison worker hostages."

A field agent, wearing a windbreaker with FBI on the chest, walked up and handed Palmer some documents. He paged through them before continuing.

"Agent Fruen, two prisoners are missing from the west wing. Go see what you can learn." Palmer continued making assignments. "Stevens, you and Rupert hang here and see where you're needed. The rest of you, build us a model, scratch it on the ground, use boxes, whatever, get it ready and we'll assess next steps." He looked at Ross. "You still here? Go!"

ROSS JOGGED to the entrance and asked for directions to the west wing. There he met a prison guard. "You have two inmates missing?"

"That's right. Follow me."

They climbed a set of stairs. At the top, the guard removed a set of keys and unlocked the steel door. It opened onto the roof. The guard relocked the door behind them and led Ross past some twisted conduits and piping. "Watch your step, it's a mess up here."

"What are we looking for?" Ross asked.

The guard led him past roof-top air conditioning units knocked off their mounts and over to the edge of the roof. Down below they could see the FBI team. In the distance, the plains of Nebraska stretched to the south. Straight ahead Ross could see the path a tornado left as it snaked across the ground, hit the prison and continued on its way. "And what are we looking for? Can you just spell it out? We're wasting time."

By the base of one air conditioning unit the guard bent over and pulled up a dirty blanket. "It's anchored here, I think they used it to climb down the wall." The guard stood and pointed south across the prairie. "And they walked away. They're out there somewhere."

Ross keyed his radio. "Boss, it's Fruen."

"Where are you?" Palmer asked.

"Look up." Ross waved at the group below.

"We don't have time for games, Agent Fruen. What have you discovered?"

"It looks like we have two prisoners who climbed down from here and escaped out through the gap in the fence. They're on the run."

Palmer waved and motioned him back. "Come on down. Looks like you, Stevens and Rupert have a job to do. Bring clothes or bedding from the escaped inmates cells. Maybe Rupert's part blood hound and can track them down."

"The Blackhawk is tied down because the weather is still unstable and unpredictable. So, the two of you, I mean the three of you," Palmer dangled his hand down for Rupert to sniff, "will be driving that old Suburban."

Ross looked at the vehicle. Rusted quarter panels, two-toned, faded paint. How far could they get in it?

"Something wrong, Agent Fruen?" Palmer asked.

"No, sir."

"It doesn't look great, but it will get you where you need to get. Four-wheel drive, full tank of gas," he paused. "And you can't hurt it. It's already in bad shape. Two on the run wearing prison uniforms will stand out. But we don't have any idea which direction they went, so what are you going to do?"

Stevens held a plastic bag stuffed with cloth. "We've got some bedding, Rupert might be able to track them."

"And we'll stop at homes and businesses circling out from here to see if there's any sign of them or if people have anything unusual to report," Ross added.

"The warden has put out a report of two escaped inmates over the radio. And he's contacted immediate homes in the area, per their protocol. The first two homes or farms in each direction. Nobody has reported anything." Palmer handed some papers to Ross. "Here's a list of people they couldn't reach. Maybe not home, or phone's out or they're holed up in storm shelters. The map marks their locations. Start with them."

Ross unfolded the map and looked at it with Stevens. "Systematic and thorough until we find something or hear something," Ross said.

"We'll start here with Rupert since we know where they came down from the roof. See if he can pick up a scent," Stevens added.

Palmer tossed the keys and Ross snatched them out of the air before Stevens could grab them. "You're Scarecrow, Stevens is Dorothy and that makes Rupert, Toto."

"Does that make you, the Wizard?" Ross asked.

Palmer laughed. "And this is Oz. We may not be in Kansas, but it all looks the same to me. Follow the yellow brick road, and bring back those flying monkeys. And bring back that Suburban."

STEVENS KNELT by the prison wall where they guessed the inmates had come down from the roof. He pulled some of the bedding out of the plastic bag for Rupert to smell. Rupert stuck his nose into the cloth. "Rupert, Zoeken." Stevens instructed.

Rupert looked up at the prison wall and then sniffed at the ground. He paced back and forth along the wall and then headed away from the prison. His nose in the dirt, tail in the air and his front paws stepping on either side of his nose. "Braaf," Stevens praised him. "Rupert, Zoeken." Stevens and Ross followed Rupert as he serpentined ahead of them, following a scent only he could smell.

RUPERT STOPPED in the middle of the road and looked around. He put his nose to the ground, and sniffed while he circled in a ten foot circle around some invisible spot on the road. "Looks like he's lost the scent here," Stevens said.

Ross looked back towards the prison, guessed they were about a quarter of a mile out, and then looked back down to the road they were standing on. "Somebody in a vehicle stopped to pick them up?"

"Or they flagged somebody down and took their vehicle."

"I'll go back and get our ride. Why don't you see what else Rupert might find."

NEBRASKA SAND HILLS

Joe stretched and turned his head, working the crick out of his neck. He had a smile on his face. He'd been dreaming of the beach and a woman with long, black hair, a señorita in a bikini. He opened his eyes and took a second to acclimate himself. He wasn't in his cell, he was in the storm cellar. He looked quickly to Tommy to make sure he was awake and then at the old couple. "How long have I been out?"

"I don't know," Tommy answered. "Maybe a couple hours. They know we've escaped. It was on the radio."

Standing up, Joe stretched his hands up and touched the ceiling. "Then we better get going. It sounds like the storm's let up outside. I'm going to go check it out."

It was cloudy, but it wasn't raining. Joe walked through the mud, climbed into the truck and turned the key. The engine turned over, but failed to start. "Come on, baby," Joe pleaded with the truck. He counted to five and turned the key again, while softly pressing a couple of times on the accelerator. "Come on." The truck turned over and then started with a roar. "Yes," Joe said to no one. He left the truck running and headed to the open hatch of the storm cellar to get Tommy.

One blast echoed from the open hatch. Joe, surprised, took a step back. A second blast echoed and Joe saw a flash of light. "Tommy!" With three quick steps he was at the open hatch. "Tommy, you OK?" Joe grabbed the hatch, ready to slam it shut.

Tommy peeked out from below. Smoke from the shots swirled in the light around him. "I'm OK."

"What the hell happened?"

"I heard the truck start and decided we couldn't leave witnesses behind."

Joe was quiet, thinking about options and how this could hurt or help them. "OK, it's done. Come on out. Bring the gun and the shells."

Tommy limped up the steps and hobbled over to the truck. Joe followed to help him into the bed. He looked in the back. It was empty. "Where's the body, Tommy?"

"I threw him out while we were driving down the road yesterday. He stunk."

"Where?"

"Not long after we got in the truck."

Tommy was so unpredictable. Joe squeezed the gun in his grasp and considered blasting Tommy and leaving him behind. "Let's go." He put the shotgun in the cab of the pickup. "I'll be right back."

Joe stood in the cellar. The farmer and his wife were on the bench where he'd last seen them. The farmer died trying to protect his wife, his body shielding her, a blast wound apparent in his back. Joe grabbed a basket and loaded it with canning jars. Then he picked up the kerosene lamp and climbed the steps. Outside he turned and tossed the lamp into the cellar. The fire would hide the scene below from any searchers. He put the basket in the pickup bed with Tommy.

Black smoke started to pour out of the cellar doors. "Mehico, here we come."

ROSS AND STEVENS sat in the idling Suburban. Two farms checked and no leads. On the radio they were listening to a weather report *"this is Hugh Hancock with a weather report. The storms that hit our region yesterday are followed by another front. Doppler radar indicates a number of hot spots, one includes the same area by the prison that got hit yesterday. Stay alert with your eyes on the sky and your radio tuned here for further updates."*

"You ever seen a tornado?" Stevens asked.

"No, but I've always wanted to. Something about the power from nature, the mystery of the spinning winds," Ross looked up at the skies. "Guess that's what gets those storm chasers out driving across tornado alley every season, trying to figure out the mystery."

"That, or they're just a little crazy." Stevens said. They both laughed.

"Why do you think they sent the two new guys out together? To get us out of their hair or as a test?" Ross asked.

Stevens looked out the open window. "Probably partly a test. I think for me, for us," he pointed at Rupert, "out in the open is a good assignment. We're used to operating out in the country."

"And me?" Ross asked.

"You know the FBI, procedures, law enforcement, operating in a city. I think we're a good team together. We can learn something from each other."

"Yeah, you're probably right." Ross looked out the window. "Palmer may know what he's doing."

The gravel road ahead of them split; two farms down the left branch, one down the right.

"Which way?" Ross asked. "Flip a coin?"

Stevens pulled out his binoculars and looked over the country side to the left, then the right. "I see some smoke this way." He pointed and handed the binoculars to Ross. "It's a sign of something. I say we go check that out first."

"We'll be able to see better from up there." About thirty yards out in the grass prairie, past a barbed wire fence, stood a windmill with a metal trough at its base for watering cattle. "How tall do you think it is, forty feet?"

"About that. Think it's sturdy after the storm?" Stevens asked.

"It's still standing." Ross climbed out of the truck. "Rock, paper, scissors to see who goes up?"

They stood in the ditch for their contest. "Three and throw," Ross said. He counted it down, pounding his right hand into his left palm. On the third he kept his fist closed. Stevens' right hand showed two fingers.

"Damn it." Stevens looked up at the windmill and swallowed. "I don't really like heights. Watch Rupert."

Ross laughed. "You don't like heights? Haven't you jumped out of planes? We flew here in the chopper."

"I'll do it. I don't have to like it."

"I'll climb it. Winner's choice. I kind of like heights." Ross stepped over to the windmill and looked up.

"Thanks. I owe you one. I'll let Rupert stretch his legs."

Ross GRABBED onto the corner post and tried to shake the windmill. It seemed sturdy. A cross brace ran at an angle from one corner post to another. The metal was rough and pitted from years of standing sentinel over the Nebraska prairie, blasted by dirt blown during summer storms and frozen in numerous winters. He grabbed it with his gloved hand, stepped onto it and started to climb and shimmy up the braces to the top.

From the top, Ross could see pretty well in all directions. He pulled his binoculars out and looked towards the smoke. A farm, or what was left of one was the source. Smoke looked like it was coming from out of the ground.

"Hey, Fruen, come on down." Stevens yelled up.

Ross looked down at Stevens. "I think we should go check out that smoke, there's a farm there," he pointed in the direction of the smoke.

Stevens waved him down. "Yeah, after I show you something."

Ross climbed down the windmill. "Where's Rupert?"

"He's over in the ditch guarding a body." Stevens started walking away. "I'll show you."

"THINK THE TORNADO DUMPED HIM HERE?" Ross asked.

"From where?" Stevens turned around in a circle. "There's nothing out here?"

Stevens and Ross stood back, looking at the body on the ground. The man was definitely dead. His head angled unnaturally from the rest of the body. He was dressed in jeans and a dirty, white t-shirt. The shirt was pulled up exposing the white skin of his belly.

Stevens walked back along the road. "I think he was left here. Maybe thrown out of a car driving down the road." He pointed at a few skid marks in the gravel. "Bounced and tumbled and ended up where he is?"

Ross pulled out his GPS unit and marked the spot. Then he took some pictures with his phone to document what they'd found. "Can't wait for the medical examiner. Check the body for ID?"

Stevens knelt by the body and checked the pockets. "No

wallet, but I have a receipt here." He held it out in his hand, Ross captured an image of it with his camera.

"Can't read the signature. But they should be able to ID it from the credit card number." He shook his head. "Still no cell signal." He pulled out the satellite phone and called Palmer.

ROSS PULLED the Suburban into the farm yard. Smoke billowed out of the ground through a storm cellar door. Laying outside of the door was a person. Ross stopped the vehicle next to the body and hopped out. Stevens and Rupert exited the other side of the vehicle, keeping it between them and the cellar door. Stevens eyed the storm cellar, his MP5 in his hands, ready to shoot. Rupert took his command and circled the site in a bigger arc. "Ross?" Stevens questioned over the roof of the vehicle.

"She's dead." Ross answered. He knelt down next to the body. She was an older woman, her skirt was partly burned. Her right shoulder, chest area was ripped open. "Looks like she was shot."

Rupert sniffed at the ground and sat. "They were here," Stevens said. "He's picked up their scent around here. Must've walked from the cellar to a vehicle."

"We're on the right track. At least we know we're going the right direction," Ross said. "They're armed."

The smoke was thinning with the fire burning itself out underground. Ross collected debris from the area around the foundation and covered the woman's body to provide it some protection from birds or animals roaming the area, until the sheriffs could get there to recover the bodies.

Their radios crackled. "Scarecrow and Dorothy, this is Oz. We've got an ID on the vehicle you're looking for. Ran the card you gave us and found who it belonged to and what he drove."

"Go ahead, Oz," Ross answered.

"It's a red Ford pickup. 1984."

"Any idea where it is?" Ross asked.

"No, but now you know what you're looking for."

"Oz, any chance of sending up a drone to scan the area for it?"

"Negative, not with this weather, and the closest one is in Omaha. Keep searching. We've got an addendum to the radio report on the escapees adding the vehicle to the watch, maybe we'll get lucky from an alert citizen."

"Oz, we've got another body, maybe two." Ross gave him the GPS coordinates.

"That's enough bodies. Go find these guys. And be careful."

"We'll keep looking, out."

SANDHILLS PUMP & GO

Sandhills Pump and Go was a two-pump station with a garage stall for repairs. An old tow truck was parked out by the road, its faded sign advertising the station on the door.

Joe pulled into the gas station and parked on the far side of the pumps to keep them hidden from the attendant in the station. He stood next to the truck and spoke with Tommy. "The pump takes credit cards. Give me a card from the guy's wallet, keep an eye on the station for any weird stuff, and we'll get gassed up and out of here."

Tommy handed Joe the card, popped the gun open and loaded two shells in it.

The pump started, the dials slowly turned. "Damn these old stations," Joe said. "They never change out the fuel filters and gas dribbles out." He grabbed the handle, stopped the flow and squeezed the handle hard again. The flow didn't change. He could hear the gas flow through the hose and watched the numbers slowly spin. "Come on."

"Do we need to fill it full?" Tommy asked.

"As long as we can get out of here without being discovered, I want to be able to get as far as we can."

"If we're here much longer, I'm going to have to take a leak," Tommy joked.

"Just hold it until we get out of here. Then you can piss all over Nebraska." Joe tapped his toe and glanced at the station. They still hadn't seen anyone and no other cars had pulled into the station. He looked up at the sky. "Think the weather has passed?"

"No, look at those clouds. They're still green and ugly. I think we're just between fronts." Tommy said. "This is one monster storm."

The gas pump stopped.

Joe returned the gas handle to the pump, snatched another glance at the station and got in the pickup. "Looks like we lucked out here."

"Mehico, here we come," Tommy answered.

Joe turned the key. The engine turned over, but didn't start. He pumped the gas pedal a couple of times and turned the key again. The result was the same.

"Try it again. It was just running."

He took a deep breath, closed his eyes and turned the key. The engine turned over, but didn't start. Joe turned the key harder, in his frustration. "Damn it."

"Joe, somebody's coming."

An attendant in blue, oil-stained coveralls walked towards them. An oval patch over his heart read, "Bill" in red stitching on a white background. He had a rag in his hands, wiping them off as he walked. He spit a stream of brown juice onto the gravel lot. "Sounds like you've got some trouble," he said as he approached the vehicle. Then he suddenly stopped, about six feet from the front of the truck. He kept his hands in front of him. "Can I pop the hood and see if we can get this started and get you boys on your way?" His jaw twitched and he licked his lips.

"Tommy." Joe said.

Tommy stood in the back of the pickup and pointed the shotgun at the attendant.

"Now if you'd be so kind to walk around to the back of the truck I think it would be best to push it over behind your garage. Get it out of the way where you can work on it," Joe said.

"Sure. Sure, I can do that." He walked around the pumps to the back of the truck.

"Anyone else inside that could help us?" Joe asked.

"Nope. Just me. Too quiet out here to need anyone else."

Tommy sat down in the bed of the truck, the gun still aimed at the attendant.

"OK, then. I'll drive and you push." Joe said. "Let's go."

"Gentlemen, go get 'em."

"Where are they?" Stevens asked into his radio.

Palmer answered, "Your victim's credit card was just used to purchase gas about twenty minutes from where you are. At Sandhills Pump and Go. Ready for the coordinates?"

Ross held the GPS unit in his hand, his fingers poised to enter the numbers. "He's ready. Go," Stevens replied.

Ross typed in the numbers as Palmer recited them. He shifted the truck into drive. "They've got twenty minutes on us, but we know they're heading south. Nowhere else to go."

"Not a lot of roads around here."

"Let's go get 'em." Ross said.

Joe stopped with the pickup hidden around the side of the garage. "Can you get this started?"

The mechanic opened the hood as far as he could. It

resisted with a screech as the old springs stretched and metal rubbed on metal. The bent hood and front panels prevented him from opening it all the way. "I'll see what I can do. If I can get you on your way will you let me be?"

Tommy stood behind him with the shotgun. "Just get it going. We need to hit the road."

From under the hood, the mechanic gave the order, "Try it now."

Joe turned the key and it turned over, but it didn't sound anywhere close to starting.

"I think the starter's fried," the mechanic said, from under the hood. "It's old and looks like you rolled it in the storm."

"Try it again," Joe ordered.

"OK, go," came the command from under the hood.

The results were the same. "Damn it." Joe climbed out of the truck. He looked out at the road, nobody was driving by. Couldn't carjack a vehicle. He turned to the mechanic, who had crawled out from under the hood and stood in front of the truck. "Can you fix it?"

"If I had another starter. But I don't"

"No vehicles in the service garage?"

The mechanic barked out a quick laugh. "One old car up on the rack I'm working on. But it's in worse shape than your truck."

Joe scanned the sky to give himself a chance to think. "How did you get to work today?"

"What?"

"How did you get here? What did you drive?"

"I didn't. My wife dropped me off."

"When's she coming back?"

"Well, usually around supper time. But with the weather and everything." The mechanic wiped his hands and didn't finish his thought.

"What?" Joe asked.

"Just thinking about my wife. Can't get a hold of her. Phone's out and cell service sucks out here." He wiped his hands again. "I'm sure she's fine. Probably be here with supper if the weather's not too bad."

"PULL OVER," Stevens said. "The station is up there on the left about a quarter mile."

Ross eased the Suburban onto the gravel shoulder.

Stevens studied the station through his binoculars. "Looks quiet. No activity."

"Let's drive by," Ross said. "We can either pull in, drive by and go back or keep going." Ross shifted the truck into drive and pulled onto the road.

"You're the boss."

The old service station was an oasis in the middle of the Nebraska sandhills. Scrubland with some brush clinging to it surrounded the station. The Sandhills Pump and Go sign flanked the highway with an old tow truck parked at its base. The gas pumps stood in the middle of the empty lot.

"Looks quiet," Ross said. He slowed the truck down to about forty miles per hour. "I don't see anybody."

They continued to roll past. "Hey, I see something. Keep going and then pull over." Stevens twisted in his seat to look back at the station. "Looks like our red pickup is parked on the side of the station."

Ross checked the rearview mirror. "See anyone?"

"Nobody outside."

"Let me know when you can't see the station anymore. Then I'll pull over." Ross kept up their speed and watched the station through the mirror.

Stevens had his binoculars trained on the station. Rupert

looked back out the window in the direction he was looking. "OK, we should be good."

Ross checked over his shoulder and turned the truck in a U-turn. He stopped on the right shoulder, the nose of the truck pointed back towards the station. "We need eyes on the station. How about you and Rupert see what you can see and I'll stay here in case they head this way in the truck."

"Sounds good." Stevens stepped out of the Suburban and checked his gear. "We'll see what we can find out." He opened the back door, grabbed his HK Sniper Rifle and Rupert bounded out.

"Stay in touch so I know what's going on," Ross said. Stevens gave him a thumbs-up, then he and Rupert took off across the hard scrabble at a trot.

RAINDROPS SPATTERED the windshield of the Suburban; a few at first, then more, with increasing intensity. The country music playing on the radio got drowned out by the rain. Ross turned on the windshield wipers. They cleared the water, leaving a trail of streaks allowing him to see forward. He knew Stevens and Rupert were somewhere out there getting wet. "Dorothy, how are you and Toto doing?" Ross asked into the radio.

After a few seconds, Stevens answered. "We're circling around back. Think we made the wrong choice, choosing to come out. We're getting a little wet." There was another break, then Stevens continued, "Have you looked out your window to the southwest?"

Ross rolled down the window, rain sprinkled his face. "What the hell is that?" he radioed to Stevens.

"You said you've wanted to see the power of a tornado."

"I don't think that's your run of the mill tornado," Ross answered.

Gray clouds had formed into a gigantic circle, like a giant yoyo spinning on its side in the sky. It was hard to tell how far away it was or exactly what direction it was going. But wherever it went, it was going to cause some destruction.

On the radio Hugh Hancock interrupted the country music, *"residents of Thompson County, if you haven't looked outside, don't. Head to your basements and shelters. A giant Supercell has formed as the warm and cold fronts we were watching have come together. It appears to be following the same path of yesterday's storm. Sit tight, stay indoors and stay safe."*

"Dorothy. I just got a weather report from our friend on the radio. I think we may want to seek the safety of that building. The storm is coming this way. And it's a big one."

Stevens answered, "We'll see what we can see, but if they're inside we may need a new plan."

THE PRAIRIE PLAYED tricks on his ability to judge how far away the storm was. Ross wiped the rain from his face and stared at the clouds, trying to judge their distance and direction. The wind picked up in intensity and he saw a wall of rain marching in his direction. "Stevens. The storm is almost here. I'm rolling towards the station."

Stevens answered. "Rupert and I will meet you there. We're heading towards the rear of the station. Don't dawdle. The tornado is on your tail."

Dawdle? Where'd that word come from, Ross thought? He turned on the headlights, took off his helmet and drove toward the station.

ROSS PARKED NEXT to the pumps, the driver's door away from the station. In the rain he couldn't see anything at the station, so they wouldn't be able to see him either. "I can't see anything from here. How about you?"

"I'm not in position where I can see them through the scope yet," Stevens answered. "Give me another thirty seconds."

"Roger, don't dawdle." Ross smiled.

"My name's not Roger," Stevens replied.

Ross laughed to himself. Keeping things loose to release some of the tension, that was a good sign. He looked again at the station. He couldn't just sit here too long. He looked back at the storm front that was closing in on them as well. Rain continued to fall pounding on the roof and hood of the Suburban.

JOE LOOKED out the rain spattered window at the Suburban parked at the gas pump. "Bill, do you recognize that truck?"

Bill glanced out the window. "Nope. Not one of my regulars."

"You can tell that quick?"

"I don't have that many customers. I know them all by name and vehicle," Bill said, pronouncing the H in vehicle.

"He's not getting out," Tommy said, as he limped nervously, pointing the shotgun out towards the lot.

Joe gazed out the window. "Could be our ride out of here, Tommy. It's old, but it's in better shape than our pickup."

Joe grabbed Bill's shoulder. "Make it so he can't pay at the pump. We need him to come inside."

Bill shuffled over to the register and pushed a couple of buttons. "I set it to prepay inside, they'll see the message on the pump."

"He's just sitting there, Joe. He's not getting out." Tommy peered out the window from around the corner.

"Maybe waiting for the rain to let up." Joe pushed Bill down into a chair. "We'll wait, but not too long. We need him to come in or we're going to have to go out and get that truck."

"FRUEN, need to find cover. That's a big ass storm and it's almost here."

The rain intensified it's pounding on the Suburban and the wind was starting to rock the vehicle on its old shocks. "My vote is the service bay on the end of the station. Just a small window, big service door, solid walls except for the service door and maybe a mechanics pit under a car hoist." Ross peered towards the station. "I still don't see anyone inside"

"Rupert and I are heading for the back door of the garage. Time for some entry and cover."

Ross could hear the storm, the jostling of the equipment and the heavy breathing of Stevens as he ran across the field. Stevens was in the open. Ross hoped he'd make it to the garage before the storm. He had to get there himself. He turned on the headlights and shifted the Suburban into gear.

"JOE. SHIT. He's getting ready to go."

"What?"

"He just turned his lights on. I think he's getting ready to go." Tommy shifted his weight from foot to foot, favoring his good leg.

"Damn it. Watch Bill." Joe ran for the door. He reached out for the shotgun as he passed Tommy, grabbed it and burst out the door at a run.

Outside, the wind and rain pelted his face. He swiped it

away with his free hand as he ran for the truck. He couldn't let it get away. It started to roll forward.

"Stop!" he yelled. He grabbed the shotgun in both hands ready to fire if they didn't stop.

THE GARAGE WAS BEHIND ROSS. He had to swing around and get to the door, enter and meet Stevens. A tumbleweed blew across the lot through the headlight beams, bouncing off into the open prairie. The signs by the gas pumps vibrated in the wind. The storm was coming.

They had two objectives; get out of the storm and capture the fugitives. Ross glanced to his right and saw the silhouette of someone running towards him. The light from the station windows showed the silhouette of a man with a rifle or shotgun in his hands. Ross punched the accelerator, the rear wheels spun, spitting gravel and then caught, launching him forward. He cranked the steering wheel to the right and the back end fishtailed pointing him towards the garage. The headlights caught a figure standing with a shotgun pointed at him.

Ross ducked to his right and pushed the accelerator to the floor. There was a loud roar and the windshield imploded. Shattered safety glass covered his lap and rain was falling in through the hole in the windshield. He chanced a peek over the dash. The garage door was ahead of him. Crash into the door to gain entry and protection? Stop short of the door, protect himself with his sidearm and see if the service door was open, if not kick it in? He glanced back to see if the man with the shotgun was following.

The back window was blown out by another blast from the shotgun. Ross swerved the truck and ran it into the garage door. He scrambled across the seat to exit from the passenger door to keep the Suburban between him and the shooter.

"Stevens, I'm taking fire. One shooter."

"Almost there."

Ross grabbed the handle of the passenger door and opened it.

The wind ripped it from his grasp and flung it to the limit of its hinges. It rebounded closed and crushed Ross' arm. "Damn."

He pushed the door open and stepped out of the truck and looked through the window at the shooter. His right hand was numb and he couldn't grab his gun from the holster.

The shooter pushed another couple of shells into the shotgun. Ross saw him approaching the Suburban. He reached for his sidearm with his left hand and struggled to pull the gun from the holster. "Stevens, where are you?"

"Approaching the back of the station."

The wind was increasing. Ross' ears popped with a change in the pressure.

A blur as something blew past him. Another tumbleweed?

There was another blast and flash from the shotgun and the tumbleweed flew into the gunman.

It wasn't a tumbleweed, it was Rupert.

JOE LINED up the barrel of the shotgun on the cop hiding on the other side of the truck. A couple of windows gone, but it was drivable. It was their way out of here. He took a step to his right, into the wind. Sand and rain struck the right side of his face, but he maintained his focus on the cop. He started to pull the trigger and boom, something ran into his side, knocking him to the ground.

The shotgun went off when he hit the ground. What the hell? What hit him?

Joe heard a growl and scrambled to his feet. The beast lunged at him again. He didn't have time to aim and fire, so he swung the stock of the shotgun around like a home run swing to hit the animal. It yelped. Joe stumbled from the blow. The strong winds just about pushed him over. Joe limped back to the station to get out of the storm and away from whatever attacked him.

ROSS RAISED up to cover Rupert. The assailant walked through the door of the service station. Rupert was gone.

"Stevens, I'm still in front of the garage. We need to take cover. The storm's getting worse."

Stevens responded in his ear piece, "I'm coming around the corner of the garage. Don't shoot me."

"You're clear."

Stevens joined Ross next to the Suburban, rocking on its suspension from the wind. Rain and sand blew into them. "They're in the station. We need to get in the garage quick, before they head there for protection from this storm," Ross said. "I'll go first, see what we've got for protection from the storm and those guys."

"Make it quick." Stevens aimed at the door of the station. "I'll make sure they don't come out this door. How about Rupert?"

"The guy outside hit him with the stock of the gun when Rupert knocked him down. I think he's OK, but I didn't see where he went."

Stevens nodded. "I lost my comm-link with him. We'll find him when this is through. You better go."

Ross slid over the hood of the truck and squatted by the tire. The garage door was pushed off the tracks, but it would be a tight squeeze through into the garage. He tried the man-door first. The knob turned. Not locked. Would it swing open? One step at a time, Ross told himself.

JOE STUMBLED INTO THE STATION.

"What the hell, Joe?"

"We have company, Tommy, and it's not some farmer." Joe pointed the shotgun at the door. "At least one guy and a dog."

"What are we going to do?"

"The storm's getting bad. We survive that in this box and maybe we find a chance to get out of here. Their truck is smashed into the garage door, but it was running." Joe motioned Bill up with the muzzle of the shotgun. "Help Tommy flip this desk over. We'll hide behind this and the back wall."

Tommy and Bill flipped the big metal desk on its side. "Why don't we go in the garage?" Bill asked. "It'll be safer."

"That's where they're going."

"I thought you said there was only one." Tommy said.

"That's all I saw. I would've had him too, if the dog didn't attack me." Joe walked around the desk and slid down into a sitting position, his back against the block wall. Rain, sand and other debris slammed into the windows facing the front of the service station. "You guys better get back here before those windows give." He kept the shotgun aimed at Bill.

ROSS PUSHED THE DOOR OPEN, slowly swinging it inward on its hinges. The wind ripped the knob from his grasp and it flew open, slamming into the wall. A quick peek around the door into the garage. Nobody shot at him. He entered in a crouch and sidestepped further into the garage. He keyed his mic. "Clear. I'm moving to the back wall away from the office. I'll cover the door."

From one knee, Ross kept his gun aimed at the door. Stevens entered and backpedaled to join him. The garage door rattled on its rails, the bent in corner started to peel a little further open.

"Into the pit," Stevens ordered. "That tornado's going to hit and we need the protection."

They both slithered into the grease pit below the car that was being serviced in the garage. Stevens covered the door to the station. "We've got great coverage here from the storm and from those guys."

"Where's Rupert?" Ross asked.

"He'll find cover." Stevens replied. "He's smarter than the two of us put together."

The garage door rattled and Ross felt the pressure change in his ears.

"Hey," he yelled. "We're the FBI! The storm's going to hit any second. Come in with your arms up and you can join us here in the garage!" He waited for an answer. None came. "You're not going to make it sitting in a glass box!"

THE MAIN DOOR of the service station flew open on its hinges, sucked out by the pressure. Papers flew around the office and rain, dirt and other debris flew in.

"Fuck!" Joe jumped behind the desk with Tommy and Bill just as one of the main windows imploded sending glass flying and more rain and debris into the station.

"Now what?" Tommy yelled to be heard above the wind.

"Ride this out and see what's next," Joe replied.

Bill curled up in the fetal position with his arms wrapped around his head.

Joe handed the shotgun to Tommy. "Keep the Feds out of here and use Bill as a hostage if you need to."

"What are you doing?" Tommy asked.

Wind and dirt continued to blow in through the open door and blown out window.

"It seems like the tornado's passed. It'll get quiet fast. I'm going to see if their truck works." Joe jumped up and limped out through the front blown out window.

OUTSIDE, he leaned into the the wind. The Suburban was still running as it rested against the garage door. If he was careful, he could make it to the truck and get in without alerting the Feds in the garage. He hopped and limped as quick as he could to the open door of the truck and climbed into the driver's seat.

Gas looked good, enough to get away. If he was going to go, now was the time. The Feds would be busy with Tommy and wouldn't have a vehicle. He shifted into reverse and gunned it. There was a shriek of metal as the truck disengaged from the door. "Sorry, Tommy!" Joe yelled as he executed a quick half circle, braked and slammed the transmission into drive.

"ROSS, somebody's taking off in the truck."

"Let's secure the office and then we'll take care of the truck." Ross walked towards the door, his back sliding against the cement block wall for protection as he approached. "FBI! Anybody in the office, put your hands above your head!"

A voice called back from inside the station office. "Stay back! I have a hostage in here."

"Listen," Ross said. "Your buddy left you behind. Give yourself up, and let the hostage go."

Stevens quietly headed for the hole torn in the garage door when the truck pulled away. Ross signaled that he'd keep talking and for Stevens to circle around to the other side of the station.

"I can't do that man. I can't go back to the Crib. I got nothing to lose here now."

"Are you Martinelli or Kelly?"

"That fucker, Joe, left me behind man. What the fuck?"

Ross eased a little closer to the door, but made sure he stayed out of site. "Hey, listen. You've had your little adventure outside the prison. Got to see a tornado close up. But, now it's time to end this. Give up, we'll catch up with Joe and you can have a little heart to heart about him leaving you behind."

"No, you listen! I want a vehicle here that I can use. My friend, Bill here, will drive until I'm sure we're not followed and then I'll let him go, unharmed. Anything funny happens, I'll shoot him."

Ross whispered into his mic, "Stevens, he's sounding a little desperate here. Tell me when you're set up. I'll leave my mic open so you can hear our conversation."

"Give me thirty seconds to get in position and another ten to get set up." Ross could hear Stevens breathing heavy and his equipment rattling as he hustled to get into position.

"Martinelli. Think about this. Nobody needs to get hurt. We end this here and now and we get you back to your comfortable cell. Then we go get Joe." Ross moved right up to the edge of the door into the office with his back against the wall. "Where were you guys headed to?"

"None of your business."

"Bill, are you OK?" Ross asked.

"Yep. I'm OK."

"I'm set," Ross heard Stevens say in his headset.

"Martinelli, I'm going to stand in the doorway here so I can see how Bill is doing and we can talk." Ross hung the HP from its sling and slowly slid into the doorway with his hands in the air. "I'm Special Agent Fruen with the FBI. Let's stay calm and talk this through."

Tommy shoved the end of the shotgun firmly into Bill's back and Bill grimaced.

"Martinelli, relax," Ross said.

"I don't think he's giving up," Stevens said. "I've got him in my sights, but the hostage is too close."

"We can do this the easy way or the hard way, Martinelli. What do you say?"

"I told you I want a ride out of here," Tommy yelled.

"You from Nebraska, Bill?" Ross asked. Bill nodded. "How about you?" Ross looked at Martinelli. He nodded.

Ross went on. "My roommate and I were talking about how people talk different, refer to things differently depending on where they're from." Ross lowered his hands and leaned into the doorframe, relaxing.

"Where you going with this, Ross?" Stevens asked.

"Here you drink red beer, maybe call the interstate the freeway. My roommate has an accent and calls every soft drink a Coke. It's ridiculous." Ross paused to see if Tommy and Bill were listening. Tommy looked at Bill's back and Ross winked at Bill.

"Or there's kids' games. We called it Duck, Duck, (he winked at Bill) Gray Duck," Ross emphasized the last Duck and swung his HP on its sling up into a shooting position. Bill dropped to the floor, leaving Tommy exposed. Stevens fired and Ross followed with a shot to the chest. Tommy fell back into the wall and then slumped to the floor, the shotgun still in his grasp.

Ross quickly stepped over and grabbed the shot gun. "Clear," he reported to Stevens over the radio.

"You shot me," screamed Martinelli.

Stevens entered, gun drawn. "What's up? He's alive?"

"I think your bullet grazed his shoulder. My shot hit his arm."

"I was aiming for his head. He moved when he dropped," Stevens nodded at Bill.

"I was aiming center mass. You want to see if you can patch him up while I cover him?"

Bill remained seated on the floor where he'd dropped. "Are you OK?" Ross asked.

Bill nodded.

"I'm glad you understood where I was going with my story." Ross reached down and offered Bill some help up from the floor. "Let's get you seated in this chair and check you out." Ross swept debris off the chair and helped Bill sit. "You're the only one here, right?"

"Yep, this is my place." Bill looked around the inside of the station. Windows were gone, water, dirt, plants and gravel covered the floor and any surface. "Guess we survived the tornado."

"Yes we did," Ross said. "Anyone we can call for you?"

Bill shook his head. "The wife's at home, but I think the phones are out."

"Just glad you were paying attention," Ross said. "We still have one on the run."

"Maybe not," Stevens said.

"What do you mean?"

"I looked down the road before I came in. The Suburban's off the road about a half mile from here."

Ross checked to see if the shotgun was loaded. "Can you handle a shotgun, Bill?"

"I've hunted birds."

"Just in case he comes back." Ross handed the shotgun to Bill. "We're going to head down the road to the Suburban."

"I don't think they had any other guns. I just saw the shotgun."

"Well, just in case," Ross said.

"Sir, you going to be OK while we go check out our car down the road?" Stevens asked. "I handcuffed this one to the desk, so he shouldn't bother you."

"I'm not going anywhere," Bill said.

Ross and Stevens started jogging down the road. Spread out. One on either shoulder of the road.

After about fifty yards they stopped. Stevens raised his rifle and looked through the scope. He laughed.

"What?" Ross asked.

"You were wondering what happened to Rupert." Stevens crossed the road and handed his rifle to Ross.

Ross looked through the scope. The Suburban was stopped against a telephone pole on the far side of the right ditch. He moved the scope to the left and chuckled. "That's quite the partner you have there." Kelly was on the ground with Rupert clamped down on his arm. "We better go back up your partner."

Joe Kelly lie on the ground. Rupert's jaws were clamped around his left, upper arm. He softly repeated his growl anytime Joe moved.

"God damn it, get this dog off of me!"

"Joe Kelly, we're FBI agents Fruen and Stevens. You've met Agent Rupert."

"Can you get this dog off me? It hurts!"

Stevens stepped over to Rupert and tapped him on the left haunch. "Rupert, Braaf."

Rupert kept his grip on Joe's arm. "Joe, I'm going to release the dog. You're not going to move. I will approach you and ask you to put your arms behind your back. Then I will handcuff you."

"OK," Joe mumbled.

Ross moved to the other side of Joe Kelly to keep him covered in case he tried to get away.

"Put your right arm behind your back," Stevens ordered Kelly. After putting one cuff on Kelly's right wrist he issued an order to Rupert, "Rupert, Laat Los."

Rupert released Joe's arm and remained standing in position, on alert.

"Joe, slowly put your left wrist behind your back." Stevens handcuffed his other wrist and issued another order. "Rupert, Erop."

"All good?" Ross asked.

Stevens pulled his sidearm from his holster. "Rupert and I have him covered. Why don't you check out the Suburban."

ROSS SCANNED THE SKIES. It was still cloudy, but not so menacing. Joe was seated on the ground with Rupert a foot or two behind him, periodically barking.

"Doesn't sound like it's going to start." Stevens said.

"Nope. Our friend here drove it into the pole hard enough to do some damage." Ross stepped over to Joe and asked, "What happened?"

Joe looked up at Ross. "I was driving down the road, thought I was getting away." He shook his head. "Then I heard a growl from the back seat. I glanced in the rearview mirror and saw this monster flying over the seat from the back end. I reacted. Cranked the wheel I guess and swerved, bounced through the ditch and hit the pole. He flew into the dash and I bailed out. I didn't get far, when I felt him attack. Every time I moved or hit him he dug in tighter and pulled on my arm, so I tried to play dead. That's where you found me."

Ross looked and Stevens. "Let's hoist him up and walk back to the station. See if we can call for a ride."

They stood on either side and helped him to his feet.

"Can I get this arm treated?" Kelly asked.

"You'll be fine," Stevens answered. "Some punctures, maybe a few tears. We'll have the prison doc take a look at you."

"How's Tommy?"

Ross answered. "He's pissed at you for leaving him behind."

"OK, Joe," Stevens said. "You lead us back to the station. Rupert will be right behind you and we'll be behind him. You try to run and you have a pretty good idea of what's going to happen."

Kelly started walking down the highway towards the station.

Stevens barked an order, "Rupert, Transport."

Rupert closely followed Kelly down the road, barking and growling to keep him moving ahead.

"You know, if we're going to be partners," Ross said, "you need to teach me some of these orders."

"Yeah, we'll see," Stevens said.

THE FOUR OF them walked across the gravel lot towards the gas station. Ross yelled out, "Bill, we're coming in. Don't shoot."

Bill walked out of the station.

"Can you hand me the gun?" Stevens asked.

Bill handed it over. "I wouldn't shoot him," Bill said.

Ross patted Bill on the shoulder as he passed him. "Yeah, we know. Just need to be safe."

"Joe, we're going to have you sit while we figure out what we're going to do next." Stevens said. "Rupert, Zit." Rupert quickly sat. "OK Joe, sit down."

Joe bent his legs and kind of fell onto his side and then sat up.

"Rupert, Erop."

"I got Zit is sit, but what was the other order?" Ross asked.

"Erop." Stevens lightly rolled the R. "It means to guard. He's going to watch over Joe until I release him and give him another command."

"Alright, let's figure out what we're going to do next," Ross said. "We got the two escapees. Wrecked our transportation. I don't see any other cars here." He looked at Bill. "Any ideas?"

"Betty runs," Bill said.

"Betty?" Stevens asked.

"Betty," Bill said and pointed out at the tow truck. "My tow truck. She runs."

"What?" Joe said. "That piece of shit runs? I thought it was your advertisement for your station. You said you didn't have any other vehicles."

"Well, I don't drive it much and forgot about her."

"Will she make it back to the prison?" Ross asked.

Bill scratched his chin. "Sure, once I get her started. Just don't drive too fast."

"We're not all going to fit in her," Stevens said.

Ross smiled. "Bill, get her started. We'll figure it out."

THE CORN CRIB

They pulled up to the prison; Ross driving, Stevens in the passenger seat and Rupert seated between them. Smoke billowed from the exhaust pipe. When they got to the HRT command post, Ross braked and rolled down the window.

"What's this?" Palmer asked.

Ross got out of the tow truck. "You said to bring back the Suburban."

"In one piece," Palmer said. Are the prisoners in better shape?"

"They're in the Suburban. One in the back seat. One in the front. They're not really getting along," Ross said.

"And they should probably see a doctor," Stevens added.

Ross unchained Martinelli from the steering wheel and got him out of the driver's seat. "Tommy here, suffered a gunshot. Or a couple. One went through, and the other grazed him."

Stevens and Rupert walked Kelly around from the other side of the Suburban. "And Kelly here has a dog bite on his arm that should be looked at."

Palmer semi-smiled and put his hands on his hips. "Nice job for three rookies on their first assignment together. Get them over to the prison and checked in with the guards there. We're wrapping things up and heading home. The prison staff has things under control and the Omaha FBI office is here to tie things up. I want to get out of here before it gets dark."

Ross pet Rupert on top of his head and looked at Stevens. "Can I try?"

"I thought you didn't like dogs." Stevens said.

"He's growing on me."

"Give her a shot."

Ross grabbed Martinelli and Kelly and pointed them towards the prison. Then he stepped back and gave the order, "Rupert. Transport."

Rupert barked and nosed the back of Kelly's leg.

Kelly cringed and yelled, "We're going!"

FBI ACADEMY - QUANTICO, VIRGINIA

Tuesday night / Wednesday morning

R oss threw his bag on his bed. "Oh man, I'm beat."

"How long have we been gone?" Stevens asked. "What time is it?"

"I don't know for sure. Which time zone? Maybe after a shower and some sleep I'll be thinking a little clearer."

There was a knock on the door. "Showers needs to wait, gentlemen. Palmer wants to see you in the shoot house. All three of you."

PALMER WAS STANDING at the door waiting for them. "Follow me."

Ross, Stevens and Rupert followed Palmer into the shoot house. The room was dark. Rupert let out a low growl.

"Rupert, Vrij," Stevens commanded.

"What's that mean?" Ross asked.

"At ease."

They stood in the dark for a couple of seconds and then the lights came on. All the members of A team were there, cheering. Rupert barked.

Palmer handed a beer to Ross and to Stevens and motioned for the team to quiet down. "I want to congratulate you all on a successful mission." He raised his bottle in the air. "And to welcome the new members of our team, agents Fruen, Stevens and Rupert."

Team members clinked their bottles together and drank.

Ross and Stevens did the same. "Congrats," Ross said.

"You too."

Palmer walked over. "I hope you enjoyed working together. I think we'll team you up on the next mission too."

Ross took another swig of his beer. "Only if he teaches me some more of those Dutch commands."

Stevens smiled. "We'll work on it."

THANKS FOR READING

SuperCell is the first novella in the FBI Hostage Rescue Team, Critical Incident series. It's born as a spin off from my first FBI Thriller – The Ninth District, where Special Agent Ross Fruen is introduced as a secondary character.

If you haven't read The Ninth District - the book that started it all, check it out.

Join the Dorow Thriller Reader list by visiting www.douglasdorow.com to stay up to date on releases, offers and other writing news. You'll get four short stories when you join.

If you enjoyed this book, one way to show it and support my writing is to leave a review at your favorite online bookstore.

Read for the THRILL of it!

AFTERWORD

People ask where I get my ideas. The idea for SuperCell - Critical Incident #1 is a mashup.

When I finished writing The Ninth District, I got some good feedback on Agent Ross Fruen from my writing group and people wondered what was going to happen to him. I decided to create a spin-off series, starting with SuperCell following Agent Ross Fruen as he joined the FBI's Hostage Rescue Team (HRT), a kind of elite SWAT unit deployed on special cases related to anti-terrorism and other crimes where local law enforcement needs the help of a team with special skills.

The idea for SuperCell itself came after I heard a news story about a jail getting hit by a tornado and some prisoners escaped. I upped the ante so I could bring in the HRT.

Rupert was in the story since I started writing it, but got some additional details after I attended the Writers Police Academy the summer of 2016. One demonstration was by a sheriff's deputy who had a canine partner specializing in searching for explosives. As he demonstrated the search around a car where he had hidden a container containing a small amount of explosives, he gave some funny sounding commands to his dog. We learned that a lot of the service dogs are trained in Dutch. I decided to bring that into the story.

I try to bring reality to my stories. I attended the Minneapolis FBI Citizens Academy in 2015 and the Writers Police Academy in 2016.

One important tip I heard at the WPA; I was talking to a woman who is a co-writer with James Patterson. She said she told Patterson that she was going to attend the Writers Police Academy. He said that was fine, but remember, "don't let the facts get in the way of our fiction".

I want to make my stories real enough to be believable while remaining entertaining.

For my family and the agents and staff of the FBI.

ABOUT THE AUTHOR

Douglas "Doug" Dorow, lives in Minneapolis, Minnesota with his wife, two children and their dogs. SuperCell is his second book.

He is a graduate of the Minneapolis FBI Citizens Academy - 2015 and the Writers' Police Academy 2016.

For more info on my writing:
www.douglasdorow.com
Doug@DouglasDorow.com

ALSO BY DOUGLAS DOROW

FBI THRILLERS:

The Ninth District - FBI Thriller #1 - SuperCell - spun off of this story. See where Ross Fruen was before joining the HRT.

Twice Removed - FBI Thriller #2

Empire Builder - FBI Thriller #3

CRITICAL INCIDENT SERIES:

SuperCell - Critical Incident #1

Free Fall - Critical Incident #2

Lost Art - Critical Incident #2

FREE FALL - A NOVELLA

Critical Incident #2

Free Fall

Critical Incident #2

A novella
by Douglas Dorow

Copyright © 2020 by Douglas Dorow

ABOUT FREE FALL - CRITICAL INCIDENT #2

In Free Fall - Critical Incident #2, Special Agents Fruen, Stevens and Rupert return as members of the FBI's Hostage Rescue team.

They are called to the wilderness of Maine to save a young girl who's been kidnapped.

Free Fall is the second in the Critical Incident series after SuperCell.

For updates on new releases, exclusive promotions and other information, sign up for Douglas Dorow's Thriller Reader list at www.douglasdorow.com and get four FREE short stories.

CHAPTER ONE

The inside of the car smelled like pumpkin pie.

Zoe sat in the back seat with her little sister, Karen, watching *The Little Mermaid* on her iPad. They each wore a pair of headphones plugged into the iPad and focused on the screen. Mom and Dad let them watch movies on long car trips, like this one, a three-hour drive to Grandma and Grandpa's house for Thanksgiving.

"Mom," Karen called out. "I have to go potty."

Zoe paused the movie.

"Really?" Dad said.

"It's been an hour." Mom said, "Isn't there a rest area soon?"

Zoe watched the trees flash by the window as they drove down the highway. This happened every car trip. Mom said Karen had a bladder the size of a walnut.

The sun was starting to color the sky. They'd gotten up early to make the drive to Grandma and Grandpa's house. Mom had wrapped up the pies and put them in the back seat. Grandma would have everything else ready to eat.

When they got there, they'd eat the Thanksgiving meal, maybe watch some more movies, play games. Zoe wanted to tell Grandma about sixth grade, what they were learning and about a couple of boys she liked.

"I could go too," Zoe added. She wanted to help Karen out. If they both had to go, Dad would be more likely to stop and complain less.

"Five minutes," Dad said. "There's a rest area up ahead. We'll stop and then see if we can make the last two hours to Grandma and Grandpa's."

"Thanks, Dad," Karen said. She fitted the headphones back over her ears and Zoe started the movie again.

THE CAR SLOWED and they pulled off the highway into the rest area. Tall trees grew on either side of the road that wound back into a parking lot. The building with the restrooms was close and a playground was next to that. Dad parked the car. "Okay, I'll meet you girls back here in five minutes."

Zoe knew that meant Dad wanted a cigarette and that it was more like ten minutes. She grabbed Karen's hand and they skipped up the sidewalk to the rest area building. Mom followed them into the restroom. Zoe picked the closest stall and went to the bathroom. She knew that it would be a while before the others were done since Mom had to go herself and help Karen.

After she washed her hands, Zoe called from outside the stall door, "Mom, I'll meet you two on the playground."

"Okay, we'll be right out."

Zoe skipped out the door and ran over to the swings. She got herself going pretty high after a few pumps of her legs.

A man walked over from the restrooms. He had on a red

baseball hat covered by his sweatshirt hood he'd pulled up. His jeans were dirty, and he wore hiking boots. It looked like he was looking for something. He was carrying a leather leash in one hand.

"Hi," the man said. "Can you help me? When I stopped to give my dog a break she jumped under the van and she won't come out. If you could come over and help me grab her, I'd really appreciate it."

Zoe put her feet down and stopped her swing. She looked towards the restroom for her mom.

"It'll be quick," the man said. "If you hold a treat on one side of the van while I go to the other, I'm sure Queenie will come to you."

"That's her name?" Zoe asked.

"Ayuh, and it fits her," the man said. "She's a diva."

"Okay, if it's quick," Zoe said. "We're leaving in a couple of minutes."

"Great, I appreciate it." The man walked towards the end of the parking lot where a dirty white van was parked. The side cargo door was open. There was a white blob under the van in the shadows.

"I think I see her," Zoe said.

The man handed Zoe a cracker. "You bend down on this side with this and I'll go to the other side and see if I can scare her to your side."

"Okay." Zoe bent over and got on her hands and knees to look under the van. "Here Queenie," she said.

As quick as she said it, she was pulled up by her coat. The zipper dug into her throat and she was thrown into the van. She landed on her side on the hard floor. The door slammed shut. What was happening? The man jumped into the driver's seat. "What about Queenie?" Zoe said.

"Hold on," the man said. He shifted the car into gear,

reversed from his parking spot, shifted again and drove out of the parking lot with his tires spinning.

Zoe looked out the back window of the van and saw something white on the parking lot. Then she saw her mom and Karen walk out to the playground.

"Mom!"

CHAPTER TWO

The Blackhawk helicopter traveled low over the trees. Team A of the FBI Hostage Rescue Team had just completed fast-roping exercises from the tower at the Quantico Marine training center. They'd climbed the tower and slid down the rope a dozen times, in different team member order, running through various scenarios when they hit the ground. Now, they were on board the Blackhawk heading back to the hangar at the FBI training academy.

Agent Ross Fruen sat next to his partners, Agents Stevens and Rupert. Since their performance in their first mission a few months ago, they'd been teamed together in training and subsequent missions. Ross and Stevens leaned their heads together to talk over the noise inside the helicopter. Their mics were off. Rupert lay at Stevens' feet and panted. "Hey, what you doing for Thanksgiving?" Ross asked.

Stevens replied, "Probably heading to Palmer's party. Nothing else to do and the food should be good. You?"

"My family wants me to come over since they're close, but since we're on travel restrictions I think I'll hit his party. I'll try to get home for Christmas or New Years."

"You want to come over to watch some football before we head over to the party?"

"Sounds like a plan," Ross said.

Stevens held out a fist and Ross bumped his gloved hand against it.

"What's with the no travel and all the training?" Ross asked. "Fast-roping today, forest maneuvers Friday."

Stevens shrugged. "You know Palmer, be prepared."

"For what?" Ross asked. "Something's going on." Their leader, Palmer, had them constantly training and shared info sparingly.

"We'll know when he wants us to know," Stevens said. "Let's finish this one up and I'll buy you a beer."

"Roger that," Ross replied.

The Blackhawk banked into a turn over the edge of the FBI Academy grounds. When it reached the landing area in front of the hangar it stopped and hovered.

Palmer circled his finger in the air over his head. The team stood up and prepared to exit. Stevens and Rupert would be the last ones out of the door. Ross was right before them.

"You going to muzzle him?" Ross asked.

"Nah, he's good with this. It's jumping out of planes where I muzzle him and put on the goggles." Stevens turned and bent his knees. Rupert stood behind Stevens panting, his tongue hanging out of his mouth. He knew the action was going to start. Ross connected two clips hanging from a harness on Stevens to the rings on Rupert's protective vest. The Belgian Malinois had completed plenty of jumps with Stevens when they were stationed overseas with the Army. The training continued with the FBI.

Team members each held a thumb in the air indicating they were ready. Palmer rolled a duffel bag out the door. A thick black rope, connected to the Blackhawk, streamed out of the bag as it fell to the ground. Palmer tugged on the rope to check the connection and tapped the first team member on the shoulder.

One by one, the members of Team A stepped out of the door, gloved hands loose on the rope as they slid to the ground. Ross moved to the open door. He knew Stevens shuffled along behind him walking with Rupert, getting dragged behind him, his paws barely touching the floor.

Ross grabbed the rope and slid to the ground. He bent his knees, absorbed the shock and rolled onto his stomach. Wind from the Blackhawk blew any loose items from the landing area. The team created a protective zone around the landing point, all looking out, guns at the ready.

Stevens hit the ground and Ross helped to unclip Rupert from the straps. Stevens gave Rupert a hand signal and the dog moved towards the hangar and stood guard. Stevens and Ross filled gaps in the circle, the rope fell to the ground, released by Palmer, and the Blackhawk flew back over the trees.

"Secure the hangar," Ross heard in his earpiece. The team moved towards the hangar as one. Before they reached the open door, Stevens ordered, "Rupert, *reveiren*" and Rupert entered the hangar to check it out. The Blackhawk landed behind them on its landing pad. Thirty seconds later Rupert returned to the door of the hangar and stood with his tongue hanging out of his mouth.

"Let's go," Ross heard, and the team entered the door to the hangar.

Once they all got inside, they relaxed. "Nice work everyone," Palmer said. "Everybody survive the descent okay?"

Nobody announced any problems and they all headed off to the conference room to debrief.

CHAPTER THREE

"Come on, Zoe, we need to get to camp before it gets dark."

Jerry walked ahead of her way too fast. She couldn't keep up. She'd run for ten steps to catch up and then walk. He made her carry a backpack that was too big for her and it was pretty heavy. It had a sleeping bag, water, and some clothes. Jerry carried a pack too. It held water, food, a sleeping bag, bug spray, sunscreen, and a pistol. He'd shown it to her to make sure she knew he had it. He also had a big knife in a sheath attached to his belt.

Besides the backpack, he'd tied a red bandana around her neck. The same one he'd tied around her eyes this morning after he grabbed her and threw her in the back of his van.

"Can we take a break? I'm thirsty," she said.

"Maybe in fifteen minutes. We have to keep going," he said.

Zoe had been on hikes and camped outside in a tent before, but not like this. They were hiking on a trail through the trees. She was kind of dressed for the hike wearing a fall-weight, down hooded jacket, fleece gloves, a stocking hat, and her new LL Bean boots. Mom gave her the boots as an early Christmas present. Her feet had grown, and Mom said she'd need the boots before Christmas. She was right.

They'd walked past a sign that said The Appalachian Trail. Roots and boulders stuck out of the packed dirt and Zoe did her best to not trip on them. She'd learned her lesson earlier in the hike when her toe got caught on a root and she stumbled forward landing on her stomach.

Jerry didn't seem to care. He'd yanked her up, got her standing again, brushed some of the dirt off her stomach and they marched on.

"I need to pee," Zoe pleaded.

"Five minutes," Jerry said. "There's a good spot to take a break a little further ahead. It has a great view and we'll be able to sit in the sun." He turned and looked back at her while he walked. "OK?"

"I can make it," Zoe said. She wasn't sure where they were going, but Jerry seemed to know where he was going. She wondered if her family was looking for her. They had to be. Karen would be worried sick, and Dad would be smoking cigarettes. Mom would be on the phone with the police.

She knew the best thing to do was to listen to Jerry until he fell asleep or something and she could sneak away or maybe they'd see some other people. He told her not to talk to anyone, but she'd see if she could whisper to them or something.

The trail curved right and headed uphill. Zoe ran a few steps to stay close to Jerry. "At the top of this hill we'll take a break," Jerry said.

Zoe struggled up the hill. At the top, it was pretty steep. She followed Jerry out onto a rocky plateau. They walked out onto a giant outcropping of solid rock. The rough surface, covered with moss and broken pieces of stone, jutted out above a valley. The sun felt warm on her face after hiking through the shadows between tall trees all day. The view was like a postcard. Zoe stopped and looked out.

"It's beautiful, isn't it?" Jerry said. He slipped his backpack off and set it on the rock. Zoe copied him.

"Where can I go to the bathroom?" Zoe asked.

"Go on the other side of those bushes," Jerry answered. He pointed to a group of dense bushes off to the side.

"Really?" She didn't want to go to the bathroom out in the open where Jerry could see or hear her.

"Yes, really," Jerry said. "It's just us here and I'll give you some privacy."

Zoe looked at Jerry and studied the trail. Nobody was coming from either direction. "Okay," she said.

"Come right back when you're done," Jerry said.

Standing on the other side of the bushes Zoe looked back to make sure Jerry couldn't see her. She pulled down her pants and leaned against a dead tree so she could pee. It felt so good after holding it for so long. Now that she wasn't worried about wetting her pants she could think about other things, like how to get away from Jerry. She pulled up her pants and rubbed her shoulders where the backpack straps had been riding. Then she heard an unfamiliar voice on the other side of the bushes.

"Hey, Sweetie. Come here," Jerry called. He didn't use her name. She was under strict orders not to tell her real name to anyone and Jerry only used it when he was sure they were alone. "Come meet this nice man."

Zoe walked out from around the bushes and saw Jerry talking with an older man wearing a dirty, floppy hat. He leaned on a long, well-worn walking stick. He was older than Jerry, maybe Grandpa's age, sixty-five or so.

"Sweetie, this is Tennessee Tom. He's hiking a big stretch of the trail here going north to south."

"Hi," Zoe said. She smiled weakly at him and looked shyly

at the ground. She wanted to be careful so Jerry wouldn't hurt him or her.

"I told him we just got here and were stopping for lunch and he's going to join us," Jerry said. "Let's take a picture here and then we can eat." Jerry directed Tennessee Tom and Zoe to stand at the edge of the overlook facing him.

Zoe turned her head and gazed back over her shoulder. She wanted to stay away from the edge. It was beautiful up here above the valley, the sun shining on the trees below. "Look here, Sweetie," Jerry said. He snapped a photo with his phone. "Okay, now turn and look out over the valley," he said.

Tennessee Tom turned, "Can you send me these if I give you my email address?" he asked. Zoe turned and stood next to him, looking out wondering where they were.

"Sure," Jerry said.

Zoe heard Jerry's feet shuffling on the granite surface and then sensed movement out of the corner of her eye. There was a shout, and Tennessee Tom flew off the ledge, his voice trailing after him. Then she heard an echo of his shout and the sound of his body hitting the ground below. She sucked in a breath and stumbled back away from the edge and fell onto her backside. "Oh my God, oh my God," she said.

Jerry stood at the edge looking down where Tennessee Tom fell. He walked back, grabbed the man's backpack and threw it over the side after him.

Zoe stared at Jerry, breathing quickly in and out. What just happened?

"Okay, you just sit there Zoe and I'll get us some snacks and water to get ready to hike to camp. We can't stop too long. We still have quite a ways to go."

CHAPTER FOUR

The Hostage Rescue Team sat around a giant circular table in the basement of The Den, a local restaurant. Empty plates of food filled the middle of the table. The Thanksgiving feast had been fabulous. Members of the team shared tales of past missions and Thanksgivings with families remembered.

Ross sat next to Stevens. "Thanks for inviting me over to watch the game," Ross said.

Stevens answered, "You know, you should let the host win."

"It was a comeback. Who knew they'd come back with a field goal at the end and cover the points. That was an unreal kick. I'll just add it to your tab."

"I'll win it back," Stevens said.

Palmer stood at the head of the table. "Okay everybody, listen up." The conversation and laughter subsided. The team focused on Palmer waiting for his next words. He held his glass in the air. "First, I offer you a Thanksgiving toast. We've had a good year with a number of successful missions and new additions to the team." The team joined in the toast hoisting their glasses and bottles in the air. He continued, "I want to apologize for keeping you from your families and hope we made up for it at least a little bit with this table of food and the company we had tonight." More cheers and shouts of thanks filled the air.

"You've been training hard the past couple of days. It isn't over." Palmer's tone changed and he became somber. The team quieted to listen. "If you've been following the news, you saw that a young girl was kidnapped this morning. Zoe White was kidnapped from a rest area as she traveled with her family for Thanksgiving. An amber alert went out. All of Maine's law enforcement resources have been on alert. The border patrol has stepped up diligence at all of the main crossings into Canada as well as the other known crossing points. The Maine and New Hampshire FBI offices have been totally engaged." Palmer paused and studied the faces around the room.

"Fruen and Stevens, I hope you didn't eat too much this afternoon."

Ross glanced at Stevens wondering what Palmer had in store for them. Stevens shrugged a response.

Palmer reached under the table and pulled out a pile of papers. "Pass these around." He handed part of the stack to a team member to his right and left. "We all have some more training and preparation to do."

Ross took a packet of papers from the stack and handed the rest to Stevens. The packet was stapled in the corner. He flipped quickly through to the end. It was about twenty pages. A picture of a young girl was on the cover page. Below the picture was her name and vital statistics: age, weight, height, hair and eye color. Twelve years old, five feet tall, shoulder-length brown hair, brown eyes. Ross waited for Palmer to continue.

"This is Zoe. We don't know who took her or why. But we

do have some information. Turn to the map on page three." A map of Maine filled the page. Small colored flags marked spots on the map. "Northwest of Portland, Maine you'll see a green marker. That marks the rest area where Zoe was kidnapped. All they found there was a small, white stuffed animal in the parking lot. It wasn't hers. They think it may have been used to lure Zoe. The orange flag marks a spot on the Appalachian Trail. A couple of hikers on the trail found another hiker at the bottom of an overlook, deceased. His pack was found with him, but based on its location; they don't think it fell with him. It was probably thrown down before or after him. The purple flag, that's where they found an abandoned van that they think was used to grab Zoe. The working theory is that they're traveling south to north on the trail and may head off into the wilderness from there. The Maine State Police, National Park personnel, and others are combing the area they can reach, talking to residents, etcetera. The Border Patrol is diverting a drone over the area between the Canadian border and this area to look for Zoe." Palmer paused. "What's our motto, Stevens?"

Stevens hit Ross on the thigh under the table. "Be prepared."

"That's right. I want you all to take ten minutes, read the packet, talk over your questions and ideas, and then we'll talk about how we're going to prepare."

After ten minutes, the team peppered Palmer with some questions and ideas. Then he launched into the preparation plan. "We don't know where Zoe is, but when we find out, we want to be ready. The northern part of Maine is pretty rugged: lots of trees, lakes, and rivers, some elevation. There are lots of cabins in the woods. They call them camps in Maine." Palmer leaned forward on the table. "We may be able to drive and hike in, maybe the Blackhawk can get us close. This time of year it's getting cold up there and the weather can change rapidly. We need to get our gear ready and continue the fast-roping practice."

Palmer's gaze shifted to Ross and Stevens. "Except for Fruen, Stevens, and Rupert, you three are going to focus on skydiving. I want you to be ready to deploy ahead of us on a search to finalize the identification of where Zoe is, who has her, what kind of situation we'll be up against when we stage a rescue operation." They both nodded their agreement. "Tomorrow morning we fly up to Portland, Maine to stage from there, if or when we're needed. Happy Thanksgiving. Now let's go get ready."

CHAPTER FIVE

It was getting colder and darker now. Jerry said they were almost there. Zoe stumbled along behind Jerry as she had been since they left the trail a little ways after he'd pushed the hiker off the ledge.

Now the trail was hard to see, if there was one. Sometimes they followed tiny paths through the trees that Jerry said deer used, other times bushes and weeds grew over some of it and it just felt like they were taking a random walk through the woods.

Once in awhile, Jerry would stop to get his bearings, check his compass and then plunge forward through the forest.

Zoe didn't look around much. She was tired and just followed Jerry.

Jerry stopped and put an arm back to stop her. "Shh," he hissed. He grabbed Zoe's hand and pulled her close. Up ahead there was a building in a small clearing in the forest. Tall trees bordered the cabin on all sides, almost like a wall surrounding it. It was getting hard to see, the trees cut off the setting sunlight from reaching the forest floor.

"Is this it?" Zoe asked. She wanted to end the hike through the woods.

Jerry studied the building through the trees, then he lowered his mouth to her ear. She felt his warm breath on her cheek and smelled it too. He needed to brush his teeth. "We'll walk slowly and quietly up to the building. If nobody's here, we'll spend the night here and finish our hike tomorrow. Come on."

He pulled her along behind him, stepping carefully on the ground to avoid dead branches and piles of loose stones. At the edge of the trees, they stopped again. Jerry studied the cabin and looked around the area. "I don't think anybody's home, but if there is, you just stay quiet."

Zoe nodded. She was afraid of what Jerry might do if she disobeyed him.

They crossed from the edge of the trees to the camp. It looked old: faded paint and bare spots on the walls, a rusty metal roof, cracked windows. When they reached the door, Jerry knocked. "I don't think anyone's here," he said. He tried the door. The knob turned and he pushed the door open. The bottom of it rubbed on the floor as he pushed. "Lucky us, they left it open."

Inside, light from the windows illuminated it enough for them to see. There was an old bed, a couple of chairs, and a wood-burning stove. "A little rough, but not a bad camp," Jerry said.

"I have to go to the bathroom," Zoe said. "Where is it?"

Jerry coughed out a laugh and guided Zoe to the open door. He pointed to a small building at the edge of the clearing. "See that little building?"

"Ayuh."

"That's an outhouse. Know what that is?"

"Like an old-fashioned porta-potty?" Zoe asked.

Jerry laughed again. "That's right. Now, you run over there

and go to the bathroom and come right back. I'll be watching."

Zoe stood and looked at the outhouse and then at Jerry. "Is there a light in there?"

Jerry shook his head. "Nope. Some light will come in through the cutout in the door and the space at the top of the wall or you can leave the door open. Now, hurry up and go and come right back. Then we'll eat something."

The outhouse had a flat wooden board to sit on with an oval cutout. Zoe pulled the door shut behind her to get some privacy from Jerry. It got darker when she closed the door, but she started to see more as her eyes adjusted. There was a rusty metal hook that fit into a metal eyelet to lock the door. She locked it, sat, and thought about her day. This was her first time alone since Jerry grabbed her. In school, they'd learned to be careful with strangers, not to get in cars, stuff like that. They didn't talk much about what to do if you got fooled and taken. She wondered what her family was doing and how they'd find her. She didn't even know where she was, she didn't know how anyone else could find her. She started to cry and felt warm tears slide down her cheeks.

She'd look for a chance to leave clues or signal somebody if she could. For now, she needed to keep Jerry happy so he'd keep her safe and fed.

"Zoe, let's go," Jerry called out from the cabin.

"I'm coming." Zoe ripped a tag out of one of her gloves with her teeth. She'd scrawled a big black Z on it with permanent marker to mark the gloves as hers last winter. She wanted to leave a clue that she'd been here. Scanning the walls in the limited light, she wanted to find a place to hide it, but also wanted it to be visible. She stuffed it into the toilet paper's cardboard tube.

"Come on Zoe," Jerry called again.

"I'm coming." Zoe stuck her glove back in her coat pocket

and walked quickly to the cabin where Jerry stood in the door.

He'd lit a couple of oil lamps giving some additional light to the inside of the cabin. "This won't be bad tonight. Right?"

Zoe kind of smiled and nodded.

"I've put some food out for you," Jerry said. An apple, a protein bar and some crackers were on a small table. "It's not quite a Thanksgiving feast, but we'll do better tomorrow night when we get to our destination."

CHAPTER SIX

The noise from the engine filled the plane's cabin. Ross sat on a bench facing Stevens and Rupert. The altimeter on his wrist read 7,000 feet. Soon they'd be at the altitude they'd planned. This jump would be different than jumps they'd done in the past. It was dark. Palmer wanted them to get close without being seen or heard. They'd decide once they were in Maine if they were jumping during the day or at night.

"Comms check," Ross heard Stevens' voice in his ear. He gave Stevens a thumbs-up. "Sounds good. How about me?"

Stevens gave him a thumbs-up in return.

"This afternoon fast-roping, tonight skydiving, what's next, horseback riding?" Ross asked.

Stevens laughed in his ear. "Be prepared."

The lights below sparkled in the night. The sky to the east glowed from the lights of the city. "How many times have you jumped?" Ross asked.

Stevens answered, "Who knows? A lot."

"How about him?" Ross pointed at Rupert. They did everything together.

"Not as many as me, but probably close to a hundred. He likes it." Stevens reached down and stroked Rupert's neck. "Is this your first night jump?"

Ross nodded. "Yes."

"Don't worry. It's different not being able to see the ground, but judge your position with the night vision."

"That makes me feel better," Ross said.

"Follow our beacon and keep an eye on your altimeter. I'll talk to you on the way down. I'll follow GPS for the target. You'll see the infrared beacon on the ground. Use that as your target and to judge the landing. And you'll see the infrared strobe on my back."

The jumpmaster signaled them to get ready. Ross stood, stepped in front of Stevens and waited for him to check his gear: first his front, then his back. Stevens tapped him on the shoulder and Ross turned to check Stevens' gear. "You're good," Ross said.

Stevens signaled Rupert to jump onto the bench. He slid a leather muzzle over his nose and strapped it around his head. Then he bent over and connected Rupert to a harness across his chest. Ross was glad he didn't have a seventy-five pound dog strapped across his chest.

"You sure you shouldn't be wearing the muzzle instead of Rupert?" Ross asked. "You're the one afraid of heights."

"Funny guy. Next time you can carry him down."

Ross followed Stevens to the open door on the side of the plane. "Beacons on," Stevens said.

Ross flipped the switch on the beacon on Stevens' back and checked it with his night-vision goggles. The flashing light would be his guide to the ground. "Check," Ross said.

The jumpmaster counted them down and signaled it was time to jump.

"See you on the ground," Stevens said, and he jumped out the door with Rupert.

Ross stepped out of the door. "I'm right behind you."

CHAPTER SEVEN

The crowded room smelled of coffee and sweat. The team came straight here after landing at the Portland airport first thing this morning. Conversations around the conference table covered the trip, the weather, the mission.

Palmer poured himself a cup of coffee and grabbed a bagel from the middle of the table. He smeared some cream cheese on it. "Okay, listen up," he said. He took a bite of his bagel and stared at the group as they got settled and quieted down. He stood at one end of the table joined by a couple of other men. Behind them on a screen was a picture of Zoe.

Ross and Stevens sat at the other end with Rupert under the table by their feet.

"Everybody ready?" Palmer asked. With no replies, he continued. "Here with me is Agent Scott from the Portland office. He knows the area, so listen to what he has to share." One man raised his hand. "And this is Agent Martin from the Border Patrol office," Palmer pointed to the second man. "Agent Scott, it's all yours," Palmer said, and stepped to the side with his bagel and coffee.

Agent Scott grabbed the remote from the table to control

the screen presentation. "Welcome to Portland, gentlemen. I wish I could tell you that Zoe had been found or that we had information on her whereabouts. We have lots of tips coming in from the Amber Alert and we're following up on them. But we don't have anything solid to share at this time. Instead, I'm going to tell you how we're preparing and the plan for today." He stepped back. "This is why we're here, gentlemen. Zoe White."

The screen changed to a map of Maine. "Border Patrol continues to monitor the crossings into Canada and various points of entry along the water."

There was a large blue circle overlay on the map. "The circled area is where we're focusing on as of now. This area of Maine is remote and rugged. There are a lot of seasonal camps, you might call them vacation cabins, and houses, in this area. Communication is spotty. Many camps don't have electricity or maybe a little solar power. Border Patrol continues to fly a drone over the area looking for people that might include Zoe and whoever took her."

Palmer aimed his laser pointer at the screen. "This spot is the last known spot where we think they were. It's where they found the hiker. But we think they're off the trail now. It's hunting season, so there are hunting parties in the woods. Maybe someone will run across Zoe and her kidnapper and let us know."

The picture on the screen changed. "This is the weather forecast," Agent Scott said. "High forties during the day. Drops below freezing at night. A weather front is moving in and may bring snow with it late tonight and over the next couple of days."

Ross whispered to Stevens, "I'd rather be cold than wet."

Palmer stepped forward. "Fruen and Stevens, Agent Scott will walk you through some additional gear he recommends for the area. I want you to be ready to fly out of the airport the minute we have a better idea where they might be. With this weather coming in we need to get you in place while we can. We don't want to get too close with a chopper or anything else that might spook them, so you're parachuting in and hiking."

Ross nodded and fist bumped with Stevens.

Palmer continued, "The rest of you, Agent Martin will tell us about the roads and the border crossing. After that, load up a couple of vehicles. You'll be heading north via the roads to be close and ready to go when we get the word from Fruen and Stevens on where Zoe and her kidnapper are and what the situation looks like." He took a sip of his coffee. "Now, get ready and be prepared to leave as soon as we know where we're going."

The team got up from their chairs and started talking. A few grabbed for the remaining bagels and coffee.

Agent Scott stepped around the table to Ross and Stevens. He stuck out his hand. "Gentlemen, so you're the jumpers?"

Ross shook his hand. "That's right. I'm Ross Fruen."

Rupert moved out from under the table and sniffed Scott's pants and hand.

"He's jumping too?" Scott asked.

Agent Stevens reached out and shook Scott's hand. "I'm Stevens. He doesn't jump alone. Though he might want to. He's strapped to me. His name's Rupert."

"Okay," Scott said. "Well, follow me. I know you have your own gear, but we've laid out a few things that you might want to bring. Things particular to the north woods of Maine."

Agent Scott led Ross, Stevens, and Rupert out of the conference room and down the hallway. "So, you guys have jumped before?" Scott asked.

Ross answered, "Just practice jumps for me. They jumped together in the Army. We're both pretty new to HRT."

"And Rupert doesn't mind jumping?" Scott asked.

"He likes it better than Stevens," Ross said. "He's a little afraid of heights."

Stevens answered, "It's not so much the height, but the thought of falling and hitting the ground."

"And you're jumping out of the plane today," Scott said.

"Yep, lucky me."

They turned the corner and Scott led them down the hall to an open door: the Supply Room. In the room along one wall, there were guns of every type behind locked cage doors. In the middle of the room, there was a table with a number of items on it. Ross and Stevens stood at the table.

"Rupert, *zit*," Stevens commanded. Rupert immediately sat. His eyes locked on Stevens.

Ross said to Agent Scott, "Rupert's commands are in Dutch and he only listens to him. Not a great partner for me." Ross smiled. "Stevens doesn't listen to me either."

"What? Did you say something?" Stevens asked.

Agent Scott chuckled. "I guess you have the firepower you need." He gestured at the guns in the cages.

"We're set there," Ross said.

"Okay, on this table we have a number of things that I recommend you consider taking with you," Agent Scott said. He lifted a black rubber bundle onto the table.

"What's this?" Ross asked.

"This is a two-person and, a one dog, inflatable kayak, I guess. There are a lot of lakes and rivers in the north and you may need this to reach an island, get across a bay instead of hiking around it, whatever." Scott looked at Ross. "Since Stevens has the dog, I'm guessing this is yours to carry. It's about forty pounds."

Ross hefted the bundle to check its weight. "I got it. It's lighter than Rupert."

"I'm good with Rupert," Stevens answered. "I only have to carry him when we jump."

"This thing won't try to bite me as we're falling towards the ground. Is Rupert going to be okay when you jump?"

"He wears the muzzle," Stevens said.

"I think you guys should trade," Ross said.

Agent Scott picked up a couple of other items. "Bear spray."

"What?" Stevens said. "There are bears? Can't we just shoot them?"

"They'll probably just run away from you," Agent Scott said. "The spray will drive them off. And with the spray, it doesn't have to be a direct hit. It disperses in a jet for aiming at the target and kind of a mist around it. Just don't spray each other or Rupert with it. It's pretty nasty. Shoot the bear with your guns as a last resort. The spray does a better job of stopping them. If you don't kill them with a gunshot, you just make them mad."

Stevens shook his head and exhaled. "Nobody said anything about bears."

Agent Scott said, "You know what they say. You don't have to be faster than the bear. Just don't be the slowest guy."

"You better take the spray," Ross said to Stevens. "I'm faster than you."

"Not if there's a bear chasing me."

"I'm sure the bears will stay away if Rupert's around," Agent Scott said. "He pushed a small device across the table. Satellite GPS to help you figure out where you are in the woods. You have a compass?"

"Yep," Ross said. "We have GPS too, but we'll take this for backup."

Agent Scott slid a small can across the table. "WD-40.

Almost as important as duct tape. It'll suck water out of things so they don't freeze, you can use it to help light a fire, and it lubricates most anything. My father-in-law also swears by it to help catch fish. He sprays it on his lures."

"Okay, we'll take it," Stevens said.

"The last thing, it's deer hunting season," Agent Scott said.

"Oh great, rednecks with guns," Stevens said.

"They should be in orange, either walking in groups, maybe on a ridgeline or in a tree stand. But, be alert. You guys walking in the woods in camouflage might get shot at by mistake if they see you first and shoot at something moving."

"Great," Ross said. "Can we shoot back?"

"Try not to," Agent Scott said. "If you do find a hunter who can tell you where his trail cameras are, or if you spot trail cameras strapped to trees along deer trails, these SD card readers will allow you to view the camera photos and videos." He handed one to Ross. "Just put the card in the slot, plug it into your phone and look at the pictures. Maybe a camera will pick up an image of Zoe and her kidnapper."

"That's great. Maybe we'll get lucky," Ross said.

Agent Scott picked up the last thing on the table. "Agent Palmer said you have satellite phones. Cell coverage sucks up there." He handed the laminated sheets to Ross. "These are topographic maps of the area. I've marked some known trails and landmarks that should help you if you need it."

"Other than the kayak, it's not a lot more stuff," Ross said. "Thanks for the info and the equipment. We'll get it stowed with our stuff at the airport and be ready when Palmer gives the go command."

Stevens looked at Rupert and said one word. "Bears."

CHAPTER EIGHT

Zoe stumbled and sprawled out on the dirt. The pack on her back pushed her chest and head into the ground. Her stocking hat got pushed sideways on her head covering one eye. She lay on the dirt, breathed in the smells of dirt and leaves and closed her eyes. They'd been hiking all day with few rests. She was exhausted. She just wanted to take a nap.

"You okay?" Jerry asked.

"Yes," Zoe mumbled into the dirt. "I think so." She rolled onto her side. "Are we almost there?"

Jerry knelt next to her. "You've done great today. I know it's been hard, but we're almost there. If we keep going, we can be at our camp in sixty minutes, tops." He pulled Zoe's backpack from her back and got her arms out of the straps. Then he gently helped her into a sitting position. He sat across from her in the dirt.

"Have some water. A short break and then we'll move on." Jerry pulled a water bottle from his pack and handed it to her. "When we get there, I'll introduce you to Barb and Buck. I haven't told you about them yet."

"Who are they?"

"Barb's a woman, maybe ten, fifteen years older than you. What, you're twelve?"

Zoe nodded.

"Buck's a dog, a husky. I think you'll like him."

"Buck, like the dog in *The Call of the Wild*?"

"You know that story? It's one of my favorites."

"We just read it in school," Zoe said. "Except he's not a husky. He's a St Bernard and something else."

"I've got the book at camp if you want to read it again."

When they got to camp, she wouldn't be alone with Jerry. That made Zoe feel a little better. There was so much she didn't know. She didn't know why Jerry kidnapped her. She was afraid to ask. She still didn't know if she should finish the journey to the camp following Jerry or try to escape. She had to be smart and stay safe for Karen and Mom and Dad. Zoe took a drink of water. She screwed the cover back on and handed the bottle to Jerry.

Jerry took the water bottle and stashed it in his backpack. "Okay, let's go."

He put out his hand. Zoe grabbed it and Jerry pulled her up to a standing position. She resettled the backpack on her shoulders, stuffed her hat in her pocket and brushed the dirt from her front.

Jerry led the way.

ZOE BLINDLY FOLLOWED Jerry as she had done for the past two days. She didn't have to think much, just keep her eyes on Jerry's back and walk.

He suddenly stopped. She almost ran into him. He turned and clapped his hand over her mouth. Then he pulled her down as he knelt on the ground. "Quiet," he said. "Don't move." He squinted and looked up ahead through the trees.

She followed his gaze but didn't see anything.

"There's a deer hunter in a tree stand up ahead about forty yards," Jerry said.

She spotted the hunter. He was up in the air higher than a basketball hoop. He had on camouflage clothing and a vest with orange panels on the front. A scraggly gray beard covered his face. He looked kind of plump. He was sitting in a camp chair on a wooden platform that appeared to be attached to the tree with a couple of wooden braces. A wood ladder running up from the ground supported the front edge of the platform. The hunter's head slumped to one side.

"It looks like he's sleeping," Jerry said. "We're going to go around him. Quietly." He shifted his gaze to Zoe. "If you wake him up, I'm going to have to hurt him. So, be quiet and follow me."

Zoe nodded to show she understood. She didn't dare make a noise. Not after what he did to the hiker yesterday. Jerry grabbed her left hand and led her around to the left. The tree would be between them and the hunter sleeping in the deer stand. Zoe watched Jerry. His focus shifted between where they were walking, avoiding dead branches and loose rocks, and the man in the tree. She reached her right hand into her coat pocket and carefully worked the stocking hat out. She held it in her hand until she was sure Jerry wasn't looking. Then she dropped it on the ground behind her. Maybe the hunter would see it when he came down out of his tree stand.

They crept along about twenty steps and stopped. Jerry glanced at the hunter. Zoe glanced at the hunter. She almost hoped he'd wake up and see them. He had a gun. Maybe he could save her. She thought about screaming but knew Jerry was crazy enough to hurt the man and maybe her. She followed Jerry as they worked their way past the hunter.

"Hey, Missy."

Zoe stopped in her tracks. The hunter in the tree stand called out from his perch.

Jerry turned and waved. "Heya. We thought you were sleeping. Didn't want to wake you."

The hunter laughed. "I shouldn't be sleeping if I want to get my deer." The man had a low, crackly voice like Zoe's grandpa.

"I guess that's right," Jerry said.

The hunter called down to them, "You two should really be wearing some blaze orange if you're going to be hiking around in these woods. I'd hate to see you get shot, somebody thinking you're a deer."

"Thanks," Jerry said. "I'm not a hunter. Didn't realize it was hunting season. We haven't heard any shooting." He walked back towards the hunter's deer stand.

Zoe stayed where she was. This might be her chance.

"It's been a little slow," the hunter said. "The reason I called out to you was your girl dropped her hat back there." He pointed back in the trees where they'd walked behind him. "Don't know if you heard, but there's a storm coming. She's going to want that hat."

"Thanks," Jerry said. He called out to Zoe. "Sweetie, this man says you dropped your hat back there a little ways. You better go pick it up."

Zoe nodded and walked back the way they'd come towards the spot where she dropped the hat. She watched Jerry and the hunter talking.

"You know," the hunter said. "I have a couple of orange rags in my pocket. If you tied them to your backpacks it'd be better than nothing. I'd feel better if you had them."

"I'll come up and get them. Thanks," Jerry said. He walked the last few steps to the ladder of the hunter's tree stand.

Zoe watched him and moved a little to her right. If he

climbed the stand he'd be directly on the other side of the tree and maybe couldn't see her. She could run away from the tree and get away from him before he noticed. She bent over, picked up her hat and stuffed it in her pocket. She took a step back away from the tree stand. Jerry kept talking to the hunter. She took two steps back. A couple more steps back.

"Stay there, Zoe," Jerry said.

The hunter peered around the tree from his perch. "Are you the Zoe from the Amber Alert I heard yesterday?" He picked up his rifle.

Jerry grabbed the ladder and pulled the legs out away from the tree. The front of the platform tilted down toward the ground. There was a screeching of nails and the crack of breaking wood.

"Run Zoe," the hunter yelled.

Zoe saw him losing his balance, grabbing for the tree. The platform tilted further. The man jumped. Zoe turned and ran.

CHAPTER NINE

Z oe heard the man hit the ground. He called out in pain.
Then he yelled, "Run!"

She didn't dare look back. She just ran. If Jerry struggled
with the hunter, she had some time to get away. The forest
was open enough to see quite a distance. She couldn't outrun
Jerry. She needed to run and find a place to hide. That was
her only chance.

A loud bang filled the air. The hunter's gun went off
behind her. It shocked her out of her daze. She couldn't just
run straight through the trees, Jerry would find her. She
turned left and ran.

After zigzagging through the tree's Zoe's lungs burned.
She couldn't go much farther. On her right, she spied a dead
pine tree lying across the forest floor. She veered towards the
tree and ran around to the other side of it. She squeezed in
among the dead branches and pushed herself up against the
trunk of the tree. Her heart pounded in her ears. She closed
her eyes and tried to control her breathing. She didn't want
Jerry to hear her.

The forest was quiet. Zoe got control of her breathing. She didn't know how long she needed to hide here. She knew it had to be a while. She had to be sure Jerry was gone.

"ZOE, COME ON OUT," Jerry yelled. "You can't stay out here. A storm's coming."

He sounded close. Zoe hugged herself tighter, closed her eyes and pushed her back into the tree.

"Come on Zoe. Another hour or so we'll be at camp. It'll be warm. We'll have something to eat. You'll have a bed to sleep in."

Zoe could tell he was getting closer. Did he know where she was? If she was able to escape Jerry tonight, would she survive the night in the woods?

"I have the hunter's rifle," Jerry said. "I could've shot you, but I don't want to hurt you. I want to get to camp before it gets dark."

The wind blew through the quiet forest. Zoe peeked and saw Jerry's boots. He was standing a few feet away from her.

"Let's go, Zoe," Jerry said. "Don't forget your hat or gloves behind. You're going to need them."

She opened her eyes and looked up. She saw Jerry staring at her. He had the hunter's rifle slung over his shoulder from a strap.

"Come on," he said.

Zoe worked her way out from under the branches and stood in front of Jerry.

"Just follow me," Jerry said. "We have to go pick up our packs. Don't run. You get lost out here you might get hurt, and it's getting cold out at night." He turned and started walking through the woods again.

She brushed the dirt and leaves off her clothes and followed him through the woods.

IT WAS GETTING DARKER. Jerry pulled a headlamp out of his pack and strapped it around his head. It lit up things better when he turned his head. Zoe didn't have a headlamp. She followed Jerry down the slope through the trees, watching the glow of light on the ground ahead of him. She could see the black outline of his back. She caught glimpses of water and islands through the breaks in the trees.

"We're almost there Zoe. Nice job on the hike this afternoon."

They reached the end of the land. Water lapped up against the shore. Jerry moved some branches off a mound on shore. Then he pulled back a net. It was covering a small, flat-bottomed boat. He threw the net in the bottom of the boat. "Hand me your backpack," Jerry said.

Zoe shrugged off her pack and gave it to Jerry. He threw it in the boat along with his. He pushed the boat partway into the water.

"Okay, get in." He held out his hand and grabbed hers to help her into the boat. She sat on the seat in the far end of the boat. She felt it rock in the water. Jerry pushed the boat a little further into the lake. Then he put the rifle in the boat at his end. He pushed the boat from shore and stepped in.

Jerry rowed the boat across the water to the other shore. He pointed his end of the boat to hit the shore first. They reversed what they did getting into the boat. Jerry got out, pulled the end of the boat up to the shore and pulled the rifle out. Then he asked Zoe to climb out. After helping her out of the boat he pulled it further up onto the shore. He grabbed their packs out of the boat and covered the boat with the netting.

"We're almost home. Follow me." Jerry walked around some rocks and up through a stand of trees. It was pretty hard to see except for what the headlamp lit up. Jerry stopped at a clearing. A cabin stood about thirty feet away. Lights from inside the cabin lit up curtains in the windows. A dog barked. "That's Buck," Jerry said. Then he yelled out, "Hello camp."

The cabin door swung open. The silhouette of a woman with long hair stood in the doorway. A dog stood by her side. "Welcome back," she said.

Jerry grabbed a hold of Zoe's hand. "Come on. Let's go in." He led Zoe across the open ground to the cabin. The dog started whining and twisting his body. "Hey, Buck." The dog ran down the steps and came over to Jerry and Zoe. He sniffed both of them and whined. Jerry pet him. "That's a good boy."

"He's missed you," the woman said. "Who's this you have with you?"

"Barb, this is Zoe," Jerry said. "Zoe, this is Barb."

"Nice to meet you," Barb said. "Why don't we all go inside?"

Zoe followed Barb into the cabin. Barb reminded her of one of her teachers. Not too old, long hair, friendly, a nice smile. Jerry and Buck came in behind them. "I'll get you guys something to eat," Barb said. She pointed at a ladder along a wall in the middle of the room. "Zoe, you're in the loft. You can check it out after we eat."

"I think I just want to go to bed," Zoe said.

"We've had a big day," Jerry said to Barb. "That's probably a good idea." He spoke to Zoe. "Your bed's to the right when you get up there. Watch your head. It's a low ceiling."

Zoe climbed the ladder to the loft. She found the bed to

the right and laid down on it without taking off her clothes or her boots. It creaked when she climbed onto it. She heard Jerry and Barb's voices, but she couldn't hear what they were saying. Her eyes closed. She popped them open again, fighting sleep, and then she gave in and closed them.

CHAPTER TEN

R oss and Stevens checked and rechecked their gear. They napped, checked maps of northern Maine, had food delivered. They'd be ready to go when Palmer told them it was time.They sat at a table playing cribbage. Stevens had taught Ross how to play a few months ago and Ross could give Stevens a run for his money now.

"Think we're jumping tonight?" Stevens asked.

"With the weather front coming in, I think it has to be tonight," Ross answered. He counted out the points in his hand and pegged eight spaces on the board. It was going to be a close game.

"I wish we would've jumped earlier." Stevens pegged his points in his hand and the points in his crib. "Daylight, even overcast would be better than the dark."

Ross dealt the next hand. "We'll get a weather update. Maybe jump first thing in the morning." He picked cards for his crib. The cut would make or break his hand.

Palmer walked into the room, pulled out a chair and joined them at the table. Rupert stood, stretched and sniffed the air. "You guys ready to go? I've got an update for you."

Stevens and Ross put their cards on the table and focused on Palmer.

He brought his iPad to life and placed it on the table where they could all see it. A satellite map filled the screen. "There's a deer hunter in the woods who didn't come home. We know he hunts in this area," Palmer pointed at the screen. "It's in the direction we think Zoe's kidnapper's taking her based on where the hiker was found yesterday."

"That's a big area," Stevens said.

"This guy likes electronics and his wife wanted to know where he might be. We've got GPS coordinates of his three favorite hunting spots for his tree stands."

"That'll help," Stevens said.

"And Agent Scott gave you something to help you view trail cameras?"

"Yep," Ross said.

"Like I said," Palmer continued, "this guy likes electronics and has cameras around, so look on trees on deer trails and around his stand. Maybe you'll see a picture of Zoe or her kidnapper. So start with finding the hunter and see what you can learn. This will get you in the vicinity for now before the storm comes in. If we learn more, we'll let you know. The drone is still up, and people are looking for Zoe."

"We're going now?" Stevens asked. "Or early in the morning?"

"I'm afraid you have to go now. There's a storm front coming in. I know the darkness has some dangers, but for time's sake, you're going now. And I think tomorrow with the winds and rain or snow it would be even more dangerous then. We've identified a couple of spots we believe are open for you to land in tonight." Palmer pointed out two spots on the map. "Farm fields bordered by trees."

"Coordinates?" Stevens asked.

Palmer read them out from the satellite map image and Stevens put them into his wrist GPS.

"Go find Zoe, gentlemen. Let me know when you're safely on the ground."

IT WAS about a two-hour flight on the Twin Otter plane to the drop zone. The lights of Portland were visible to the south. It was a dark, moonless night to jump.

Ross and Stevens sat quietly, each getting ready for the jump and the mission in their own way. When they got closer to the drop zone the plane flew in blackout mode. The exterior wing lights went out, internal lights went out. The only visible light came from the cockpit instrument panel and a couple of red lights on either side of the door.

The jumpmaster opened the door. The wind buffeted around the edges, vibrating nylon straps and loose clothing causing the only sound besides the rumble of the engines. The jumpmaster stood off to the side following their path and altitude on the glow of his screen. He communicated with the pilots getting updates and verifications of jump time.

Ross spoke into the microphone around his neck, "Why do this if you're afraid of heights?"

"I told you, it's not the height. It's the potential hard landing."

Ross laughed. Stevens stood to Ross' right with Rupert, seventy-five pounds of muscle, hanging across his stomach, attached by a harness hanging from his shoulders and wrapped around his waist. Rupert's tongue hung out of the side of his mouth, visible through the leather muzzle strapped over his snout. Goggles covered his eyes to protect them from the wind.

Stevens stood a little farther back from the door than most jumpers did, and he had a death grip on a nylon strap hanging from the ceiling.

Ross went over the mission in his head, rehearsing their actions from the jump out the door to acquiring their landing spot, landing and what they would do after that. Stevens was the sniper, responsible for observations, shooting if needed. Ross was his spotter, recording Steven's observations, providing breaks and protection. Rupert was along for area protection and reconnaissance.

The jumpmaster signaled them; two minutes to jump. Ross and Stevens checked their own gear and rigging and then went over each other's, making sure all straps were where they belonged and all buckles were closed properly.

They turned and looked out into the blackness. Their target was somewhere below them. Ross would have preferred to jump when it was light out. They each lowered the night vision monocle over their right eye. Stevens checked the altitude and GPS on his wrist. He gave Ross a thumbs-up. Ross returned it. They each turned on infrared beacons hanging from their gear so they could see each other in the fall and on the ground after they landed.

A new light shone by the jumpmaster. He held up a finger. One minute. Rupert whined in anticipation.

They planned to jump from 11,000 feet so they wouldn't need supplemental oxygen. They would jump about a mile and a half from the targets to land in a field. Once out the door, it would be about thirty seconds of thrill and terror.

Stevens stepped to the door. Rupert whined and stared out, or was that Stevens whining? Ross stood behind them, in position to follow them to the ground. He said a short prayer, the same one he said before every jump, "God, please make it a safe jump and a safe landing," and then waited for the signal.

The jump light turned green, and the jumpmaster gave a thumbs-up to Ross. Ross tapped Stevens on the shoulder. Two quick steps and they were out the door. Ross followed.

CHAPTER ELEVEN

It was an eerie feeling. Ross knew he was falling, but there were few signals for his visual senses. The air resistance signaled he was falling through the air, pulling on his limbs. He felt the cold air on his cheeks and around the neck of his jumpsuit. He saw the plane continue on its regular path and disappear into the night. Stevens' beacon hovered below him, falling as fast as he did, so it felt like they were barely moving. He checked the altimeter on his wrist. He'd deploy his chute at 3,500 feet above the ground, Stevens and Rupert were going to deploy at 3,000 feet, giving them a little buffer from each other.

Ross checked on Stevens' beacon, its regular signal blinking in the night. He checked his wrist again, five seconds. He deployed his chute.

The sudden arrest of his fall signaled he'd been falling and that the chute had deployed correctly. He checked his steering for control and scanned the darkness for Stevens' beacon. Its speed changed, indicating that they were deployed and in a similar glide to the target.

The area around the landing spot was dark to both of

Ross' eyes. There was no visible light and he didn't spot any objects through the night vision monocle that didn't belong. Ross followed Stevens in towards the landing spot. Stevens would glide and land. Ross would land short of his beacon.

There was no real depth perception, no way to gauge the distance to the ground, other than the altimeter and Stevens' beacon. Ross bent his knees and drew his legs up towards his chest. About fifty feet short of the landing spot, he flared his chute into a stall and dropped to the ground. He absorbed the landing and shed his chute before dropping to one knee, automatic rifle at the ready, he surveyed the area behind him and to the sides. He knew Stevens would be doing the same ahead of him and that he'd release Rupert to survey a circle around them.

Ross spied Rupert out about fifty yards circling their position counterclockwise, nose to the ground capturing scents, looking for what didn't belong. Rupert doubled back and froze. He'd spotted something and quietly sat to observe. There was no bark of warning or a whine. Ross slowly lowered to a prone position on the grass and searched for what Rupert had sensed. He softly grunted into his throat mic to let Stevens know something was up. He steadied his breathing and tried not to listen to his heartbeat in his temples, focusing on the noises of the forest around them.

There was a rustle of leaves off to his right. He swung his rifle in that direction. An object moved. Rupert rose up to advance. A deer froze and then plunged away from them through the trees once it became aware of Rupert in its path.

"All clear," Ross said into his mic. He gathered up his chute and harness and met up with Stevens to stow their gear on the edge of the field and make plans for the next move of the night.

∼

ROSS COULD SEE STEVENS' outline in the dark. He spoke in a quiet voice, "You want to let Palmer know our status? I'll figure out where we're going."

Ross knelt in the leaves and pine needles and studied the topographic map for elevation changes. Based on their location and the first GPS target it looked like a circuitous route to avoid a pond and a large hill was their best bet. A straight line might be the shortest route, but it wasn't always the easiest or safest.

Stevens joined him. "Nothing new from Palmer."

"Think we're good with headlamps?" Ross asked.

"Sure," Stevens answered. "At least until we get closer to the hunter's location. The kidnapper is either there or farther north."

Ross turned on his headlamp illuminating the map. "The first spot to check is here," he stabbed the map with his gloved finger. "It's about a mile that way," he pointed through the woods with his arm. "But I think we should follow this creek bed and then cut off this way," he traced a route with his finger. "Something to follow in the dark, easier walking. I make it about three-quarters of a mile longer."

Stevens stood and stretched. "You good?"

Ross folded up the map and stuffed it in a front pocket of his vest. "I napped a little on the plane. I'm good." He pointed at the black bundle on the ground. "Think we need it?"

"Scott seemed to think so. Lots of water up north."

"Who's carrying it?" Ross asked. "Rock, paper, scissors?"

"I got Rupert," Stevens answered.

Ross groaned. "Okay, I'll start with it, but you'll get a turn." He picked up the bundle and Stevens helped him attach it to his pack. "You just want to slow me down if we see a bear."

"I'm not stupid," Stevens said.

They worked their way through the trees following the light of their headlamps towards the creek, a few hundred yards to the west.

THE WALKING WASN'T bad next to the creek. For portions of it there were well-traveled animal paths with just some rocks or fallen trees to watch out for as they walked. About thirty-five minutes in, Ross checked his GPS. Then he pulled out the map and scanned it. "This is a good point to cut in. We'll get to the first spot, check it out and move on if we need to. Rest, water and fuel when we're there."

"Sounds good," Stevens said.

They didn't make much noise as they walked through the trees. No chatter. Ross led the way. He heard Stevens following behind him. Rupert switched between following Stevens and exploring smells out to their sides. He was never far away.

Ross led them up an incline. They turned their headlamps off as they approached the peak. Ross stopped just before the top. "Spread out here. Send Rupert ahead to scout it out. We go down the other side of this and the tree stand should be about eight hundred yards out."

"Agreed," Stevens replied. Rupert sat to his left, ready for instructions. Stevens dropped his night-vision goggles down over his eyes and gave Rupert the search command, "Rupert, *reveiren*." He jabbed his arm out twice in the direction of the tree stand.

Rupert took off in the direction Stevens pointed. Stevens followed.

Ross put his night vision goggles over his eyes and followed Stevens, staying about ten feet to the side in case someone shot up the hill. He didn't want to get hit by a shot that missed Stevens. The trees glowed in the goggles.

At the bottom of the hill, Ross circled to the left before advancing towards the coordinates for the tree stand. He saw Stevens to his right weaving through the trees. Rupert would be sniffing and circling through the trees looking for someone that didn't belong there.

Ross heard Stevens click his throat in his earpiece. He dropped to a knee, pointed his assault rifle in the direction of the target and waited. He knew Stevens would move forward to connect with Rupert or assess the situation. He waited for Stevens to update him on what was going on.

"All clear," Ross heard Stevens announce. He rose from his position and walked forward to find Stevens and Rupert.

He found them about forty yards ahead. Stevens had Rupert stationed out to the north about twenty yards for security. Stevens stood by a pile on the forest floor. There was a body and some pieces of wood. "Our hunter?"

"He's dead," Stevens said. "He didn't fall out of his tree stand. It looks like he was in it and someone pulled the ladder out." Stevens pointed up.

In the green glow of the goggles, Ross saw a wooden platform hanging from the tree with two-by-four braces hanging in the air. "What killed him?"

Stevens pointed at the body. Ross could see the dark stain of blood on the shirt. "He was shot," Stevens said. "Don't see his gun anywhere. I'd guess our kidnapper got spotted by the hunter, took down the tree stand, got a hold of his rifle and shot him."

Ross turned his back to Stevens. "Get this kayak off me, would you?"

Stevens unclipped the pack and put it on the ground.

"Thanks," Ross said. "We should check for ID. Make sure it's him. Document it first?"

"We're probably good with headlamps for light. I'd guess the kidnapper is long gone with Zoe."

Ross and Stevens raised their night vision goggles onto the tops of their helmets and turned on their headlamps. The light allowed them to verify what they had seen in green before. Ross pulled out his cell phone and took some pictures.

When he was done, Stevens patted down the hunter and found a wallet. He searched it and found a driver's license. "It's him."

"Damn," Ross said.

Stevens held the license in the palm of his hand and Ross took a picture of it.

"I'll send these pictures and coordinates to Palmer," Ross said. "What should we do with him?"

"I guess we cover him with the lumber as much as we can. Keep any critters from getting at him tonight. Someone should be here tomorrow to get him."

"The cold weather tonight should help."

They put the hunter in a resting position on his back and covered him with pieces of wood and brush. When they were done, they both said a silent prayer.

CHAPTER TWELVE

Ross lit up a few of the trees around them with his headlamp. "This guy's supposed to have some trail cameras out here. Let's see if we can find any."

Stevens turned away and lit up the forest in the direction the hunter had faced in his tree stand. "I'll head out that way and see if there's anything out there."

"I'm going back and see if I can find a game trail he might have put a camera on," Ross said. The dead hunter was a pretty big clue that the kidnapper came by here, but pictures on a camera would really solidify it. Ross reached a narrow bare trail running through the trees. He headed left, back the direction he and Stevens had come from first. At each tree along the trail, Ross scanned his light up and down looking for a camera. He didn't think a camera would be too far down the trail.

After about twenty trees he was ready to turn around and go back up the trail the other direction. Three more he told himself. The first was empty. He quickly scanned the second and took a step to move on, but then scanned it again. There it was. A camouflaged box strapped to the tree at about chest height. He tried to figure out how to undo the straps. He decided it would be quicker just to cut them. He unsheathed his knife and sliced through the two straps. "Bingo. I found one," he said over the radio to Stevens.

"Great," Stevens responded. "Nothing here yet. I'm going to keep looking for a while."

"I'm going to head the other way on this game trail and see if there's another one." Ross backtracked on the trail and then started scanning trees when he got to his starting point. He knew what he was looking for now. He lit each tree up and down as he walked by. On the seventh tree, he spied another camera.

"Hey, I got another one," Ross said. He cut this camera's straps. "I'll meet you back at the tree stand."

"See you there."

Ross carried the two cameras. He hoped one of them held an image of Zoe. As he walked through the trees, they all looked the same to him, but he could see Stevens' headlamp up ahead and walked towards it.

They rendezvoused back at the tree stand. Ross sat on the kayak pack and put the two cameras on the ground. "You have the adapters handy to connect to these?"

"Yep." Stevens put his pack on the ground and rummaged through a pocket to find the equipment. "You know what you're doing?"

Ross reached for the cords, "I can do it." He connected the first camera to his cell phone. Files transferred and he was ready to look at the photos. "This is the first camera I found. It was south on the game trail."

Stevens stood behind him to get a view of the pictures on the phone.

"There should be a shot every time the camera sensed movement and each picture should have a timestamp," Ross said.

"Let's see what we got."

Ross started with the most recent, it was him approaching the tree.

"Nice selfie."

He scrolled back to the next shot. A shot of a doe appeared on the screen. "This was earlier tonight before we got here."

Stevens said, "With the timestamps, we should be able to go back to when Zoe and the kidnapper should've walked through. Sometime this morning or yesterday? Depending on how fast they were traveling."

Ross kept scrolling back. "I'm wondering if we'll see a bear."

"Shut up," Stevens said and pushed him in the back.

"Not a lot of photos on here. Must be a quiet hunting season. There're no people pictures."

"Except yours," Stevens said.

Ross disconnected the camera and hooked up the other one. "This one was farther north on the trail. It was pointed the other direction so there shouldn't be a picture of me."

The first photo was a doe. "The deer we saw on the other camera just strolling down the trail," Stevens said.

Ross pulled up the next photo. "Hey, look." On the screen, there were two people. Closest to the camera was a shorter person in a coat, carrying a backpack. "Is that Zoe?"

"I think so," said Stevens.

Ahead of Zoe walking up the trail was a taller person with a backpack and the barrel of a rifle sticking up in the air. "And she's following the kidnapper up the trail. Looks like he's got a rifle."

"Probably the hunter's."

.   .   .

ROSS SENT Palmer the videos and a message with where they found it and the direction Zoe was heading. He thought it would give Palmer and the Border Patrol some info on where to focus the drone search. "Based on the timestamp they came by here a few hours ago."

"You ready to go after them? Or should we take a break?" Stevens asked.

"Let's go." Ross stowed the satellite phone and trail cameras in his pack. "You got the kayak?"

"I'll take it for a while." Stevens turned around. "Hook me up."

Ross lifted the kayak bundle and connected it to Stevens' pack. Stevens headed towards the game trail. "Come on. Let's go." Ross followed. Rupert trotted through the woods alongside them.

When they reached the game trail, Stevens stopped, facing the direction Zoe and the kidnapper had gone. "You ready to go?" Stevens asked Ross. "We're going to have to move quick."

"Ready."

"Rupert, *plaats*," Stevens commanded. Rupert sat to Stevens' left. He stared at Stevens ready for his next order. Ready to go to work. Stevens reached into a pocket on his vest and pulled out a plastic bag. He held the open bag in front of Rupert's snout.

"He got a good whiff of Zoe's scarf? Think he'll be able to track her?"

"I think so," Stevens said. "The trail's been dry. Not a lot of traffic besides the deer." Rupert whined, waiting for the next command. "Rupert, *zoeken*," Stevens said and pointed up the trail.

Rupert bounded ahead, nose to the ground.

CHAPTER THIRTEEN

Ross and Stevens jogged after Rupert on the game trail. He stopped a couple of times, circled and sniffed the ground, turned back to Stevens and then bounded ahead. After a half-hour, Ross felt the sweat dripping down his back. He'd pulled the gloves off his hands earlier to try and cool off. "How long can he keep this up?" Ross asked.

"He'll keep going until he finds something, loses the scent or I call him off."

"I suggest we take a break soon. Check where we're at. Check in with Palmer."

"Heard you," Stevens said and continued jogging after Rupert on the trail.

Ross imagined Zoe walking on this trail after the kidnapper. She must be afraid, not knowing what's going on, worried for her family, wondering if anybody is looking for her. The kidnapper had proved he was violent, capable of hurting people. Had he hurt Zoe?

The light from his headlamp bounced around lighting up the trail, the trees, Stevens' back. "Rock," Stevens called out.

Ross aimed his light down at the trail, spotted a large rock in the trail and stepped over it.

"Stopping," Stevens said.

Ross almost ran into him. "What's up?"

"He lost the scent on the trail." Rupert came back towards them on the trail, nose down. He started circling looking for the scent. "Rupert, *kom heir.*" Rupert stood in front of Stevens, panting, tongue out to the side. "Rupert, *af.*" The dog lay down as commanded and waited for Stevens to tell him what to do next.

"Check in with Palmer. I'll give Rupert some water and then we'll see if we can find the scent again. It's not like Zoe flew from here. I just think they veered off the trail." Stevens set his pack with the kayak attached on the ground, bent down, cupped a hand and poured some water for Rupert to drink from it.

Ross put his pack on the ground and pulled out his cell phone. He powered it up. The screen lit up after twenty seconds. "No bars for cell phone."

"You had to check? Expecting a call? A woman calling you back?"

"No." Ross pulled the satellite phone out and called Palmer. "Checking in, boss."

"Where you at?" Palmer asked.

Ross read off the GPS coordinates for Palmer.

"You've made some progress."

"Rupert's on a scent. We've been running after him for a while. Looks like we're going to go off the game trail now into the forest. The scent seems to be strong. No other signs of Zoe or the kidnapper."

Palmer responded, "The drone's identified three locations with heat signatures, hot chimneys. We'll try and see what we see in the daylight, but the weather front with heavy snows is supposed to roll in around sunrise now."

"What time is that?" Ross asked.

"It should lighten up around six-thirty, sunrise at seven-thirty-six."

"What are the GPS coordinates for the hot-spots?"

Ross wrote them down while Palmer read them out. "Based on where you're at and how fast you've moved, you should be able to reach at least one of the hotspots by sunrise."

"Okay, boss. We'll check in with you then. We better get moving," Ross said.

"Out," was all Palmer said and the call ended.

"I say we follow Rupert as long as he stays on Zoe's scent," Stevens said.

"Agreed. I'm betting he leads us to one of the hotspots Palmer gave us," Ross said.

Stevens reached for his pack.

"I'll take the kayak now," Ross said.

"No arguments here." Stevens disconnected it from his own pack and hooked it to Ross'. He put on his own pack and called Rupert over to give him another whiff of Zoe's scarf. "Rupert, *zoeken*." Stevens pointed towards the north.

Rupert started searching for the scent. With nose down, he circled the trees. He passed once, twice over a spot and then took off through the trees.

"Let's go," Stevens said.

Hiking was harder off the game trail. They wove through the trees, around large boulders. If they could get to the spot Zoe was being held by sunrise they'd have time to set up an observation post and see what was going on, who they were up against, if Zoe appeared to be in immediate trouble or not.

"HEY, WAIT A MINUTE," Ross called out to Stevens. Ross stopped and studied his GPS. He pulled the top map out of his pocket.

"Rupert, *kom hier*," Stevens commanded and walked back to join Ross. "What's up?" Rupert ran back to them and walked around them in circles.

"The first GPS mark is that way," Ross pointed into the forest, "about a half-mile."

"He ran right by it," Stevens said, nodding his head at Rupert. "He's still hot on a scent to the north. How far to the next spot?"

"About three miles. A camp on an island."

"I say we keep going as long as Rupert's on the scent. We'll see if he leads us there or beyond. We can come back."

"Agreed," Ross said. "Just thought we should talk it through."

"At the pace we're going, we'll beat sunrise," Stevens said. He knelt and gave Rupert some water.

Ross used the break to drink water too. "Ready when you two are."

"Rupert, *zoek*," Stevens commanded. Rupert took off through the woods on the path he had been on before. "You going to keep up?" Stevens asked before he took off at a trot after Rupert.

SNOW STARTED TO FALL, and the wind blew harder from the north. They jogged up a hill and stopped before the peak as they did before. "Rupert, *kom hier*," Stevens said in a loud whisper. Rupert stopped, turned around and ran back to Stevens. "*Braaf.*"

Ross and Stevens pointed their headlamps towards the ground. Ross checked GPS coordinates and pulled out the topo map, holding it in the glow of the lamp. "The next spot is on the other side of this hill. It drops down to the water and then there's an island. They may be there."

"That kayak you've been hauling through the wood may come in handy," Stevens said. He walked around Ross and unhooked the bundle from Ross' pack. "We'll leave it here for now until we see if this is the spot. Assuming it is, we can get an observation nest set up."

"Let's see what we've got," Ross said.

They turned off their headlamps and moved the night vision goggles into position.

"Gotta keep Rupert close now," Stevens said. He attached a ten-foot lead to Rupert's vest and commanded him to track. "Rupert, *zoek*"

"I'll follow further behind," Ross said.

Rupert, nose to the ground, led Stevens up the hill, pulling the lead tight as Stevens worked to keep his movements slow.

They disappeared from Ross' view as they went down the other side. Ross followed them down a few steps and then went to a knee to keep from sticking out at the peak and to observe and back up his partners. He knew Stevens would be focused on Rupert, so he scanned the hill and the water. There were no visible lights in the darkness.

After a couple of minutes, Stevens and Rupert came back up the hill. Ross signaled Stevens and they joined him at his position. "Rupert lost the scent at the water," Stevens said. "I'm guessing they used a boat or canoe to get over to the island. Whatever, it looks like we're at the right spot."

Smoke wafted out of the cabin chimney and there were traces of light from the windows. Ross checked his watch. "We have about three hours until it starts to get light. Let's get set up before anybody's awake and check in with Palmer."

~

"IT'S SNOWING," Ross said. Big flakes blew through the air, swirling around them.

"We need to hurry and get set up," Stevens said. "The snow will help hide us, but it could also give us away if we leave tracks in fresh snow. It'll be more work to get close." He walked along the top of the hill. "If we set up along here, we're high enough that anyone on the island won't see our tracks and we'll have a good line of sight to them." He shrugged his pack off and set it on the ground. "Get a bunch of big branches. We'll build a mound, cover it with our ghillie suits and if the snow keeps coming down we'll just be a snowbank to anybody looking up here." He pointed along the ground. "We'll enter and exit back here at the top of the hill, run the nest down the hill a little ways and we'll watch them out the front."

The snow was really coming down. Ross couldn't see the cabin across the water, so he knew if there was anybody in the cabin, they couldn't see them up here either.

CHAPTER FOURTEEN

Zoe opened her eyes. She could see the ceiling; wooden beams with painted boards running between them. A spider web glistened in the sunlight in one corner. Where was she? She heard voices.

Oh yeah, now she remembered.

The past two days had been exhausting following Jerry through the woods, not sure of why he took her or what he was going to do to her or with her. Jerry had killed two men, but he hadn't hurt her since he grabbed her at the rest area.

The voices she heard had to be Barb and Jerry talking down in the kitchen. She couldn't tell what they were saying, but she knew the sound of their voices. The smell of bacon and coffee filled the air. Somebody had taken her coat and boots off last night and covered her with a heavy quilt. Her tummy rumbled.

Zoe couldn't stay in the loft forever. She had to go to the bathroom and she was hungry. She threw back the quilt. The chilly air made her shiver. It wasn't cold, but it wasn't as warm as she'd been under the quilt. She climbed out of the bed.

The wood floor was cold on her feet. She pulled on her boots and looked for her coat.

"Hey, Zoe. Are you up?" Barb called up from below.

Zoe walked over to the loft railing. Barb smiled up at her. She and Jerry sat at a wood table eating breakfast. Buck looked up at her and barked a quiet hello. "Do you know where my coat is?" Zoe asked.

"I hung it by the door," Barb answered. "Come on down and have some breakfast. You can sit by the stove and stay warm.

Zoe worked her way down the ladder, the right foot on a rung, her hands gripping the smooth sides of the ladder. She put her left on the next rung down. At the bottom, she stood and faced Jerry and Barb. Light from the windows gave her a better look at the cabin. It wasn't a lot of space, but it looked comfortable; the small kitchen, a table, a couple of chairs and a small sofa. A black, wood-burning stove sat in the corner. She could feel the heat flowing into the room. Buck came over and sniffed her hand. "Hey, buddy," Zoe said. She scratched him behind the neck and along his back. His coat was soft and thick. His eyes were ice blue. They almost glowed in the light.

"He likes you," Barb said. "He's a husky. This is his favorite time of year. With that thick coat, he could live outside. Ready to eat?"

Zoe shifted her weight from foot to foot. "I really have to go to the bathroom." She smiled at Barb. Jerry watched her without saying a word. He just slowly ate his breakfast.

"Oh, right. I'm sure you do." Barb pushed her chair back from the table. It screeched across the floorboards. "Come over here." She led Zoe to the door and grabbed her coat off a wooden peg sticking out of the wall. She held it out for Zoe. "Put your arms in." After Zoe had her arms in, Barb knelt in front of her to zip it closed.

She smiled at Zoe. "You'll be surprised what it looks like outside this morning. You two made it back just in time last night. I bet we got two feet of snow."

"Really?"

"Yes. It's a winter wonderland out there this morning. Enjoy it while you're out there. It's beautiful." Barb said. "You have your hat and gloves?"

Zoe pulled them out of her coat pockets. Buck sat next to her on the floor at attention.

"Put them on. The sun's shining and it looks nice, but it still feels cold. The wind let up since last night, so that's good." Barb pulled Zoe's hat down over her ears. "Buck will go out with you. He loves the snow. Just follow the path to the outhouse. We both walked out there this morning," she nodded at Jerry, "so the snow should be pretty knocked down for you."

Barb opened the door and Buck launched himself out and into the snow. Zoe followed him onto the deck. "Hurry up. Breakfast is still warm," Barb said as she closed the door.

Zoe puffed out a frozen cloud of breath and squinted, the sun reflecting off of the field of white in front of her made it almost impossible to see. It was beautiful. A white fluff covered the ground only marred by the path to the outhouse and where Buck had run, rolled or dived in the snow. Trees by the water were draped in snow and it covered the trees and the hill across the water.

Her bladder reminded her why she came outside. She saw the path through the snow to a small building and followed it. Though the snow was packed from Barb and Jerry walking out here, it was still soft. Buck ran by, bounding through the white powder, diving snout first into the drift and then plowing a path through the snow. Zoe smiled. He showed pure joy in the cold and snow.

At the outhouse, Zoe pulled the door open. The inside

was similar to the one at the other camp she and Jerry had stopped at. This one had a regular toilet seat to sit on other than the bare wood. She lifted the lid, dropped her pants and sat down. She sucked in a breath when her bare skin touched the cold seat.

When she exhaled, a cloud of her breath floated around her head. She couldn't sit here all day, but this was the only privacy she had. She knew her family was searching for her, but she'd be hard to find. She left the tag in the other outhouse, but who knew when or if anybody would ever see it. She tried to leave her hat until the deer hunter saw her drop it and look what happened to him.

A tear ran down her cheek and into the corner of her mouth. She had to stay safe and look for other opportunities to escape or leave clues until she was found. Barb seemed nice. Buck liked her. Jerry's the one she's afraid of.

CHAPTER FIFTEEN

They'd done a good job building the nest. To a casual observer, they'd just be a snowdrift. It was actually kind of warm, like an igloo, with the heat from their two bodies and Rupert's. They'd slept for an hour or so, confident that nobody else was around and if a bear or cougar came around, Rupert would alert them.

Ross took his turn observing the camp through the scope on the sniper rifle. The postcard setting was easy to watch; the cabin in the snow, surrounded by trees, frosty windows, smoke wafting up from the chimney. They had to be warm, rested, probably had a hot breakfast.

Earlier, Stevens had seen a man come out of the cabin and walk through the snow to the outhouse. He was average size, wore an oily Carhartt jacket and faded jeans. The red and black trapper hat with the earflaps down covered most of his head. The only identifying thing was his brown beard.

He returned to the cabin and a female made the same walk. She wore a blue air force parka, the hood up, the fur around the edge covering her face. All they could tell was she appeared to be twenty to thirty by her size, narrow hips, skinny, tight jeans. She moved easily through the snow, making the path wider.

She'd returned to the cabin and they waited. That's what they did; wait, observe, gather intel, get the info back to Palmer.

"Agent Scott didn't give us snowshoes," Ross said.

"He couldn't think of everything," Stevens responded. "And I don't think we wanted to carry any more equipment."

"Probably not."

"You even know how to snowshoe?"

"No," Ross said. "Not a lot of time in locations with a lot of snow.

"Thought you were in Minnesota before your HRT assignment."

"I was in the Minneapolis office from spring until fall."

"Oh, that's right," Stevens said. "You were lucky to get out when you did."

"Right, look at me now," Ross said. "So lucky."

They waited.

"Think the bears come out in this?"

"Oh sure," Ross said. "They have to fatten up before they hibernate. And they like to find caves and nooks to hibernate in. Like this nest."

Stevens flipped the bear spray from hand to hand. "I'm ready for Smokey if he wants our nest."

"Just be careful with that. It goes off in here and we're in serious hurt."

Ross spied some movement through the scope. "Got something," he said. The door to the cabin opened. "I think it's the female you saw earlier. No coat. Twenty-something. Blonde hair pulled back in a pony-tail."

Ross blinked and adjusted the focus on the scope. A dog bolted out of the cabin and dove into the snow. He followed it with his scope. "A dog. A big husky."

"Shoot," Stevens said. "A dog's better than a security system. We need to stay away and downwind."

Ross swung the scope back to the door of the cabin. "There's a girl coming out. Shorter than the woman. Maybe five feet tall. Hard to tell. Based on her coat, boots, hat, size, I think it's Zoe."

"Time to check in with Palmer," Stevens said.

Ross watched Zoe walk through the snow. The dog ran around her and dove into the snow. "She must've just woken up. She's heading to the outhouse. Walking okay. Doesn't appear to be hurt."

The satellite phone was on speaker, the volume down. The call went through. Ross and Stevens had used the phone enough to know how it worked, the delay from speaking to receiving. The signal traveling from their unit to the satellite 400 miles up, and back down to Palmer. They had to speak slowly and clearly and wait. A response would come and they'd repeat the process. Take turns, no interrupting.

"Palmer here. Status?"

Stevens spoke, "Subject acquired at point beta. Appears to be okay. Two other individuals: a male and a female, both adults and a dog."

"You're on your own for a while. With the storm last night, the team is delayed getting through. Roads are blocked. Maybe tonight or tomorrow before they get there."

"Roger that. We'll continue to observe from our outpost. South of camp, on top of the hill. Water between us and them."

"If status changes, take care of the girl. We don't have any identification on the kidnapper yet, assume it's the male."

"We only saw tracks for two people."

"Adult female's a question. Observe and see what you can figure out. Partner with male or another victim?"

"Roger," Stevens said. "Observe and report. The girl is the priority. Weather report?"

"It's a bluebird day today. Clear night tonight. Maybe some clouds and flurries tomorrow."

"Thanks, boss. Out." Stevens ended the call.

Ross continued his observations through the scope. "Zoe's walking back to the cabin." She stopped and pet the dog and threw a chunk of snow. The dog chased it and dove nose first into the fluffy snow. "Husky seems friendly, at least to Zoe."

"Good to know," Stevens said. "Maybe it'll listen to her if we need it to."

"She's back inside." Ross took his eye from the scope and watched the scene below without enhancement. "She seems okay. Interesting thought that Palmer brought up. That the other female might be a victim."

"Hard to get off the island," Stevens said. "She might be stuck there. Or maybe there's a relationship. We'll keep watching and see what we can figure out."

CHAPTER SIXTEEN

The glare hurt her eyes when Zoe stepped out of the outhouse. She closed them and then squinted to see where she was going. It was better through the slits of her eyelids. Buck ran up to her through the snow and danced around her, whining with excitement. Zoe dropped to her knees and Buck sniffed her neck and licked her face. "Hey, buddy. You waited for me." She ran her hands through his thick fur and scratched him behind the ears.

Her eyes adjusted to the bright sunlight. It was time for some breakfast. Barb said it was still warm. After breakfast maybe she could figure out what's going on. Maybe Barb could tell her something.

Zoe trudged through the snow-packed path back to the cabin with Buck jogging along behind her. Barb opened the door for her when she stepped onto the deck. "Come on in, Zoe. You ready to eat now?"

"Yes, please," was all she said.

Barb took her coat and hung it on the peg. She grabbed Zoe's hand and led her to the table. "Sit down and eat. You have to be starving." In front of her was a bowl of oatmeal and a plate with toast and bacon on it. Next to the oatmeal were some smaller bowls with some chocolate chips, brown sugar, and dried berries or something in them. "I didn't know how you liked your oatmeal so there are some things you can add to it. There's a pitcher of maple syrup too. And I assumed you liked bacon." Barb tossed a piece to Buck. "He likes it."

Jerry sat in a chair by the wood-burning stove. He seemed to be focused on the rifle he'd taken from the deer hunter yesterday.

"This looks good," Zoe mumbled. She ate a piece of bacon and took a bite of toast. She wasn't a big fan of oatmeal but figured she needed to eat it if she didn't want to go hungry. She added a little of each of the things in the bowls to the top of her oatmeal and then stirred them into the mush. "Can I have something to drink?" she asked.

"Oh sure," Barb answered. "We just have water." She poured Zoe a cup of water. Then she sat down across the table from Zoe. She drank out of a ceramic mug. "Or you could have some tea if you like it. It's good with honey."

Zoe smiled and ate. The bacon tasted great and the oatmeal loaded with the extras wasn't too bad. She wondered what her family was doing, what they were having for breakfast. Probably grandma's pancakes. They had to be going crazy not knowing where she was. Not knowing if she was safe.

"I'm going outside to chop some wood while it's still nice outside," Jerry said. He grabbed the rifle and walked to the door where he threw on a light wool coat, his bomber hat and grabbed his leather chopper mittens. "Let's go, Buck."

Cold air from the door enveloped Zoe when Jerry opened the door. Buck ran outside and Jerry followed him out.

Zoe relaxed a little now that Jerry was gone.

"You want to try some tea?" Barb asked. "It's nice to have something warm to drink."

"Okay," Zoe said. "I don't think I've ever had tea."

Barb walked into the kitchen. "Come here. I'll show you what we're going to do."

The kitchen was just an extension of the room, but it was its own little area with a sink, a stove, a small refrigerator, and some cupboards. Zoe joined Barb at the counter next to the sink. On the counter were a couple of mugs and a glass container with some purplish leaves in it.

"Let me show you," Barb said. "We fill the teapot with some water and put it on the wood-burning stove to heat up, as long as we have a fire going." She filled the silver teapot with water and handed it to Zoe. "Go put this on the stove. It'll whistle when it's done."

When Zoe returned to the counter, Barb continued, "Now we put some tea leaves in these silver things, they're tea infusers, and put them in the mugs." She did that. "When the water's hot, we pour it in the mugs and let it sit for a few minutes, take out the infusers and we sip our tea. This is a berry mixture of tea, non-caffeinated. I think you'll like it."

Barb seemed nice, showing Zoe how to make the tea. She wanted to ask her some questions.

"Now, we need to do some things around here while the water boils and after," Barb said. "Jerry's out chopping wood for the fire. We all have to do our part. We'll clean up the table and do the breakfast dishes." She handed Zoe a silver pail. "Take this out and fill it with clean snow, where it's new and fresh, and we'll melt it on the stove to use to wash the dishes."

Zoe put her coat on and went outside with the pail. It was still bright out, but the light was different now. The sun was higher in the sky. It moved over the hill across the water. There was a pounding sound from around the back of the cabin. Zoe trudged through the snow to investigate and saw Jerry swinging an axe, chopping logs into smaller pieces. His head was bare and his coat was open. Steam floated around his body. He swung the axe and split another log, the pieces falling to either side of the large stump he used to hold the logs. He didn't see Zoe. He was focused on his work.

She stepped back around the corner of the cabin out of Jerry's view and walked back out in front. A large white field of snow spread out between the cabin and the water. It was a perfect blanket, except where Buck had run through it. Zoe spied him trotting through the snow along the shore sniffing the ground around the trees. She walked out into the snow with her pail and plunged it into the snow, filling it to the brim.

Buck plowed through the snow and danced around her. "Buck, I think you like me." He rolled in the snow and lay on his back. Zoe pet his stomach with her mittened hands. "I bet you never get cold. We're in our own wilderness out here, aren't we?" Zoe stood and lifted the pail. It was heavier full of snow. She used two hands and trudged back to the cabin, completing her first job of the day.

Barb had the teapot and poured water into their mugs. "Put the pail on the stove. When it's melted we'll do dishes. Until then, let's enjoy our tea." She carried the mugs to the table and put them down across from each other. "Come sit with me."

Zoe sat down and put her hands around the mug to warm them. The tea smelled sweet and flowery. Barb blew on her tea and Zoe copied her.

"Let's get to know each other," Barb said. "I'm sure you have lots of questions."

Where to start? Zoe had so many questions. "Are you and Jerry married?"

Barb smiled and shook her head. "No, we're not married."

"How did you get here?"

"I came out here with Jerry at the end of the summer, like you."

"You were kidnapped, thrown into a van?"

"Oh, no," Barb said. "I came out here for an adventure. To live off the grid."

"Off the grid?"

"Out here we're disconnected from the world. No phones, no internet. We use solar power and batteries for the electricity we need for the water pump, the fridge, the stove when we use it, some lights. It's a simpler life. Less stressful."

It was peaceful out here. And maybe if you came here by choice it would be okay, but Jerry had kidnapped her. He'd tricked her and thrown her in the van and taken her from her family. "I don't like Jerry," Zoe said.

"He'll grow on you. He's a nice guy."

"He can be nice," Zoe said. "But, he kidnapped me and hurt two men on the way out here. He's mean."

"He didn't hurt you, right?" Barb asked.

"Not after he grabbed me."

"He had to hurt those men to protect you."

"Protect me?"

"Jerry only has your best interests in mind. He wants you to be happy. Be out of the stressful world," Barb said. She reached across the table and lifted the infuser out of Zoe's mug by its chain. "Blow on it again and try it. I think you'll like it."

Zoe bent over the table and blew on her mug. She inhaled the aromas again. "It smells good."

"It tastes good too." Barb sipped her own tea and Zoe copied her.

"It is good," Zoe said.

"If you need to, you can add a little honey to it. Make it a little sweeter."

Zoe shook her head.

"Any other questions?" Barb asked.

Zoe sipped her tea again. The tastes played around on her tongue. "How old are you?"

"I'm twenty-six."

"Can you leave if you want to?"

Barb studied Zoe over her mug while she took a drink. She placed her mug on the table. "If I wanted to I could. But, it wouldn't be easy. We're on an island a long way from civilization. You know the hike. Jerry hikes into town every week or so to get supplies." Barb reached across the table and grasped Zoe's hand. "Together we can survive out here. Live a life that's simpler. I'm glad you're here."

Zoe liked Barb's touch but wasn't sure what she was saying. It sounded like they were never leaving.

"Finish your tea and we'll do the dishes," Barb said.

CHAPTER SEVENTEEN

"I'm going to go take a leak and then we can plan the day." Ross backed out the end of the nest and crawled on his hands and knees through the snow until he was sure he was far enough from the peak that he wouldn't be seen when he stood up. He stretched and found a tree to relieve himself on. He twisted and bent over to touch his toes and did a few jumping jacks to loosen up the muscles after being cramped in the nest all night. He grabbed a handful of snow and put it in his mouth and let it melt. Then he scrubbed some on his face to really wake up.

Ross crawled back into the nest, squeezing by Rupert, who wouldn't move, and took up a position beside Stevens.

"The girl went back in the cabin," Stevens said.

"You know, we're not really sure what's around here and what's on the other side of the island except what we've seen from the satellite photos. I think one of us should do some recon so we know the surroundings better and what they might have on the other side of the island. The other stays here on observation and then we regroup and make a plan."

"Sounds good to me," Stevens said. "Rupert and I can go do recon."

"I thought we'd throw for it," Ross said.

"Sure." Stevens rolled onto his side to free up an arm.

They each made a fist and Ross count it out and pumped his arm up and down, one, two three, show. "Damn it, I never win." Ross held out his right hand with two fingers for scissors. Stevens had a fist for rock. "Give me the rifle. I'll observe."

"Winner's choice, right?" Stevens said.

"You want to observe?"

Stevens laughed. He handed the rifle to Ross. "Rupert and I will go exploring. It'll feel good to stretch the legs." He backed himself out towards the end of the nest.

"Regular radio check-ins," Ross said.

"Roger that," Stevens answered.

ROSS WONDERED what this whole situation was.

A guy kidnaps a twelve-year-old girl, marches her through the woods, kills two people and brings her to this remote camp. And now they find a woman and a dog here. The setting is good to keep the girl in place. An island surrounded by cold water. She wasn't going to swim across it, but in a month, it would probably freeze and then she could run for it. There had to be a boat down there. The guy got the girl across the water somehow.

If they kept watching, maybe they'd figure it out. Or Palmer might come up with some more info. Ross settled in to watch the camp.

The cabin door opened and the male came out. The dog came out after him.

Ross acquired the guy in the scope and followed him, the crosshairs on his body. Wearing less clothes, Ross was able to pick out some more distinguishing features: hair color, length, approximate height, and body type. He had a beard, shaggy brown hair, not a huge guy, but kind of wiry. He had a rifle hanging from a strap over his shoulder.

The guy walked around the end of the cabin to a pile of wood. He set a piece of wood on a stump and swung an axe over his head and into the wood to split it. The log split and two halves fell from the stump. The sound of the axe hitting the wood reached Ross a second or so later. The man repeated the process and the sound of another log being split traveled over the water and up the hill to Ross.

Ross radioed Stevens. "The guys outside chopping wood around the side of the cabin. Dog's out too. The man has a rifle."

"Roger," Stevens answered. "We're heading around the west side of the island. Everything's quiet."

"Be careful."

The sound of wood chopping told Ross what the guy was doing. He studied the rest of the camp with and without the scope trying to put together options for getting to the cabin and saving Zoe. A bright light got his attention. The sun reflected off the cabin door window as somebody opened it. Zoe came out of the cabin carrying a pail. The dog came out with her and ran into the loose snow.

Ross studied Zoe through the scope. She appeared okay, focused. She carried the pail out into the snowfield and filled it. The dog bounded over to her and she pet him. She smiled. *At least she has something to smile about.* She picked up the pail and struggled to carry it back to the cabin.

Another update to Stevens. "Zoe came outside. Appears to be okay."

"Roger," Stevens replied. "Back in an hour or so. We'll be checking in."

Ross returned to observing the camp and thinking through options for rescuing Zoe.

CHAPTER EIGHTEEN

Zoe put the last of the dishes away where Barb directed her to put them. "Nice job, Zoe. You're learning your way around the kitchen." Barb pulled out a chair by the table. "Come sit here."

Not sure what was going on, Zoe did as she was told. She sat in the chair and Barb handed her a book.

"Jerry said you'd like this."

It was *The Call of the Wild*. "We talked about it. Buck's named after the dog in this book."

"Why don't you read it while I take a look at your hair. Jerry thinks we should cut it a little shorter."

"What?" Zoe put a hand up to her head.

Barb gently pushed her hand down. "Out here it will be easier to take care of if it's a little shorter."

"But your hair's long," Zoe said. She looked at Barb's blonde hair pulled back into a ponytail.

"Jerry likes me with my hair longer. But, it's harder to take care of." Barb put a towel over Zoe's shoulders and started to brush her hair. "We'll just get these snarls out from your hike and sleeping on it the last couple of days and trim it up a little."

Zoe gave in. If it would keep Jerry happy, she'd let Barb cut her hair. She opened the book and concentrated on the story while Barb brushed her hair. It felt good and reminded her of times with her mom on Sunday nights when she'd brush her hair to get her ready to go to school Monday morning. They talked during these sessions about school, family and her friends.

In *The Call of the Wild*, Buck didn't know about the trouble brewing for him. Zoe felt like Buck, taken from a safe, comfortable life he knew, to a dangerous one he didn't. Tears ran down her cheeks. A couple dripped from her chin onto the pages of the book. Poor Buck.

The sound of the scissors cutting her hair brought her out of the story. She sniffed back the tears and rubbed them from her cheeks.

"Are you okay, Zoe? It'll be fine. I think you'll like the haircut," Barb said.

Zoe sniffed again. "It's fine. The story's making me sad."

Barb cut another length of Zoe's hair. "I've never read it. Maybe you can tell me about it tonight."

"Sure," Zoe said. She went back to reading the book and ignored Barb pulling on her hair and cutting it. She decided she was going to be strong like Buck. She'd take on the problems that came her way and stay safe until her parents or the police found her or until she found a way off the island.

"I think I'm done," Barb said. She pulled the towel off Zoe and handed her a mirror. "Take this, see what you think."

Zoe studied her reflection in the mirror. She looked like a younger version of herself, back a few years ago when she had shorter hair. She turned her head and studied the haircut. "Thanks," she said to Barb. "It looks good." Her head felt lighter and she felt the cool air on her neck now that it wasn't covered with hair. "Can I go outside and explore while it's sunny and nice out?" She stood and handed Barb the mirror.

"Sure," Barb said. "Don't stay out too long. We'll have lunch soon. Be careful out there, especially around the water. It's cold and deep. And no screaming or yelling."

Zoe grabbed her coat and went out the door. A day like this would've been a great one to go sledding with Karen and her family. There was a hill just a few blocks from Grandma and Grandpa's house. The island was pretty flat, but maybe Jerry and Barb would take her across the water in the boat to the hills surrounding them.

Rounding the corner of the cabin she saw Jerry. He had quite a pile of wood on the ground now from all of the chopping he'd been doing. He looked up and spied her. "Nice haircut," he said. "Barb has some pretty good skills. You like it?"

Zoe weakly smiled and nodded her head.

"Can you help me stack this wood?" Jerry asked.

"Barb said I could go exploring around the island for a little bit before lunch."

"That's probably a good idea." Jerry swung the axe and planted it in the stump. "When you come back, I'll have some loaded in this box." He pointed to a wooden box with a rope attached to it. "Haul it over to the deck when you come back for lunch and we'll get it inside and put it by the stove." He turned his head and scanned around the area in the distance. "You should take Buck with you. Where is that dog?"

Zoe joined Jerry in looking around them for a sign of Buck.

"Can you whistle?" Jerry asked. "That's how I usually try to call him. Not a real loud whistle, just a short, quieter whistle. If he's around, he'll hear it and come running."

Zoe puckered her lips and whistled out three short tweets.

"That's pretty good. You work on that with him while you're out. Whistle and call his name and he'll figure out they mean the same thing." Jerry whistled a long tone followed by two short ones. A couple of seconds later Buck came blasting through the snow from the bushes behind the cabin.

Zoe called Buck over and gave him a hug around his thick furry neck. "Does he ever get cold?" she asked.

"I don't think so," Jerry said. "He's built for this weather. What we need is a sled for him to pull."

"He'd like that," Zoe said.

Jerry picked up a couple of pieces of the split wood and stacked them next to the other logs. "You two go out. Just not too long. I'll be ready for lunch soon after all of this chopping."

Zoe took a couple of steps to the north. "Come on, Buck," she said. The dog barked and ran past her. She let Buck lead the way, his nose taking them on a path towards the shore on the east side of the island.

CHAPTER NINETEEN

oss watched Zoe through the scope as she walked over
to talk with Jerry. She looked different. He studied
her. Her hair was shorter. They were trying to change her
appearance. She wore the same coat, boots, mittens, hat.
They probably didn't have other clothes for her. Was her
kidnapping a random act? She hadn't been a predetermined
target? A moment of opportunity. Ross guessed the man had
gone hunting, looking for the right opportunity to grab a girl.
The man probably had a size or age range in mind. Ross still
didn't know what they were doing here at this camp.

The location was one to hide at. Were they planning to
move after a while? After the heat died down a little? Canada?

Ross' radio chirped in his earpiece. "Hey partner," he said.

"Checking in," Stevens said.

"Good timing. Zoe's out again. They've cut her hair
shorter She and the dog are heading west away from the
cabin. If you're over there, stay alert."

"If she's alone should I attempt contact?"

Ross thought through the options and repercussions.
"Let's talk it through," he said. "If you can yell at her across

the water, make sure it's her, let her know we're here, she'd feel better, but she might act differently. We can learn something directly from her. The dog sees you and starts barking, you don't have much time to talk and have to hide." Ross let Stevens think about it. "I'm guessing there's no chance to get her across the water."

"No. Maybe if I had the kayak. The water's freezing cold. I couldn't get her to swim across. And I don't think it works for me to go over and back." Another break. "And there's the dog."

"He'll bark. Shoot him, they'll hear it," Ross said. "I think we leave things as is unless you find a great opportunity to talk with her. I'm afraid if you make contact and she goes back, the guy will sense something's up and put her in more danger."

"I agree," Stevens said. "I'll watch for her and keep scouting and be back to the nest after that."

"Roger," Ross said.

He watched the guy finish stacking wood, go to the outhouse and then go back into the cabin. The guy must be pretty sure Zoe can't or wouldn't get off the island to let her wander around. Ross swung the gun to the west to find Zoe. She and the dog continued to walk through the field of snow and along the shore. Zoe threw a snowball into the water. The dog ran to the edge, stared at the water and ran back to Zoe. Maybe he's not a swimmer.

Not a lot of new observations today. They had a better picture of the kidnapper, got another look at his gun. Zoe appeared to be okay. When Stevens got back they'd call into Palmer and see if he was able to get any more info on the kidnapper and maybe who the woman with him might be.

They needed a plan. Even if they waited for Palmer and the team to get here, they needed a plan.

CHAPTER TWENTY

The cabin smelled delicious when Zoe opened the door. She and Buck returned from their walk both tired, hungry and thirsty. Buck headed right for his water dish and lapped up some water.

It was good to get outside and explore, but it didn't give Zoe any hope for escaping. She'd continue to try and find ways to signal the outside world that she was here, but for now, she'd just try and keep Jerry happy to keep herself safe.

"You must be hungry," Barb said. "Sit down there next to Jerry and I'll get you both some soup and bread."

"It smells good," Zoe said. She sat next to Jerry and poured herself a glass of water.

"Find anything interesting outside?" Jerry asked.

"No, Buck and I just went exploring."

"It's a beautiful place, isn't it?" Jerry asked.

"It is. Especially with all of the new snow and surrounded by the hills and trees. It's very private."

"That's why I like it," Jerry said. "I've never been much of a city guy. I like the outdoors and taking care of myself."

Barb ladled some soup into Jerry's bowl, then some into

Zoe's. "It's chicken, rice and vegetable soup. I'll bring some buns over to eat with it."

Jerry bent over and inhaled. "Smells good."

Barb returned to the table with her own soup and a basket of buns. Zoe said a silent prayer for her family and herself and picked a bun from the basket.

"Did you remember to pull the wood over?" Jerry asked.

Zoe nodded. "Ayuh, I pulled it over to the stairs. It was pretty heavy."

"Well, you've proved you're pretty tough over the last couple of days," Jerry said. "We'll bring it in after lunch."

Over lunch they talked about the weather, Jerry told a couple of jokes and Barb brought up *The Call of the Wild* book. They talked about Buck's life and Zoe talked about the movie with Harrison Ford. It would be fun to see that together. Maybe Jerry could get a copy and they could figure out how to have a movie night in the cabin. Jerry showed Zoe the other books they had to read in the cabin through the winter. If she had any suggestions, he'd see if he could pick up some more on his next trip into civilization.

After lunch, they cleared the dishes. Barb had already melted a pail of snow on the stove and she asked Zoe to wash up the dishes since she'd cooked lunch. Zoe'd discovered that they were all expected to work.

As she washed the dishes she thought about her morning. They gave her some freedom. Exploring the island with Buck had been fun. If there was something she wanted to do, she'd have to bring it up herself, volunteer to do it. She'd find out if there was anything she could do for Buck: feed him, exercise him, walk him. If she could hang out with Buck, maybe she could avoid Jerry. She'd talk about it with Barb tonight.

"Zoe, can you bring me some water, please?" Jerry asked. He sat in a chair reading a book by the window. Barb sat at the table with paper and pencil, sketching.

Jerry liked cold water. She took a glass container from the fridge and poured water into a cup. She carried it carefully and offered it to him. Nervous she held the cup in two hands trying not to spill any of the water. Jerry took the cup from her. "Sit down," he said, pointing to the other chair by the window.

Zoe sat stiffly in the chair, her butt on the edge of the chair, her back straight, away from the back of the chair.

"Relax," Jerry said. "Sit back, get comfortable." He leaned forward and put his hand on her knee.

Zoe slid back and rested against the back of the chair. Her hands gripped each arm of the chair. She twisted her legs away from him so he couldn't reach her leg. She didn't want him touching her. What did he want?

"There, that's better." Jerry sat back in his chair, closed his book and set it on the table between them. "I just want to know how you're doing. We've got a beautiful place here. The three of us, four with Buck, will do great out here. It's comfortable, life is simple, we have what we need." He turned his head and gave Zoe a questioning look. "What do you think?"

Zoe crossed her arms and brought her feet up onto the chair and wrapped her arms around her knees. "It's nice here," she said.

"Do you like it? Want to stay?"

Zoe nodded. She missed her family but didn't think she should tell Jerry that.

Jerry reached into his pocket and pulled his hand out in a fist. He leaned forward. "Give me your hand," he said. "I have something for you."

Zoe held out her right hand, palm facing up.

He held his fist over her hand. Then he opened it, palm down. "Close your hand." Zoe closed her hand around something Jerry had left in it. He lifted his hand and sat back. "Go ahead. Look," he said.

Zoe brought her closed hand in front of her and opened it. She quickly closed her hand and looked at Jerry. He smiled. Fear, disappointment, hopelessness welled up. She couldn't breathe. Then a wail escaped from deep in her chest. Zoe fell out of her chair, stood up and ran for the door. She threw the door open and ran outside. Down the stairs she went. She ran through the snow, her tears blurring her vision. Her throat tightened and a small squeal escaped. She fell to her knees and screamed, a high-pitched scream of a twelve-year-old girl.

"Noooo," she cried, her hand still in a fist.

"ZOE, WHAT IS IT?" She felt Barb put her coat over her shoulders. She knelt next to Zoe and put her arm around her. Zoe leaned into her for support, a feeling of security.

"What is it?" Barb asked.

Zoe held out her fist and opened it. The tag from her mitten that she'd left in the outhouse a couple of days ago, the one with the big black Z, sat in the palm of her hand. Nobody is ever going to find her.

BARB TOLD her to be strong and helped her stand. Zoe wiped the tears from her cheeks and walked back to the cabin with Barb. When they got inside, she went straight to the ladder and climbed up to the loft. She laid down in bed and stared at the ceiling. Her attempts to leave clues had failed so far. The deer hunter saw the hat she dropped, and Jerry killed him. She thought she'd left her mitten tag to be found. It was a long shot, but it was something. But Jerry showed he outsmarted her and had the tag.

CHAPTER TWENTY-ONE

Ross waited for Stevens to return. The camp below him was quiet. The only thing that moved was the smoke rising from the chimney of the cabin. A warm fire would feel good. His eyes closed, he opened them. He sucked in a quick, deep breath through his nose and shook his head. Maybe a nap when Stevens returned. Or a quick walk through the woods to wake up.

He used some tricks to try and stay awake. He bit his tongue, he tried to pick out new details around the camp through the scope. He called Stevens on the radio. "Hey, partner, talk to me. I'm getting tired."

"We're not too far away, maybe fifteen minutes."

"Learn anything?"

"The cabin isn't in a good defensive position. We'll have the advantage. It's surrounded by high ground on the south and west. Water to the north and east. When the team gets here, we can put some of them on the west side."

"Let's call Palmer when you get back," Ross said. "See how they're doing." He watched the cabin through the scope.

"Sounds good."

"See any bears?"

"Funny guy. Just deer tracks."

The cabin door flew open and Zoe ran out. Ross watched her through. He saw her scream and then the sound reached him in the nest a second later, like a badly dubbed Japanese movie. "Just a second partner."

Zoe knelt in the snow without a coat, sobbing.

"What's up?" Ross heard Stevens ask through his earpiece.

"Zoe's run outside screaming, upset. Something's happened." Ross watched the woman walk out of the cabin, follow Zoe's path through the snow. She put a coat around Zoe's shoulders and knelt next to her, talking calmly to her. Zoe showed her something in her hand. Ross swept the scope back to the cabin and saw the man standing in the doorway, the dog sitting next to him, a hand on the collar to keep the dog in place. The man had a smile on his face. He turned and pulled the dog with him back into the cabin.

Ross could've taken him out with a shot while the man stood there in the doorway of the cabin. He moved the scope back to Zoe and the woman. They were still talking. Zoe's shoulders jerked as she cried. The woman hugged her tight, gave her a kiss on her head and helped her stand. Hand-in-hand they walked back to the cabin and closed the door.

If only they were closer or had a microphone in the cabin. Ross would love to know what they were talking about.

"COMING IN," Ross heard in his ear. Rupert crawled in and sniffed Ross' neck. "Hey, buddy. Welcome back."

Stevens crawled in after him.

"You going to sniff my neck too?" Ross asked.

"I didn't miss you that much," Stevens said. He crawled in next to Ross. "What's the situation?"

Ross handed the rifle to Stevens. "All's quiet since Zoe ran out crying. Not sure what happened. The woman comforted her and got her calmed down and back inside. The guy just had a smirk on his face as he watched Zoe crying in the snow."

"Asshole."

"I'm going to get out and stretch. I've got a plan I want to talk over when I get back," Ross said.

"Take your time. We'll be here on overwatch."

ROSS JOGGED through the snow away from the nest. He had to get his blood flowing. He stopped and stretched his arms, pulling one elbow across his chest, then the other. He leaned against a tree to stretch his legs and twisted to stretch his back. It felt good to move. His body missed the regular workouts he did as part of the HRT team.

The forest was quiet. The snow muffled any noise, but nothing really moved except a few birds flitting through the branches of the trees. Ross had a plan in mind to share with Stevens. He wondered what he'd think. He didn't think he'd like it, but after what he saw this afternoon it looked like Zoe needed to be rescued.

Ross slipped into the nest and crawled up next to Stevens. "I feel bad leaving the kid over there," Ross said. "You should've seen her this afternoon. I don't know what happened, but it wasn't good. I could hear her screaming up here. It sounded like total despair."

"What do you have in mind?" Stevens asked.

"I think we need to go over there and get her. Let's talk it through."

Ross and Stevens talked through options while Stevens kept watch on the cabin through the scope.

CHAPTER TWENTY-TWO

She'd be strong. She wouldn't give up. She'd be smart and escape or be rescued and see her family again. Zoe got up and climbed down the ladder.

Jerry and Barb played cards at the table. Zoe stood at the end of the table and waited for them to give her their attention. "Do you want to play?" Barb asked.

"No," Zoe said. She took a deep breath and looked past them to the other end of the table. "I just want to apologize for how I reacted."

"Thank you, Zoe," Jerry said. "You're a very mature twelve-year-old. The past couple of days have been tough, but it'll get easier."

"It'll get easier," Barb echoed.

Zoe smiled weakly. "Can I go outside with Buck while it's still light outside?"

"Go ahead," Jerry said. "Throw a stick for him and try and tire him out while you're out there."

~

Zoe put on her coat, grabbed her hat and mittens and opened the door. "Let's go, Buck," she said. The dog ran out ahead of her and Zoe followed. She picked up one of the smaller split pieces of firewood and threw it ahead for Buck to find. The dog sprinted to the spot where the log landed and stuck his nose deep in the snow. He came back up with it in his jaws and ran back to Zoe and past her.

"Come on, Buck," Zoe said. "You need to give me the stick if you want me to throw it for you again."

Buck wiggled up to her, whining with excitement.

"Buck, sit." The husky plopped his rear into the snow. "Drop it." Buck dropped the log into the snow. Zoe picked it up and continued walking towards the water. Buck trotted alongside and stared up at her, waiting for her to throw the log again. Zoe threw it ahead again and Buck took off after it.

They repeated this exercise a couple of times until they reached the water. Zoe walked along the edge of the water until she reached the boat she and Jerry had used the other day. She pushed on it to see if she could move it. She tried to lift the end of it. It was heavy. She barely moved it.

Zoe stared across the water. How far was it? Farther than the length of the swimming pool she took lessons at. Maybe three times as far? Buck stretched his nose out from shore and lapped up some water. "Don't fall in, Buck."

The end of the boat hung just off the shore over the water. Zoe took off her mitten and pushed up her right sleeve. She grabbed the edge of the boat with her left and reached out to feel the water. It was cold. She left her hand in to see how long she could stand it.

When she got to forty in her head, her fingers felt numb. She pulled her hand out of the water and pulled herself away from the edge of the water, using the boat for leverage. The fingers of her right hand tingled. She couldn't use them to pick up her mitten. She picked up the mitten with her left hand, stuck it in her pocket and jammed her right hand inside her jacket to warm it.

Zoe headed back towards the cabin with Buck running ahead. The sky was clear. She spied the contrails of a jet overhead. She ran past the cabin into the open field of snow behind it. She took off her jacket and waved it over her head. She doubted anybody on the plane saw it, but she had to try.

Be strong, be smart. Zoe knew she had to be positive and come up with ideas to escape or stay safe until she was rescued. She knew her family wouldn't give up looking for her, no matter how long it was. She put her coat back on and stuck both her hands in the mittens.

"Come here, Buck." Zoe stood in the field of white and threw the log for Buck. She'd tire him out if that's what Jerry wanted. Buck chased the log and Zoe followed. They repeated this over and over in the field of snow until the sun started to set.

"Buck, Zoe, come on in. It's time to eat." Jerry stood by the pile of wood next to the cabin and waved.

Zoe picked up the stick and waved back to show Jerry she'd heard him. "Come on, Buck. Let's go in."

CHAPTER TWENTY-THREE

"Hey," Stevens said. "Zoe's coming out. Just her and the dog." He still had the rifle and scope trained on the cabin.

Ross watched her and the dog coming towards them through the snow. "What's she doing?"

"Playing with the dog."

"I want to let her know we're here. Give her some hope," Ross said. "If we had the kayak inflated, we could cruise over and get her now."

"That's something to think about."

They watched Zoe and the dog work their way over to the water. She pushed and pulled something, a boat, trying to move it.

"She's not giving up," Stevens said. "Now we know how they got to camp."

They watched her check the water. "She's thinking of swimming?" Ross asked.

"She's getting desperate if she's thinking of swimming across in that cold water."

Zoe and the dog headed north and went past the cabin. She took off her coat and waved it in the air.

"She's trying anything," Ross said. "She's waving to that passenger jet flying overhead."

"I hope the guy doesn't see what she's doing," Stevens said.

"We gotta go tonight." Ross picked up the satellite phone. "I think it's time to check in with the boss and tell him what we're doing."

"You tell him, I'll listen."

Ross pushed the button to place the call. "Hey, boss. We're checking in."

"What's new? You guys ready for some more weather?"

"Why don't you tell us about the weather, and we'll tell you what's up."

"Another front is moving in tonight. Gusty winds and blowing snow."

"Zoe's getting a little desperate, looking for ways off the island," Ross said. "Something happened this afternoon that upset her. They've cut her hair short, physically she seems fine, but I think the mental stress might be getting to her."

"Her parents say she's a tough kid, she's an older sister, but she's twelve. We still don't know who the guy or woman with him is."

"The woman seems to be taking care of Zoe."

"Ideas?" Palmer asked.

"Let me tell you what we're thinking," Ross said. He relayed the plan to Palmer while he watched Zoe and the dog run through the snow on the other side of the cabin.

❧

THE SIDES of the nest pushed in and out from the gusty winds like it was breathing. "I'm going to go out and inflate the kayak," Ross said.

"Don't let it blow away in this wind," Stevens said.

The changing weather had brought blowing snow, low clouds and poor visibility with it. The gods were looking down on them tonight. The wind created noise to cover Ross' travels. "You want to come out and help?"

Stevens groaned. "Okay, I'll help, but you'll owe me one."

Ross crawled out the south end of the nest. Rupert followed him, Stevens, after him. It was a good time to stretch. Stevens would keep an eye on the cabin door to see if anyone exited, but at this time of night, the chances of that were low. Nobody would come out in this weather if they didn't have to.

Ross and Stevens opened the bundle and removed the kayak, the foot pump and the two halves of the paddle. The black kayak stood out on the white backdrop of the snow, even in the low light of a stormy night.

"We should've tried this back in Portland," Ross said, "in the light."

"We'll figure it out."

Rupert walked around them in the snow, as if he wanted to help.

Ross pulled a roll of paracord out of his pack. He unrolled about a ten-foot length of it and cut it off. He tied one end to a D-ring on the kayak and the other to a tree behind them.

On his knees, Stevens poked around the end of the kayak. "There's an opening here with a cover. Bring the pump over."

Ross carried the pump to him and held out the end of the hose. Stevens unscrewed the black cover. It was connected to the boat by a short string. He grabbed the end of the hose, fit it in the opening and turned it to lock in place. "Ready," he said to Ross. "Start pumping."

Ross put the pump on the snow and stepped on it. It sunk into the snow. He exhaled heavily in frustration.

"Nice one, Einstein," Stevens said.

"Just a sec." Ross found a couple of long branches on the snow that had broken off in the wind. He laid them side-by-side, stepped on them to force them down into the snow. He put the pump on his newly constructed base and started pressing the pump up and down with his foot. "This is going to take a while," he said.

"I'll switch out with you in a bit," Stevens said. He stood by Ross to talk to him. "With this fresh snow, they might see your tracks."

"I'll stay in the footpaths they've made. If we get this thing filled up fast enough, I can get over there, get in place and the wind should cover up my footprints. And, with luck, they're too tired in the morning to notice."

"You know I don't like to rely on luck."

Ross switched legs and kept working the pump, pushing down and letting the pedal up, over and over. "Well, I'll say a prayer."

"I'm not that religious either. But if it will help."

Ross kept working the pump to inflate the kayak.

"You know I'm also not happy you're going over there alone," Stevens said.

"With you up here on the hill you'll have almost the entire field of fire covered with your rifle. That's better than being down there."

"But, it's just you down there and the two of us," Stevens gestured at Rupert, "up here."

"If you'd teach me some Dutch and if he listened to me, maybe I'd take him with me."

"Let us go," Stevens said.

Ross shook his head. "Thanks, partner. But you know

you're a much better sniper than I am. This plan will work. We'll rescue Zoe. Get her home to her family."

"I don't like it, but I'll do it."

Ross stopped pumping the kayak up and checked how full it was. He'd made some progress. "Your turn," he said to Stevens.

CHAPTER TWENTY-FOUR

Ross dragged the inflated kayak over the snow. If he moved far enough east, Stevens told him it looked like there was a small washout down to the water and his footprints would be out of view from the cabin in the morning. He found a dead branch leaning on a tree with a black strap wrapped around it, just like Stevens said he'd left for him to mark the way down the hill.

He checked the kayak again. It was still full of air. He dragged it behind him down the hill to the water. Now he had to figure out how to get it in the water and get into it without tipping over. They should've practiced.

Ross pushed the nose of the kayak into the water, climbed into the open middle and jabbed the end of the oar into the snow. He shifted his weight and levered the paddle to slide the kayak off the snow. The first push moved him a couple of inches. The second got it sliding off the bank and into the water.

Freed from shore, the kayak rocked from side to side and Ross used the paddle to steady himself. If he tipped over and went into the water, the plan would be aborted. He couldn't make it through the night soaking wet. "Thanks," he whispered to nobody.

"I've launched the kayak and it's floating," he radioed to Stevens.

"That's good. Stay dry," was the reply.

He had some experience on the water. He was no expert, but he'd kayaked, paddle boarded and canoed before. He used the double-bladed paddle to maneuver himself away from shore and then paddled east before crossing to the island. The wind pushed the kayak more than he anticipated. It was like a giant hand took a hold of it and pushed it back to the shore. He leaned into his strokes and pulled hard to paddle into the wind across the choppy water.

"I'm almost to the island," Ross said into the radio.

"The camp is still quiet," Stevens replied.

When he got closer to the other side, the land blocked the wind as he sat low on the surface of the water. The kayak slipped silently through the black water. Ross bumped the end of the kayak into shore. The water surface was about a foot below the snow-covered island. "I didn't think about how I'd get out of this thing. We should've practiced."

"You keep talking this practice thing. Figure it out. Stay dry."

Ross maneuvered the kayak so it was broadside to shore. He grabbed onto exposed roots and pulled. They supported him. He took the loose end of the paracord and tied it to one of the roots. He didn't want the kayak to float away. It would be more hidden floating on the water than it would be if he pulled it up on shore. His MP5 hung from a strap and he swung it around to his back. Then he started to pull himself slowly out of the kayak, holding onto roots and rocks. He wriggled himself half out of the boat onto his stomach on the snowy shore. He used his elbows and dug them into the ground and pulled himself forward until his knees were on the ground. "The eagle has landed," he said into his headset.

"I thought I was watching a sea lion at the San Francisco pier. Rupert had it at even money that you'd fall in the water."

"Let him know he owes me." Ross crawled forward on his hands and knees.

"Still clear," Stevens said. "Just keep the outhouse between you and the front door and they shouldn't see you if anyone comes out. If they do, I'll let you know, and you drop."

"Roger," Ross said. "Moving forward." He stood, moved his MP5 to his front and held it at the ready. He walked slowly towards the outhouse. The snow on top was new. The wind blew it around. Underneath, the snow was a little firmer, crunchy from melting in the afternoon sun and refreezing with the night temperatures. Ross hoped the new snow and the wind muffled any sound. He didn't just walk with a regular gait to the outhouse. The man or the dog might hear walking sounds and wake up. Instead, he took a step and waited. Then he took two steps and waited. He broke up the pattern. To move faster, he took longer steps.

"You're still good," Stevens reported. "It's still dark in the cabin."

Ross continued until he got to the outhouse. He leaned against the wall. "I'm there."

"Take a break and prepare," Stevens said. "When you come out from behind there you'll be exposed. You need to minimize your time in the open. Let me know when you're ready and I'll focus on the windows."

Ross whispered into his microphone. "I'll walk in the footprints already in the snow from them walking around out here. The wind should blow snow to cover up my fresh steps before they wake up."

"Roger."

His watch said a little before oh three hundred. Everyone

in the cabin should be sleeping hard, including the dog. Ross pulled the small can from his vest. He'd wrapped it in tape so it wasn't so slippery in his gloved hands. He walked through the next steps in his head. He also thought about moves to cover and safety if Stevens alerted him. After a couple of deep breaths he reported to Stevens, "Ready."

"Good luck. No changes in the cabin. Count it down and execute."

Ross peaked out around the corner of the outhouse to make sure nothing was in his way. He glanced at the ground for existing footprints to step in. He ducked back behind the outhouse, sucked in another breath. "I'm ready," he said. "Three, two, one, go."

He stepped out from behind the outhouse and took quick, big steps around it. He looked at the cabin. Nothing moved. It was still dark. He sprayed the upper hinge on the outhouse door with the WD-40 and repeated it on the second. It should help with any potential squeaking. Lifting up on the handle of the door to help take any weight off the hinges, he slowly pulled the door open. There was a tiny squeak. He sprayed the upper hinge again. Then he pulled the door until the opening was wide enough for him to fit through. Inside, he lifted up on the door handle and slowly pulled it closed.

He found he'd been holding his breath. He inhaled. "I'm in," he reported to Stevens.

"Looks clear," Stevens reported back.

Ross sniffed the air. "It smells in here," he said. "But I'm out of the wind."

"You can sit and wait until we see who comes out."

Ross sat on the toilet seat. He'd be here a while. "Let me know when somebody comes out."

CHAPTER TWENTY-FIVE

Ross mixed sitting and standing in the outhouse to try and stay ready. He was careful not to bang anything into the walls or the door. He needed to remain quiet. He was prepared for when the first person came out to do their morning duty. He had the other can out of his vest, also wrapped in tape and he made sure his Glock was in place. "Talk to me partner, it's been a long night. I've been in here so long I'm used to the smell now."

"It's probably permeated your gear. We may need a bonfire after this mission."

Ross smiled. Stevens was a good partner. He kept things light, but he had the skills and experience to keep Ross safe. He wished that he had been able to bring Rupert with him for another resource at the camp to take on whatever came his way.

"Bets on who comes out first?" Stevens asked.

"I'm betting it's the guy. With the dog or without?"

"Easier without the dog."

"Can you do it if you have to?" Ross asked. He knew that as a dog handler, Stevens had a soft spot for dogs. He always said it wasn't the dog, it's the master. The dog just does what the master or the alpha of the pack tells it to do.

"If it's you or him, I can do it. I just hope I don't have to."

"Me too." Ross flexed his gloved hands to keep his fingers ready. He couldn't afford for them to be slow or unresponsive because they were cold or stiff.

"You ready to double-date with Maria and her friend?"

"You have to tell me a little more about her," Ross said. Stevens had been trying to fix him up for a month since he met Maria at a dance club.

"What's to know? She's smart, beautiful."

"Why's she unattached?"

"You should meet her and find out."

"Maybe New Year's Eve if we're not on duty then."

"It's a date," Stevens said. "I'll contact Maria as soon as we're done with this mission. You'll owe me."

"Okay, I'm awake. I think I'll go silent until it's go time."

Ross played through the next scenarios in his head. Does he let the guy open the door and surprise him? Does he open the door as the guy approaches? He needed to decide one way or the other. He had to rely on Stevens to tell him what was happening on the other side of the door. He decided he'd open the door before the guy got to the outhouse. He didn't want to be trapped in here. He might need some room to maneuver.

"Oh six hundred, partner," Stevens said. "I think it'll be soon."

"I can't see through the door, so you're my eyes," Ross replied. He stood up and slowly moved from foot to foot. He held the Glock in his left hand, the can in his right. He hoped this worked. They wanted to save Zoe, save or apprehend the other woman and take down the guy without killing anyone, including the dog. "Let me know who's coming and distance on the approach. I plan to open the door when they're close and catch them by surprise."

"Roger," Stevens said. "It's almost like I'm there with you. Wish I was."

"Me too," Ross said. He listened and waited. The wind still blew, but it sounded like it was calming down. He put a pair of clear safety glasses on and pulled a buff up to cover his chin.

"Head's up," Stevens said. "Cabin door's opening. Male subject heading your way. Wool coat, bare head, bare and empty hands."

Ross tried to control his breathing. He pulled the buff up over his mouth and nose. His glasses fogged a little when he exhaled. He stayed still, weight evenly displaced so he didn't move and didn't cause anything to creak.

"Thirty feet. Head down. Not nervous about his surroundings. Just coming out for his morning piss."

Ross wished he could see outside.

"Ten feet, six feet, go."

On go, Ross launched himself forward and drove his left hip into the door. It swung open and he stepped out of the outhouse. The door rebounded and started to swing back at him. He stopped it with his foot.

The man's head shot up. He looked right at Ross. His arms reflexively swung up, palms facing Ross to stop whatever was coming towards him.

"FBI," Ross yelled. He pressed the plunger on top of the can with his right index finger and a stream of bear spray shot out at the man. It hit him in the face. Ross dropped the can and shifted his Glock to his right hand.

The man screamed and brought his hands to his face.

"Get down on the ground," Ross yelled.

The man wiped his sleeves over his face and stumbled in the snow. Ross used the opportunity to push the man down, face first into the ground. "Hands behind your back," he ordered.

"My eyes, man. I can't breathe," the guy cried.

Ross kept his Glock pointed at the man's back. He put a knee between his shoulder blades, slapped a handcuff on his left wrist and pulled it behind his back. "Put your right hand behind your back."

"I can't breathe, man. My eyes are burning."

"Female subject exiting the cabin," Stevens said in Ross's ear. "Knife in her right hand. I've got her."

Ross glanced up at the woman on the deck. "FBI, ma'am. Stay where you are." He bent over and said to the man, "Right hand behind your back. I have a Glock pointed at the back of your head."

"What are you doing?" the woman screamed.

The man moved his right hand behind him, and Ross secured his wrist with the handcuff.

"What are you doing?" the woman screamed again.

Zoe stepped out of the cabin with a hand holding the dog's collar. The dog started barking and pulled Zoe out the door. "Buck, quiet," she said. "Sit." The dog continued to bark, but he sat on the deck next to Zoe.

"Zoe, I'm with the FBI. Are you okay?" Ross asked.

Before she could answer, the woman stepped behind Zoe, put her left arm around her and hugged Zoe to her body. She held the knife to Zoe's throat with her right hand.

"Barb, what are you doing?" Zoe asked. The look on her face was confusion and fear. The dog continued to bark at Ross.

"You let him go," the woman said. "Or I'll hurt her."

The man continued to squirm under Ross' knee. He was rubbing his face back and forth through the snow.

"I can't let him go," Ross said.

"I have a shot," Stevens said in his ear.

"I'm not leaving without Zoe," Ross said to the woman. "Hey, buddy," he said to the guy on the ground. "You want to tell your girlfriend to put the knife down before someone gets hurt."

"Let us go," the guy said.

"I'll hurt her," the woman said.

Zoe started to cry.

"Send it," Ross whispered.

The woman was standing there with a knife at Zoe's throat one minute. The next, her head jerked to her left and she fell to the ground.

Zoe stood in place, holding the dog.

"Don't move," Ross said to the guy. He shifted his focus to Zoe and stood. "Zoe, look at me. I'm an FBI agent. My name's Ross and we've come to rescue you." Zoe started to look back where the woman had been. "Look at me, Zoe." Ross locked his eyes on her. He pulled the buff down from his chin so she could see his face. Is there anybody else here besides the three of you and the dog?"

She shook her head and weakly said, "No."

Ross holstered his Glock. "Okay, I want you to turn to your left, don't look around you, and take the dog with you into the cabin while I finish up out here. Can you do that?"

Zoe nodded.

"Great. You're safe now. We'll get you out of here in a little while and get you back with your family. They've been worried about you. You go in the cabin with the dog and close the door. I'll come in and talk to you in a few minutes. Okay?"

Zoe turned, and pulled the dog with her into the cabin and closed the door.

CHAPTER TWENTY-SIX

S he was saved. She couldn't believe it. Zoe sat on the floor with Buck and stroked his fur to calm him down. The FBI agent said she'd be back with her family soon.

She saw Agent Ross had Jerry on the ground and was putting handcuffs on him. He was going to jail. She couldn't believe Barb grabbed her and threatened to hurt her.

Zoe laid her head on Buck's side and hugged him while she waited for Agent Ross to come in and tell her what was going on.

CHAPTER TWENTY-SEVEN

"The girl's okay?" Stevens asked.

"Yep, she's fine. A little shocked, but I think she'll be okay." Ross grabbed the man and stood him up. His eyes were red and watery. His face was red from the bear spray and scratched from him scrubbing it in the snow. Ross walked him over to the outhouse. "You're going to wait in here," he said. "You come out without me asking you to, and my friend on the hill will shoot you. Got it?"

"I got it."

"Okay, sit down," Ross said.

The man stepped into the outhouse and sat down. Ross closed the door. "Sorry you had to shoot the woman," Ross said to Stevens over the radio.

"You called it," Stevens replied. "She was going to hurt the girl."

"You want to call Palmer and tell him to come and get us? He should be able to land the chopper right here in front of the cabin."

"I'll call him," Stevens said. "What about me and Rupert? We're stuck over here."

"When the team gets here, someone will row over in the boat and pick you up. I'm going to take care of things over here and sit with Zoe."

"I'll let you know what the boss says," Stevens replied.

Ross pulled out his phone and took a series of pictures of the area including the woman, dead on the deck. He cracked open the door. The dog barked. "Can I come in?" he asked. "Will the dog be okay?"

"I'll hang onto him and let him know it's alright," Zoe said. "Come on in."

Ross entered the cabin and closed the door. He kept an eye on the dog. It was warm in here with the fire going. Ross slipped off his helmet and put it next to the door with his MP5. He put his hands out to show he wasn't a threat. "You're okay, right?"

"I'm fine," Zoe said.

"You know, we had to hurt the woman. You called her Barb?"

Zoe nodded.

"I'm going to cover her with a blanket to be respectful and I'll be right back." Ross grabbed a blanket off of the closest chair and stepped back out through the door.

Ross covered the body with the blanket and tucked the loose ends under so it stayed in place.

"Boss says they'll be here in twenty minutes," Stevens said.

"Sounds good. Give me a little time to calm Zoe down and get her ready to travel. You listening to our conversation?"

"As long as you keep the channel open."

Ross stepped back into the cabin and closed the door. "Hey, Zoe. What's the dog's name?"

"He's Buck."

"You like dogs. You two have been getting along." Ross smiled. "We've been watching you the past couple of days making sure you were safe and trying to figure out how to save you."

"Watching me?"

"Yeah, come here." Ross stood by the window. Zoe and the dog came over to join him. The dog sniffed his legs. "Look up there on the hill." He pointed out the window. "My partner, Agent Stevens and I and his dog, Rupert, have been watching you from up there. Stevens can hear us now talking through our radios. Hey, partner," Ross said. "Wave something so Zoe can see you."

Ross and Zoe watched as Stevens stuck a hat out the front of the nest and waved it.

"You have a dog, too?" Zoe asked.

"Yep, Rupert. He followed your scent through the woods and led us here. You'll meet him soon." Ross suggested they sit at the table and talk.

Ross spoke calmly. "We found two people hurt along the way: a hiker on the Appalachian Trail and a deer hunter in the woods."

"Ayuh," Zoe said. "Jerry hurt them."

"Did anybody else get hurt?"

Zoe shook her head.

Ross decided to change the subject. "Have you ever ridden in a helicopter?"

"No."

"Well, today's the day," Ross said. We have a helicopter with some of the other people on our team coming to pick us up." He looked around the cabin. "Is there anything you want to bring with you? We should get it ready."

Zoe looked at Ross with pleading eyes. "Can Buck come?" She had a grip on the dog's fur.

"For sure," Ross said. He put his hand down and let Buck sniff it. "Anything else?"

Zoe looked around the cabin and shook her head. Then

she held a finger in the air. "One thing." She went to the table and picked up the book and held it out to Ross. "Can I take this? It wasn't mine."

"*The Call of the Wild*. Sure, it's yours now." Ross handed it back to Zoe.

"The hero of the story is a dog named Buck."

"Perfect," Ross said. "There should be a character named Zoe in it too. You're a strong hero as well."

The sound of a helicopter filled the air. "Let's watch it land through the window," Ross said.

THE HELICOPTER LANDED SENDING a cloud of snow into the air. The FBI Hostage Rescue Team disembarked and went to work. Stevens and Rupert came down the hill and waited for a ride across the water. The woman was put in a body bag and carried to the chopper. Two members of the team fetched the prisoner from the outhouse and walked him to the chopper. Palmer walked to the cabin.

There was a knock on the door. "Come on in, boss," Ross said.

Palmer entered the cabin. "Nice and cozy in here. You must be Zoe," he said. He pulled off a glove and put out his hand.

Zoe shook his hand. "And this is Buck."

Palmer knelt and ran a hand through the dog's fur. "Nice dog." He looked into Zoe's eyes. "Your parents are looking forward to you coming home and they're looking forward to meeting Buck."

"I get to keep him?" Zoe threw her arms around the dog's neck.

"I spoke with your parents and arranged it already," Palmer said. "So, the three of you ready to go?"

Ross looked at Zoe. "Ready?"

She nodded.

The four of them walked out of the cabin and closed the door. As they approached the chopper, Ross said, "You can meet Stevens and Rupert. We better work out introductions of the dogs."

Stevens stood with Rupert outside the chopper door.

Ross, Zoe, and Buck approached and the dogs sniffed each other. Buck growled. "Buck, sit," Zoe commanded. Buck immediately sat. Rupert did the same.

"What?" Ross said. "Rupert'll listen to her and not me?"

Stevens laughed.

"Thank you for finding me, Rupert," Zoe said, and she hugged the dog. She let loose of Rupert and hugged Agent Stevens around the legs. "Thanks for saving me."

"You're welcome, Zoe. We're just glad we could do it."

"Okay, let's go before the boss gets mad," Ross said. "This is Zoe and Buck's first helicopter ride." Ross helped Zoe into the Blackhawk and settled her in a seat. He fastened her seat belt and put a headset on her so they could talk. "You ready?" Ross asked.

"I'm ready," Zoe answered.

The Blackhawk rotors started.

"Did you see my sign?" Zoe asked.

Ross didn't know how to answer.

"We saw it this morning, Zoe. That was a pretty smart and brave thing to do," Palmer said.

The Blackhawk lifted into the air. When it got high enough, it swung around and over the cabin. Zoe pointed out the window. In the field of snow behind the cabin the letters

H E L P Z O E

were stamped into the snow to be seen from above.

THANKS FOR READING

Free Fall is the second novella in the FBI Hostage Rescue Team, Critical Incident series.

SuperCell is the first in the series

Lost Art is the third in the series.

If you haven't read The Ninth District - the FBI thriller that started it all, check it out.

Join the Dorow Thriller Reader List by visiting www.douglasdorow.com to stay up to date on releases, offers and other writing news. You'll get four FREE short stories when you join.

If you enjoyed this book, one way to show it and support my writing is to leave a review at your favorite online bookstore.

Read for the *THRILL* of it!

AFTERWORD

People ask where I get my ideas.

The idea for Free Fall - Critical Incident #2 came by combining a real story of the Hostage Rescue Team rescuing a kidnapped girl in the wilderness of Oregon - I moved it to Maine, and wanted to show Stevens and Rupert jumping out of a plane together.

I try to bring reality to my stories. I attended the Minneapolis FBI Citizens Academy in 2015 and the Writers Police Academy in 2016.

I want to make my stories real enough to be believable while remaining entertaining.

For my family, my readers, and the agents and staff of the FBI.

ABOUT THE AUTHOR

Douglas "Doug" Dorow, lives in Minneapolis, Minnesota with his wife and their two dogs.

For more info on my writing:
www.douglasdorow.com
or email me at
Doug@DouglasDorow.com

Read for the *THRILL* of it!

ALSO BY DOUGLAS DOROW

FBI THRILLERS:

The Ninth District - FBI Thriller #1

SuperCell - spun off of this story. See where Ross Fruen was before joining the HRT.

Twice Removed - FBI Thriller #2

Empire Builder - FBI Thriller #3

CRITICAL INCIDENT SERIES:

SuperCell - Critical Incident #1

Free Fall - Critical Incident #2

Lost Art - Critical Incident #3

LOST ART - A NOVELLA

Critical Incident #3

Lost Art

Critical Incident #3

A novella
by Douglas Dorow

Copyright © 2020 by Douglas Dorow

ABOUT LOST ART - CRITICAL INCIDENT #3

In Lost Art - Critical Incident #3, Special Agent Val Martinson, a member of the Art Crimes Team, is introduced and partners with the Hostage Rescue Team to recover some stolen paintings.

Lost Art is the third in the Critical Incident series after SuperCell and Free Fall.

For updates on new releases, exclusive promotions and other information, sign up for Douglas Dorow's Thriller Reader list at www.douglasdorow.com and get four FREE short stories.

CHAPTER ONE

B ruce and Clark found the last painting on the list. It wasn't in the first gallery they checked, where they were told it would be. They found it in the gallery on the second floor. The painting on the wall was the biggest one they'd been asked to take. It was about six feet tall and eight feet long. It depicted a battle at sea; two large sailing ships firing canons at each other, smoke filling the air. They lifted it off the wall and set it on the floor.

"Man, that's heavy," Clark said. "What do you think this weighs?"

"I don't know."

"How much is it worth?"

"Shut up, Clark. Let's just get it to the loading dock. It's worth a lot or we wouldn't be taking it." They were friends, but sometimes Clark was just too much for Bruce to handle, always asking questions, like a little kid.

Bruce and Clark weren't their real names, but that's what everyone called them since they picked out the Halloween costumes to wear for this heist: Batman and Superman, also known as Bruce Wayne and Clark Kent.

Nobody on this team used their real names. They were all using aliases. They had a crew of six guys for this job, and Bruce and Clark were friends chosen for this job because they had some connections in the museum. Over the past six months they'd made a few trips to Salem to scout out the area, make notes and connect with their old friend, Norm, who was working in operations in the museum. Over drinks one night, they offered him some money for some info. Another night he delivered some invoices, schedules, and maps. Finally, he got them inside.

Now Norm was dead. Tony, or Iron Man, shot him when they'd rounded up museum personnel at the start of the heist.

They carried the painting between them horizontally, holding it by the wooden frame. Bruce faced forward and led the way, and Clark followed, holding the other end.

"We have to haul it all the way to the loading dock?" Clark asked. "We couldn't be any further away."

"Let's get it down there and get out of here," Bruce said.

Bruce stopped and glanced at the emergency exit. The backup spotlights over the door were on. A red light flashed between the two spotlights on the box.

"When did those lights came on?" Clark asked. "Is the alarm triggered?"

"I don't know," Bruce answered. "Let's go."

They made it to the freight elevator. "Set it on its side," Bruce said. "We'll slide it in." He lowered one side to the floor, and they stood the painting on its edge. He pushed the down button and heard the elevator start. The door opened and Bruce pulled and lifted the ornate frame while Clark pushed and they got it in the elevator. "Hit the first floor button," Bruce said.

The motor kicked in, and the old elevator shook. Bruce thought about the emergency lights. Something didn't feel right. The bell dinged, the elevator door opened, and they slid the painting out into the hall.

"Where is everybody?" Clark asked. "Hello?" he yelled.

"Lean the painting against the wall here," Bruce said. "We'll figure out what's going on." Something was wrong. There should have been a truck backed up to the loading dock door for them to load the painting into and then they were all going to go. "Stay here with the painting. I'll be right back." Bruce walked to the end of the hallway and looked out the safety glass window of the service door leading to the parking lot. He pulled his head back. "There're cops out there," he called back to Clark.

"Where is everybody?"

Bruce leaned against the wall. "I think they left us." He couldn't believe Tony and the crew had left them behind. On purpose, or did they have to leave in a hurry? Tony hadn't sent anyone to find them in the museum and hadn't called or texted. Tony left him here with Clark, one person who wouldn't be of much help to him. When Bruce got out of here and found Tony, there'd be some trouble.

"Friggin' massholes," Clark spit out. "Now what're we gonna' do?" He pushed his plastic Superman mask up onto his head. "Tony killed Norm and we're left here to take the rap."

"Pull your mask back down," Bruce said. He turned his head and looked for cameras on the walls.

"I thought the cameras were off," Clark said.

"They were supposed to be, but I'm not trusting what Tony said right now. We've got a room full of hostages. We'll figure something out. Follow me." Bruce led the way down the hallway.

CHAPTER TWO

Bruce and Clark walked from the loading dock back towards the conference room where the hostages were locked in. Their shadows stretched out in front of them from the emergency spotlights behind them at the exit. As they passed a vending machine, Clark asked, "You have any money?"

"What?"

Clark stopped in front of the vending machine. "I want to get some chips and something to drink."

"Oh, mother," Bruce muttered in reply. He pushed Clark away from the front of the vending machine, pulled the handgun from the back waist of his pants and smashed the plastic front of the vending machine with the butt of the gun. The plastic cracked. He hit it a second time and made a hole in the front. "There. Get the chips you want." He did the same thing to the soda machine and pulled out a Coke for himself.

"Thanks." Clark grabbed a bag of Fritos and a Coke and followed Bruce.

Bruce pulled his cell phone out of his pocket and hit a

pre-programmed number. He waited for an answer. He heard a message, and it rolled to voice mail. "Damn it."

Clark pushed the mask up on his head and jammed Fritos into his mouth. "Who you calling?"

"Tony."

"What are we going to do?" Pieces of chewed chips flew from Clark's mouth.

"We're on our own." Bruce said. He reached out and pulled Clark's mask back down over his face. "Let's go talk to the staff."

Bruce led the way, and they walked through the museum to the conference room that was used for presentations. Earlier the team had gathered the staff working in the museum and forced them all into the room. After shooting Norm, Tony locked the staff in with the dead body, running a chain through the handles of the double doors to the room and padlocked it.

Purses and phones were piled on the floor outside the room. The six people inside cowered along the wall on the other side of the conference room table, as far from the door as they could get. Bruce pulled out his pistol and showed it to them through the window and spun the dial on the combination lock securing the chain. He turned to Clark. "You have your gun?"

Clark pulled it out of his waistband. "Right here."

Bruce whispered, "Don't shoot anybody. It's just for show. To keep them under control." He popped open the lock and pulled the chain through one of the handles so he could open the door. "Stay out here. Just in case." He pulled the door open and slipped inside. Norm's body was laid out against the wall inside the door, covered with a couple light jackets.

Everyone looked so scared. Bruce held the gun behind his back to keep it from their view. Maybe they'd be a little more comfortable. "Can anyone tell me when the rest of the team left?"

Six pairs of eyes looked up at him. Some were red from crying. Nobody said anything.

"Anyone?" Bruce repeated. He waited for an answer.

A couple of people whimpered.

"Anyone? When did the rest of the team leave?"

A mumbled response, "Maybe twenty minutes ago?"

They must've taken off right after they sent him upstairs with Clark. They were left behind to keep the cops busy while the team got away. Clark was right. They were massholes. "You guys sit tight. We don't want anyone else to get hurt. We just need to figure out how we can get out of here." Bruce stepped out of the room and leaned against the glass doors. The hostages were museum employees. Maybe one of them knew a way out of here that they could use without being seen. Or they could pretend they were hostages too, but someone would give them up.

A noise down the hall by the loading dock grabbed his attention. A door opening? A voice yelled, "Answer the phone," and a black case dragging a cord slid from the hallway into the lobby. Bruce heard the door slam shut.

"What's that?" Clark asked.

The box started beeping. Bruce walked over to inspect it. It was a hard black case attached to a cord that led back down the hallway. He followed the cord and saw it led to the door he'd looked out earlier. The black box continued to beep. Bruce walked back to the case, knelt down and opened the case. A phone handset lay in a compartment. He lifted it and the beeping stopped. He moved it to his ear. He didn't say anything.

"Good morning, this is Captain Kiley with the Salem police department. Who am I speaking to?"

Bruce just held the handset to his ear. How did the police know they were there? Why the phone instead of entering?

"Hello?" the voice from the handset said. "Are you there?"

"I'm here," Bruce said.

"We understand that there are hostages and someone may be injured. Is there anything I can do to help you at this time?"

"How do you know that?" Bruce asked. He covered the mouthpiece of the handset and looked at the cameras around the lobby. "Clark. Get something to smash those cameras."

"I thought they were off," Clark said.

"I just want to make sure," Bruce said. He held the phone to his ear again. "How did you know there were hostages here?"

"Are there?" Kiley asked. "Can you let the injured out?"

"They killed him," Bruce said. "We didn't do it."

"Who killed him?"

Bruce squeezed the handset. "I need some time to think," he said and placed the handset back in the case.

CHAPTER THREE

"What a beautiful day to be a pirate!" Tony yelled from the cockpit of the boat as they skimmed over the water. "Right boys?"

The team: Dick, Barry and Arthur, cheered in response and raised their bottles of beer. Tony turned up the music. They were just a bunch of friends, four guys dressed as pirates, out having a party on the water, if anyone paid any attention to them.

Tony steered the boat into the bay on the west side of Misery Island and drifted to a stop among other boats anchored there. Music from several boats in the bay filled the air, each group having their own party. After dropping the anchor, Tony joined his team to celebrate the success of the morning's operation.

The four of them sat on the cushioned benches in the rear of the boat, two on each side facing each other. Tony left the music playing to cover up their conversations. The four of them all leaned forward so they could hear each other. Between them, four wooden cases were stacked on the floor. Tony set his beer on top. "Nice job you guys," he said. "This morning couldn't have gone better. Now, we need to move on to the next phase."

"You sure Bruce and Clark can't give us up?" Dick asked.

"I'm sure," Tony said. "They don't know anymore than I wanted them to know. They know we were headed to the wharf, so we need to keep moving." He handed a duffle to Barry. "Here's your and Arthur's share of the money. After we move some of the art to my boat, Dick will take you to your boat. Then you're gone."

Barry unzipped the duffle and peeked inside. He held it open and showed it to Arthur, who nodded. Barry zipped the duffle.

"Now you three go ditch the pirate costumes," Tony said.

When the three disappeared, Tony pulled off his pirate costume and slipped on a pair of shorts, a t-shirt and a New York Yankees ball cap. While the others were changing, he raised the anchor and started the boat.

He slowly idled over to another anchored boat.

"Dick, take the wheel," Tony said.

Dick took his place and Tony leaned over the side of the boat. "Barry, help me here. Grab a hold and keep us together." With the boats side-by side, Tony stepped over the side and onto the anchored boat. "Arthur, hand me the cases." Arthur passed each of the wooden cases to Tony, one-by-one, and Tony grabbed the metal handles and set the cases in the bottom of his boat. "Gentlemen, it's been a pleasure," he said and gave them a tip of his ball cap. "Dick, I'll see you on the other side of the island."

Tony placed two hands on the boat and gave it a push to separate it from his. "Now get out of here."

While Dick drove his boat over to another anchored boat to drop off Barry and Arthur, Tony pulled up his anchor and started his boat. He laughed and looked up into the sunny sky. They were almost done.

. . .

TONY SLOWLY DROVE his boat around Misery Island. It was a beautiful day to be out on the water. He'd have a lot more days like this when they sold the paintings. He didn't know where he was going, but it would be someplace warm on the water. The Caribbean? Mexico? He'd heard good things about Cabo. He'd have to learn more Spanish.

On the east side of the island, Tony looked for a spot to leave the other boat. If Dick didn't know who he really was, he would've left him and the boat behind. He found a spot far enough from other boats and shifted to neutral, letting the engine idle.

The larger boat pulled up next to him. "What do you want to do?" Dick asked.

"Anchor here," Tony said. "It's as good a spot as any. No other boats around."

Dick turned off the engine and tossed Tony a line. Tony pulled the boat close to his and tied the line to a cleat. He waited for Dick to drop the anchor. He glanced at his watch. "Come on, Dick. We need to shove off."

"I'm ready." Dick walked into the back end of the other boat. "Kind of a shame to leave this art behind after we went to the trouble to take it."

"We have the pieces that count," Tony said. He bent over a black plastic box in the back of his own boat, opened the top and got it ready, connecting wires and flipping the power switch. He flipped the top closed, stood and lifted the box. He set it on the side of the boat. "You ready?"

"Good to go," Dick said.

Tony handed the box across to Dick in the other boat. "Just set it in the back by the engine."

Dick took the box, set it in place and then climbed across

from the other boat to Tony's. Tony sat in the driver's seat and started the boat. "Cast us off," Tony said.

Dick untied the line from the cleat and tossed the loose end into the other boat. "Ready to go, Captain."

"I think it's time to do a little fishing," Tony said. He steered his boat away from La Fiesta. "I feel like a nice surf and turf dinner tonight." When they got a few hundred yards away, Tony slowed the boat and handed Dick a fishing rod. "Let's see who catches the first fish."

CHAPTER FOUR

A bus picked up the FBI Hostage Rescue Team at the Logan International Airport in Boston after they flew up from D.C. The team quickly transferred gear to the bus and boarded. The Massachusetts State Police had a vehicle in front and behind them, lights flashing, ready to escort them to their destination. The door closed behind the last member to board the bus, and they started moving.

Palmer, the team lead, stood at the front of the bus. "Listen up! We have about twenty minutes. We have stolen art and a hostage situation at the Peabody Essex Museum in Salem, Massachusetts. The regional SWAT team's busy with an overnight domestic situation and this is high profile with the value of the art in the museum, so the Boston field office spun us up to help. We believe there are a number of hostages and one has been killed. We're not sure how many perpetrators are in the museum. Local PD deployed a throw phone and has spoken to one bad actor initially. But he quit talking. They can't get him to answer their calls.

"There's a Maritime Festival taking place at the waterfront wharf area about a half mile away from the museum. Salem PD is locking down the area around the museum. When we arrive, I'll connect with them and the Boston FBI agents on site." Palmer bent over and glanced out the front window of the bus, asked the driver a question and turned back to the team. "Use the next fifteen minutes to plan with your partners, check your gear and be ready to hit the ground running when we arrive."

Agent Ross Fruen sat across the aisle from his partners, Agent Stevens and his K-9, Rupert. They'd been partnered in their first assignment months ago, it went well, and Palmer had them working together on subsequent deployments. They'd be working together today.

Everyone was dressed for action in green gear: tactical pants, shirts, ballistic vests with FBI on front and back and with pockets to store additional supplies, helmets, gloves and an assortment of weapons. Stevens sometimes got called upon to be a sniper. Today, Ross and Stevens each carried the HK 416 assault rifle and the Springfield 1911 pistol. Ross used to carry a Glock, but Stevens talked him into the Springfield. He said when he drew it from its holster the skies opened; the sun shone down, and the gun became one with his hand. Ross hadn't had that experience, yet.

Rupert wore a ballistic vest and panted in the seat next to Stevens, waiting for directions from his master.

Ross checked his vest pockets and weapons, making sure everything was ready. The HRT team trained constantly and was always ready to go.

The bus turned a corner and slowed. Outside the window people were dressed in older period costumes, long flowing dresses, and as witches and pirates.

"Where are we?" Ross asked.

Stevens answered. "Looks liked we've gone back in time. Salem witch trials?"

"Maybe we should've dressed differently."

"Yeah, we'll stand out a little," Stevens said.

The bus turned another corner and stopped. Palmer stood. "Everybody off. Grab your gear. Let me find out the situation from the police chief and the Boston FBI team on site. Be ready to deploy."

Rupert whined, ready for action. Stevens scratched him behind the ears. "Just a couple more minutes, buddy."

The team filed off the bus and kept it between them and the museum. They grabbed their bags from the luggage compartment under the bus and laid it out on the ground in groups based on need and experience. There wasn't a lot of talk. The Hostage Rescue Team was like a football team before a big game: each knowing their role, practiced and ready to improvise as needed. Ready for the whistle to start the game.

Ross scanned the surrounding area. The only costumes in this area were other uniforms of emergency personnel. Police cars were parked at the intersections. A firetruck idled at the end of the block.

The sun was high in the clear sky. The sound of quiet music, from the festival at the docks a few blocks away, filled the air along with the hum of the crowd's voices. They partied on, aware or unaware of what was going on a few blocks away.

Palmer and a uniformed police officer joined the team. "Listen up. This is Captain Kiley. His team has the perimeter under control. There's been no communication with anyone inside the museum since the first contact. This morning they got an anonymous call that the museum was being robbed, that there were hostages and one casualty."

Looking out over the team, Palmer said, "Stevens, get the camera up and running on Rupert. We'll need to send him in for reconnaissance. Maybe deliver a radio so we can communicate with whoever is in there. Davis, grab your rifle. Up to the roof." Palmer pointed to a high-rise apartment building on the next block. "And Gronowski, there's a parking garage on the other side of the museum. Top level is your outpost. Get moving."

Davis and Gronowski each took off at a jog to their respective spots to give overhead coverage to the team.

"Captain, do you want to get the museum director over here?" Palmer asked. "See if he has some copies of the museum map for us." He turned back to the team. "When he gets here, we'll ask for options to get Rupert in. We need to know where the perpetrators are and how many. Then we can put an attack plan together."

Ross joined Stevens as he knelt next to Rupert and attached the camera to the back of his vest. Then he clipped an earpiece to Rupert's ear and pushed it into the ear canal. Rupert shook his head. "He still doesn't like that," Stevens said.

"At least he leaves it in." Ross said. "Need any help?"

"We're just about ready. Come with me." Stevens walked a few steps away. "I like to leave him by himself for a little bit while he gets used to the equipment and then I'll test it." He pulled his phone from his pocket and launched the app.

Ross stood next to him to see how things looked. Even though they'd been partnered together since they joined the HRT, he was still amazed how Stevens and Rupert worked as one. Sometimes he thought it was a psychic connection.

The screen showed the area ahead of Rupert. "Camera. Check." Stevens said. He turned up the volume on the phone to check the microphone. They could hear the team talking. "Mic. Check. Let's see if he can hear me." Stevens hit the button to unmute the phone and quietly delivered a command, "Rupert, *Blaffen*." Rupert barked. "Rupert, *Zit*." He sat. "Rupert, *Kom Voor*." Rupert quickly stood, ran to Stevens and sat in front of him, facing him, waiting for his next command. Stevens knelt and scratched Rupert's neck. "*Braaf*," He said. He turned to Ross, "We're ready."

Ross keyed his mic. "Boss, Agent Rupert is ready for recon."

"Come on over," Palmer answered.

"Let's go, guys." Ross, Stevens and Rupert hustled over to meet up with Palmer.

"Where's the museum director?" Palmer asked.

The police captain scanned the area, "They said they were coming over." He pointed across the street, "Here they come."

The largest agent Ross had seen walked towards them. He wore a grey waffle knit shirt, black tactical pants and a dark blue ballistic vest with FBI across the front. His Glock and FBI badge hung from his belt. He led another man, forty-some years old, in khakis and a dark blue shirt, - both pressed, brown hair gelled in place and modern looking glasses with blue-tinted frames. He carried an iPad and shifted it nervously from one hand to the other. The second man wasn't short, he was probably close to six feet tall, but he was six or seven inches shorter than the FBI agent.

"Boston FBI?" Palmer asked.

The giant answered, "Right, and this is Doctor Lewis, the museum director."

Palmer said, "Doctor Lewis, this is some of the team. They'll be trying to enter the museum, get a better sense of the situation and rescue the hostages. What information can you share about entering the museum and what to expect when they get inside?"

"Thank goodness you're here," Doctor Lewis said. He turned his iPad so the team could see the screen. He showed them the Google maps satellite view. "If you get up on the roof and move over to this roof access door, you'll be able to enter. The staff uses the door for smoke breaks." He swiped to open another view. "This is a drawing of the upper level. There are stairs down to the second floor and then the lobby."

"May I?" Palmer asked and took the iPad from the director. He studied it and handed it to Ross.

"I just can't believe this happened this morning," Doctor Lewis said. "I'm worried about the art and my staff. And the Captain said the phone caller said someone had been killed." Doctor Lewis swiped a palm over his forehead and pushed back his hair. "I'm here to help you anyway I can."

"How do we get up on the roof?" Ross asked. The museum had multiple wings, two and three floors high.

"Captain?" Palmer asked.

"The fire department has a ladder truck we can deploy from Essex Street."

Palmer answered. "Sounds good. Fewer windows and if we have police visible, anybody inside will be back and have a hard time seeing. The roof's covered by Davis and Gronowski. Get up there via the ladder, deploy Rupert to get us eyes and ears inside." He gave a hand-held radio to Stevens. "See if he can leave this close to a bad guy inside so we can hear them and maybe talk to them. They haven't been talkative on the throw-phone. Bring ropes in case you need to get down fast. Once Rupert's safely deployed, we'll both have a view of the video and put a plan together."

"Roger," Ross said. He and Stevens grabbed ropes and left for the ladder truck. Rupert followed. When they got to the truck, Stevens knelt and hoisted Rupert across his shoulders. "You sure you don't want me to carry him?" Ross asked. "You're not the best with heights."

"I got him," Stevens answered. "Just follow us up and keep me moving."

Ross radioed the team watching the roof, "All clear up top boys?" The all clear sign came back from both snipers and Ross and Stevens climbed the ladder to the roof, Ross following Stevens and Rupert to the top.

CHAPTER FIVE

M usic from the waterfront floated up over the sound of the idling firetruck. People gathered behind the barricades and watched the operation unfolding at the museum. At the top of the ladder, Ross squeezed by Stevens and led the way onto the roof. He covered the area with his assault rifle and gave the all clear signal to Stevens.

Stevens lowered Rupert onto the roof and all three of them took a ready position, Ross and Stevens with rifles ready to fire.

"The door's by the air-conditioning units," Stevens said.

"Watch the door and I'll drop the ropes," Ross said. He took the two ropes and tied them to a metal stand pipe. He uncoiled the ropes as he walked to the edge of the roof and dropped them over the side. Then he rejoined Stevens and Rupert. "We're set," he said.

"Let's go," Stevens said.

"Overwatch, we're moving," Ross radioed to the snipers.

Stevens gave Rupert a command to stay and he and Ross moved across the roof, walking quietly. They moved as one, from experience, each covering a sector and protecting the other. They avoided skylights so they wouldn't be seen from inside. Stevens called for Rupert and sent him to check the door, to smell if anyone was on the other side. Rupert didn't signal for human or explosive scents. "Looks clear," Stevens said.

"I'll prop it open so Rupert can get in," Ross said.

"I'll cover the door while you open it." Stevens positioned himself behind one of the AC units, with Rupert by his side.

Ross approached the door. This was it. He trusted Rupert, but there could always be a surprise. Maybe they booby-trapped the door. He tied a rope to the handle. Then he pushed on the thumb lever to disengage the latch and used a piece of duct tape to hold it in place. Holding the rope, he backed away from the door, letting the rope slide through his gloved hand. He laid on the roof to minimize his exposure, aimed his rifle at the door and pulled on the rope with his left hand.

The rope grew taught. The door didn't budge. Ross pulled harder, and the door opened with a pop and slowly swung open.

When it was open about a foot, Stevens said, "Hold it," over the radio. "Looks clear. Hold it there. I'll send Rupert over to check it out." He put the hand-held radio in Rupert's mouth and issued the command to hold on to it. Then he pointed him to the door and Rupert trotted over and slowed as he approached it. Stevens commanded, "Rupert, *Af.*" Rupert laid down facing the door about ten feet away. "Rupert, *Dik-By.*" Rupert crept closer to the door.

"I don't see anything on the screen," Stevens said to Ross. "I think we're good." He issued a command, "Rupert, *Blif.*"

"Tie the rope to something to keep the door open," Stevens said.

Ross tied the rope to a metal equipment support to keep the door open so Rupert could get in. He and Stevens stayed in position watching the door. "You guys have Rupert and us covered?" Ross asked the sniper. He heard two "Rogers" in reply.

"We're ready, Boss," Ross said. "Rupert's in place and ready to enter."

Ross joined Stevens, and they studied the image on his phone. Ross knew Palmer could see the same image.

"Send him in," Palmer said. "Let's see what we're up against."

Stevens issued the command, "Rupert, *Reveiren*." He rolled the R's of the word.

On the screen they watched the image change as Rupert stood and entered the building to begin his search. Rupert worked his way down the stairs and through the building. Stevens issued him additional commands in a soft voice, guiding him left or right or having him stop so he could listen for voices or other sounds.

"RUPERT, *HALT,*" Stevens commanded. Rupert must've been on a stair landing based on the image angle. The image bounced a little as Rupert panted, moving the camera up and down.

"What've we got?" Palmer asked. On the screen was an image of someone in a Superman costume. Behind him they could see Batman inside a conference room. He was holding a gun. Past him in the conference room they could see a group of people.

"You seeing what we're seeing?" Stevens asked Palmer. "Superheroes."

Superman looked right at them and turned to Batman.

"He saw Rupert," Stevens said.

Palmer said, "Wait."

They watched as Superman went to the conference room

door and spoke with Batman. Superman turned and headed for Rupert.

"Drop the radio and get him out," Palmer said.

Stevens issued a command, "Rupert, *Loslaten*. Rupert, *Kom Hier*." The image on the screen changed as Rupert turned and headed to the roof.

"Watch the roof, boys," Ross said into the radio for the snipers. "Rupert's coming out of the door and somebody might come out behind him." He hustled to the spot where he'd tied the rope holding the door open and readied himself.

"He's coming. He took a couple of wrong turns," Stevens replied.

Ross got ready to let the door close after Rupert exited.

"He's getting close," Stevens said. "I see light in the stairwell."

Ross watched and waited. He cared about this dog, one of his partners. He'd get out okay. Where is he? Rupert exited the building and Ross pulled the rope, undoing the slip knot he'd tied. The door swung shut.

"Rupert, *heir*," Stevens said. Rupert ran over to him. "*Braaf*."

The door stayed shut.

CHAPTER SIX

Clark knocked on the glass conference room door. "Bruce, come here." He motioned wildly and glanced back across the lobby. "Bruce!"

Bruce stepped out of the conference room. "What's up?"

"There was a friggin' robo dog out here."

"What are you talking about?"

"I saw a robo dog or something over there. A dog in a vest, maybe a camera strapped to his back."

"Where?"

Clark nodded across the lobby. "Over there. On the stair landing."

"Go check it out. I think it's time to get out of here."

While Clark walked over to the stairs, Bruce ran the chain through the door handles in preparation to lock it again. He needed to figure out what they were going to do. He looked at the people cowering in the room, Norm dead on the floor. Tony was going to answer for all of this when they caught up with him.

Clark joined Bruce outside the conference room. "The

dog disappeared, but I found this." He held out a walkie-talkie. "It was on the floor."

"Go up the stairs, make sure we don't have any company." Bruce took the radio from Clark. It was on. A red light flashed on the top next to the stubby black antenna that stuck out of the top. Somebody wanted to communicate with them. He hadn't answered any ringing phones earlier and stayed silent on the phone the cops threw in earlier. He depressed the talk button and let it up again.

A few seconds later a voice came over the radio. "Hello, is somebody there?"

Bruce held the radio, debating if he should answer or not.

"Hello, this is Special Agent Palmer with the FBI. I'd like to speak with you about getting you and the museum staff out of the museum safely."

Bruce listened without answering.

"I don't want to talk if you can't hear me. Can you say something or key the radio again so I know you're there?"

Clark rejoined Bruce. "Nobody. No dog on the stairs." He bounced from foot to foot and nodded at the radio. "It's the Feds? What are we going to do?"

Again, Bruce just held the radio and listened. He put a finger to his lips to shush Clark.

"Just let me know you can hear me and we'll put together a solution to get you and the hostages out of there."

Bruce toggled the Talk button with his thumb.

"Thanks. I appreciate the gesture," the voice said over the radio. "We understand that somebody's been injured. Can we start with getting them out of there to get them medical attention?"

Clark threw up his hands. "What are we going to do? It's going to be bad when they find out he's dead, not just hurt. We have the others. We can use them as bargaining chips."

"Nobody else is getting hurt today," Bruce said. "This was

supposed to be an easy job. Get the art, get it out of here. Get paid." He glanced through the glass into the conference room. He had to figure out how to work out a deal to let them go or they'd be going to prison. Hostages?

"What do we do, Bruce? We're effed."

"I think the truth might just set us free," Bruce said.

"Can we work something out?" the voice on the radio asked again.

Bruce started pacing across the floor. He'd formed a plan to propose to the FBI. He held the radio up to his mouth and pushed the button. "I have a proposal for you," he said.

"Is this Batman or Superman?"

"It's Batman," Bruce said. "Wait. How do you know we're Batman and Superman?" He looked around the room for cameras.

"We had a camera on the dog that your partner saw. He just delivered the radio you're holding. He's gone now."

"Listen," Bruce said. "The art is gone. I think our partners left us behind to keep you busy while they got away. All I want to do is get my buddy and me out of here safely and I'll tell you where there're going."

"Do you know?" Clark whispered.

Bruce nodded.

The answer came over the radio. "Batman, if what you say is true, that the others got away with the art. I can't just let you go too, can I? I have no leverage that you'll tell me where they went."

"Well, we need a solution," Bruce replied. "Figure out a way to get us out of here or we'll have to get more aggressive. We have hostages. People and the art that's left here. We don't want to harm either, but we will. You have fifteen minutes to figure out a solution. Let us go and I tell you where the art went. Don't let us go and it's on you."

"Can you move the injured person to the door so we can

extricate them and get them medical attention?"

"He's dead. Someone from the crew that got away killed him. Fifteen minutes," Bruce said.

"I need thirty to review the options and put together a plan for you."

"Fifteen."

"Okay, fifteen. Don't hurt anyone else."

Bruce unlaced the chain from the conference room door handles and stuck his head in. The museum staff was quiet, just sitting along the wall. "Who has a car by the loading dock?"

Nobody answered. A couple of people looked away, not wanting to make eye contact. A couple just stared at him. Less afraid than the others. Maybe just pissed off.

"If I can get a car by the loading dock we're out of here and the police will come and get you after we leave." Bruce waited for an answer. He tapped the barrel of the gun against his leg. "Who has a car?" he yelled. He and Clark had to get out of here.

A woman with grey hair raised her hand. "I do."

"What is it?" Bruce asked. "Where are the keys?"

"It's a dirty white Subaru wagon. The keys are in my purse."

"Which purse is yours?"

"It's red."

Bruce picked up a red purse in the pile by the straps and held it up so she could see it. "This one?"

The woman nodded.

He closed the door and dumped the contents of the purse on the floor. Geez, women carried a lot of crap. He pushed the items around and picked up a black key fob with the Subaru logo on it and a mess of keys attached to it by a big metal ring. He tapped the glass and held them up for the lady to see. She nodded her head.

CHAPTER SEVEN

P almer, the radio channel open to everyone on the team, started barking orders to his team members and the Boston FBI agent who had joined them. "Get on the cameras around here: traffic cameras, ATM's, businesses, and see if he's telling the truth. Did another crew leave earlier with the art? When and where can we track them to?"

Agent Ramirez from Palmer's HRT team said, "I got it."

"Fruen and Stevens. You're on the roof with Rupert?" Palmer asked.

"Roger," Ross replied.

"Be ready to reenter the museum. I'm sure we just have the two bad guys inside. We know you can enter from there. We'll send Rupert in first, I'll monitor the video along with you and we'll decide on when to go. I'm sending the Boston FBI agent up with you." Palmer paused. "Boston, grab a shield. I'd prefer three on two going in. You're big and can go over the top of the shield and they can go from either side. Grab a helmet and get up to the roof."

"Yes, Sir," the agent replied.

. . .

THE BOSTON FBI agent climbed off the firetruck ladder onto the roof. He held the ballistic shield by its handle with his left hand. Ross gave the agent a fist-bump. "I'm Ross Fruen, that's Stevens and Rupert. Just follow us."

"I'm Martinson," the big agent said. He shook hands with Stevens.

"Ten minutes left," Palmer said on the radio. "See if Rupert can get a view of the two guys and the hostages. We need an idea of the situation. Some of this will be your call."

Ross relayed the message to the Martinson.

Ross and Stevens went through the same motions again to open the door. Stevens sent Rupert ahead down the stairs. Since all was clear, he nodded his head towards the door and slowly entered while he watched the image on his phone. Ross followed him and signaled Martinson to fall in behind them.

THE AGENTS STOPPED on the stairs. Stevens checked the image on his phone and whispered commands to Rupert to get him to move into a position that allowed the camera to view the two costumed figures and see into the conference room. He directed Rupert into the shadows of the stair landing. "Hopefully he's far enough back where just the camera is visible to those two," he said to Ross and Martinson.

"We're in position," Ross radioed to Palmer.

"Can you hear what they're saying?" Palmer asked.

"No, but you can see they appear agitated. They're still separate from the hostages. I think we can surprise them," Ross whispered.

"Can you move them away from the hostages so they aren't in your line of fire?" Palmer asked. "I'm radioing

Batman in five minutes. Maybe you can catch them off guard while I'm talking to him."

"We'll run through a couple scenarios. Let us know when you're going to call him."

Ross gathered Stevens and Agent Martinson with him on the stairs, up around the corner of the landing so the bad guys couldn't see them. "The boss is going to radio them in a couple of minutes. Our goal is to move them to our right, away from the hostages and take them."

"Options?" Stevens asked. "Use Rupert? Flash bang?"

Martinson stood holding the shield. "What else do we have?" he asked. "Alarm system, lights, fire extinguishers. We can't just shoot them, right?"

"Not if they aren't threatening us or the hostages," Ross said. "Can one of us sneak down the stairs and move to the left ahead of time to change the angle? They'll move away from pressure. The goal is to move them away from the hostages."

Palmer pinged Ross and Stevens on the radio. "Time's up. I'm going to see if I can get them to move towards the loading dock. That should create a gap between them and the hostages."

"We're ready," Ross said. He told Martinson to get ready with the shield. When Palmer got the dynamic duo to move, the three agents would move down the stairs behind the shield and maybe fan out from there. Stevens would monitor the video feed and signal when they were free to move.

"Save the hostages, save the art," Palmer said

"Roger that," Ross replied. "Save the hostages, save the art."

CHAPTER EIGHT

Bruce glanced at the clock on the wall. Time was up. He wiggled the radio in his hand, willing the FBI agent to call.

"Is he going to call?" Clark asked.

"He'll call." Bruce had used the fifteen minutes to create a plan. He held a few chips. He had the hostages. He had the art in the museum. He could offer up the heist team and the art they'd taken, maybe. He knew some of the details and options of plans they'd discussed for when they got away. The plan probably wasn't accurate, but the FBI didn't know that.

A voice from the radio said, "This is Agent Palmer. Let's talk."

Bruce thumbed the button and replied, "We have hostages and art in here. We can hold out for a while, but the rest of the crew got away with the major pieces. The longer we debate, the farther away they get. Too long and you'll never get the art back."

"What do you propose?" Palmer asked.

"We have keys for a car in the parking lot. Let us drive away and I'll tell you where the crew went."

"Why would I trust you?"

Bruce shook his head and growled into the radio, "Because they abandoned us here."

"I let you go. And you'll call me and tell me where the art they took went," Palmer said. "That's not a lot of leverage."

"Tick Tock," Bruce replied. "They're getting farther away while we talk."

"Give me a few minutes," Palmer replied.

Bruce and Clark stood facing each other. With the masks on they couldn't see each other's faces, but Bruce could tell Clark was nervous: he paced around and fiddled with the pistol in his hand. "Clark, this is a gamble. If they let us go, great. If they don't, they arrest us and we're in a position again to bargain. Less prison time for giving them info. We didn't kill Norm, we don't have the stolen art. We can trade info for leniency."

"I'm not a snitch," Clark said.

"Listen," Bruce said. "We're trapped here. Left behind to take the rap. We don't owe those guys anything. We might get out of here, but we're probably going to get caught. We don't have anything for our troubles, no money or anything. All we have is info."

"We can't just give up," Clark said. "We've never given up anything without a fight."

"We'll talk with this Palmer and see if we can work something out." Bruce tossed the car keys he'd gotten from the hostage in the air and caught them. "There's a chance."

"This is Agent Palmer," the voice on the radio said. "Come to the parking lot door and we'll work something out. I'll leave a cell phone for you on the stairs. We'll move back and let you get to the car. If."

"If what?"

"If you give me a name. Come to the door and give me the

name of the leader and you'll have a path to the car. Then in fifteen minutes you call me with the other info."

"We'll need to trust each other," Bruce said. "We're moving to the door."

CHAPTER NINE

Ross readied his assault rifle. "Get ready," he whispered. "They're going to move." He glanced at Stevens, who watched over the scene of the two thieves on his phone. Martinson lifted the ballistic shield, his left arm holding it in front of him, his right holding his Glock.

"We'll see if we can get down the stairs to the floor without them noticing us," Ross said. "Then we announce and take them. Save the hostages, protect the art."

"Roger," Stevens answered.

Martinson nodded.

The three of them inched up to the corner of the stairwell. Ross stood on Martinson's right side and placed his left hand on his arm to move him to the left a little. Stevens stood on Martinson's left. When Stevens gave them the signal, they would move down the stairs and onto the floor together, protected by the shield and their body armor. Rupert must've sensed the tension. He repositioned himself and rose slightly.

"Rupert, *Stil*," Stevens commanded. "Let's go."

They silently swung around the corner and descended the

stairs. Martinson led the way, aiming his Glock over the top of the shield. Ross scanned the main floor. The costumed characters were moving away from the conference room. They each held a handgun. A large painting leaned against the wall. Batman appeared to be talking on the radio. They didn't notice the FBI agents coming down the stairs.

Martinson reached the main floor and took a few steps forward. Ross joined him and peeked out from the right side of the shield. His aim on Batman on the right. He knew Stevens did the same on the left, aimed at Superman. "FBI, drop your guns!" Ross yelled.

"FBI!" Stevens echoed.

Superman's head jerked around to the right. He grabbed the frame of the painting, pulled it and swung it around in front of him. It screeched as it slid across the concrete floor. Hiding behind it, his arm stuck out along the edge, and he fired. Ross felt like he was in the painting, cannons from two ships firing at each other, smoke filling the air.

Batman was behind the painting. No shots came from him. Ross changed his aim to Superman, looking for a shot. Four shots rang out rapidly in succession from close by. Four holes appeared in the painting to the right of the frame, right about where Superman stood behind it. The shooting stopped: both from Superman and from the FBI agents. The painting wobbled and fell forward onto the floor with Superman laying on top of it.

Batman was left standing and put his hands in the air. He dropped to his knees. "Don't shoot. Don't shoot," he yelled.

Rupert ran forward and bit down on Superman's right arm, the gun still in his hand.

"Martinson, cover us," Ross said.

Stevens joined Rupert and took the gun from Superman.

Ross approached Batman. "On your stomach," he ordered. "Hands out to your sides."

Batman lay on the back of the painting and reached his hands out to either side.

"Left hand behind your back," Ross ordered. He placed a handcuff around his wrist. "Now your right hand." Ross handcuffed the other, locking Batman's wrists together behind his back. He pulled his mask off. "We've got control," Ross radioed to Palmer. "Send in medical. We have one apprehended and one with multiple gun-shot wounds needing attention."

"We're coming in," Palmer replied.

Ross motioned to Agent Martinson. "Come here and watch this one. I'll attend to the hostages."

"I have the combo," Batman said.

"What?" Ross asked.

"The conference room doors are chained shut and locked with a padlock."

"Okay. What's the combo?"

Batman told Ross the combination. Ross unlocked the padlock and got into the conference room. "Hey, folks. I'm Special Agent Ross Fruen with the FBI. Everyone okay in here?"

The hostages got up from the floor. One man came over and embraced Ross. "You're all welcome," Ross said. "If you could all sit at the conference table here and face away from what's going on out there, we'll have someone come in and talk to you, get some information and then we'll give you some time to contact your friends and family. Are there more bad guys?"

"We've only seen the two since the others left," a man answered.

A member of the HRT team joined the group in the conference room. Ross went back out to talk with Palmer.

"Stevens, you and Rupert take Gregor and Lawrence with

you and clear the museum. Make sure nobody else is here," Palmer said.

"Is Superman going to make it?" Ross asked.

"He'll make it," Palmer said. He looked down at the painting lying on the floor. "Save the hostages, save the art. Some simple instructions." He looked up at the two of them, Ross and Martinson, standing by the painting and directed his gaze at Agent Martinson. "The hostages are saved. But this painting didn't make it. Do you know Agent Val Martinson from the Boston office with the Art Crime team? I haven't seen her yet."

Ross smiled, and a laugh escaped.

"What's so funny, Agent Fruen?" Palmer asked.

Ross pointed at the large agent next to him with his thumb. "Let me introduce you to Agent Val Martinson."

"YOU'RE AGENT VAL MARTINSON, our art expert?" Palmer asked.

Val stood the ballistic shield on its end and leaned an arm on it. "That's me."

"You shot the painting."

Special Agent Palmer stood in front of the agents, Fruen and Martinson, and shook his head. The painting, with four bullet holes through it and blood splattered all over the back, lay on the floor. Paramedics were putting Superman on a gurney to transport him to the hospital. Batman sat against the wall, his hands handcuffed behind his back. An agent watched over him.

"I shot Superman through the painting. He was shooting at us."

"Okay," Palmer said. "But you had to shoot through the painting?"

"I was protecting myself and the other agents. It'd be a

little harder to fix us. They can fix the painting." Val paused. "If they want too."

"If they want too?" Palmer stared at Agent Martinson. "I think they'll want to," he said. "And probably charge the FBI for the cost. I'm recommending the Boston office pick up the tab."

Val shifted his weight and smiled. "It shouldn't cost much."

"I think it'll cost plenty. Specialized skills, experts, etcetera. It's not just some tape and a touchup."

"The painting's a fake."

Palmer stared at Martinson and narrowed his eyes. "A fake?"

"It's a good fake," Val said. "The museum probably thinks it's an original. But the real one is still floating around out there somewhere." He lifted his hand and circled his finger through the air.

Palmer shook his head. "A fake." He inhaled and blew out a long breath. "You can tell the museum director. Follow me. Both of you. We're going to go find out what they took and talk to Batman."

STEVENS AND RUPERT returned after clearing the museum. They joined Agents Martinson and Ross and sat on one side of the conference room table where the hostages had been sitting earlier. They faced the door and watched the activity outside of the room through the glass walls. The damaged painting was being moved. Batman sat against the wall. Palmer and the shaken museum director, Doctor Lewis, went up the stairs.

Rupert lay under the table at Stevens' feet. The three agents waited for another agent to bring in Batman so they could interrogate him and for Palmer to come back with the museum director, who was inventorying the works to determine what was missing.

"So, it's a fake," Ross said.

"Yep," Val answered.

"Glad you knew and shot Superman."

"I'm glad he wasn't bulletproof."

"I dated a Val once," Stevens said. "Luckily she didn't look like you."

"You're better looking than some of his dates," Ross said.

"Shut up," Stevens said. "So, where'd Val come from? Family name?"

Val shook his head. "No. My mom was a fan of Val Kilmer in Top Gun."

"Hmm," Stevens replied. "A good movie. You must get that question a lot."

"Yep."

"So why art?" Ross asked.

"I played football in college and I liked art. Did some painting. Studied art history. Got hurt playing football, wasn't good enough to go pro and my art skills are good, but not that good. So, I applied to the FBI and offered up my art knowledge. I've been on the art crimes team since I came out of The Academy. Searching for lost art and returning it to its rightful owner. Interesting and rewarding work. I can't stand people who buy great works of art and keep it for themselves. It should be enjoyed by all."

"What was going on here today?" Ross asked.

Leaning forward, his elbows on the table, Val answered, "I'm hoping Batman can tell us. But, my guess is either these idiots decided to rob a museum, thinking it would be easy to find a buyer for the paintings, or, the more probable, some rich collector wanted some paintings for his private collection and these guys were hired to get them."

"They took hostages and killed somebody," Stevens said.

"That's why I think it's the second." Val said. "I want to hear what's missing from the museum director." He stood up from the table. "We need to get Batman in here to find out where the stolen art went and who took them."

"Here he comes," Stevens said.

The conference door swung open, and the agent escorted Batman into the room.

A growl rumbled from under the table. "Rupert, shh," Stevens commanded.

Val sat in the middle with Ross on his left, Stevens on his right.

Ross asked the agent escorting Batman to remove the handcuffs and guard the door. Then he directed his gaze to the prisoner. "Just sit there." He pointed at a chair across the table from the three of them.

Val leaned forward towards Batman. He knew his being an FBI agent, a large FBI agent, often intimidated people. Before he could ask his first question, Batman blurted out, "How's Clark?"

"We can find out," Val said. "He was alive when the paramedics wheeled him out." He paused.

"I'll tell you whatever you want to know," Batman said. He leaned forward towards Val. The agent behind him stepped forward and put a hand on his shoulder. He sat back in his chair. "Tony killed Norm, and they left me and Clark here to take the rap. I'm hoping you'll give us a deal if we help, but I just want to get Tony for leaving us here."

"Who's Tony?" Val asked. "You know his full name? Is Tony his actual name?"

"Geez, I don't know. He's just Tony." Batman drummed his hands on the table and blew a breath towards the ceiling. "He planned this thing. I can answer all of your questions, but you gotta go get him before he gets away."

"You know where they went or where they're going?" Val asked.

"He said they were going to the wharf. They had a couple of Amazon delivery trucks to haul the paintings away and those big sailing ship statues, the carvings on the bow."

"Figureheads," Val said.

"Yeah. Okay. The figureheads. Whatever. Tony said they were hauling them down to the wharf."

Val stood. "Let's go." He looked at agents Fruen and Stevens. "Come on. We have to get to the wharf." He looked at the agent by the door and pointed at Batman. "Cuff him. He's coming with us."

CHAPTER TEN

Val grabbed Batman by the elbow and guided him towards the loading dock door. They'd handcuffed his hands in front of him. Agents Fruen, Stevens, and Rupert followed. Their steps echoed off the concrete floor. "What's your name, anyway?" Val asked.

"It's Bruce."

"No, really, your actual name. Not Batman's name, Bruce Wayne."

"Really, it's Bruce. Bruce Miner."

"Really? Okay," Val said. "That should be easy to remember."

Ross called out from behind them, "Hey, Martinson, I told Palmer we got Batman and we're going after the stolen art. He said don't wreck anymore of it."

"How we getting to the wharf?" Stevens asked.

"I have a vehicle," Val answered. He pushed the exit door open and pulled Bruce out behind him. "It's over on the other side of the bus." They hustled across the parking lot. The sun shone high in the sky and Val felt a light breeze when they cleared the building. The heavy beat of an amplified bass from the party at the waterfront echoed off the storefronts.

After swinging around the bus, Val pushed the button on the key fob and the rear gate of the black Suburban automatically opened. "Come on, Bruce. You're riding shotgun." He guided Bruce to the front passenger seat.

Stevens issued a command, "Rupert, *Stap in.*" Rupert jumped into the rear of the vehicle and Stevens pushed the button on the door to close it. He and Ross each climbed into the back seats.

Val started the Suburban, squawked the siren, hit the lights and drove over the park grass to the street. "You know how to get to the wharf?" he asked Bruce.

"It's close. Take a left here and then hang a right on Congress."

The Suburban tires lightly squealed when Val cranked the wheel to the left. He honked the horn as he approached the next corner and turned right onto Congress Street. Pedestrians stepped back from the curb and watched them cruise by. He hit the siren and cars ahead of him pulled over.

A sign on the left said Pickering Wharf Marina. Big white tents filled an empty lot and people dressed in costumes wandered around, lined up for food and drink or watched the band playing on the stage in the center of the block. Val turned left and slowed because of the people filling the street.

"Where are they, Bruce?" Val asked.

"I don't know. The plan was to drive the vans to the wharf. That's all I knew."

"Damn it." Val stopped the Suburban. He thought about what they knew and didn't know. The gang had taken large paintings, figureheads and probably some other items. Disguised as super heroes. "Tony isn't Tony, is he? What was his costume?"

"Ironman, Tony Stark," Bruce answered.

"Let's see if we can find a couple of Amazon delivery trucks and people dressed as superheroes."

"Umm," Bruce said.

"What?" Val asked.

"They aren't wearing their superhero costumes now. We wore pirate costumes under these." Bruce tugged at his own Batman costume.

"You gotta be kidding me." Val looked out the windows of the Suburban at the crowds. Half the people were dressed as witches or pirates.

"CAN YOU BELIEVE THIS?" Val looked in the rearview mirror at Fruen and Stevens in the back seat.

Fruen let out a breathy laugh. "Whoever this Tony guy is, he's a smart guy. He planned, timed and executed this heist well."

"What do you think we should do?" Val asked.

"Let's roll over to the docks on the other side of these tents and see what we can see. We're behind them on the timeline. But we should check it out."

Val shifted into Drive and slowly moved ahead. Pirates drinking beer gave him the finger and moved out of the way. Fruen was right, Tony was smart. He'd planned this heist during the festival, left Bruce and his partner to stall the authorities. Val needed to quit reacting and start thinking.

They rolled onto the wide walkway that ran between the storefronts and the water. Boats of all sizes were tied along the edge. People partied on the boat decks, laughing, drinking, eating.

"Up there," Stevens said. He pointed over the seat.

Ahead were two Amazon delivery vans parked on the walkway, one in front of the other. Val rolled forward and stopped about thirty yards behind them.

"We'll check them out," Stevens said. "Pop the back open to release Rupert."

The back gate swung open, and Rupert jumped down to the sidewalk. Stevens and Fruen each exited the vehicle and stayed behind the open doors on either side of the vehicle for protection. Ross called to the people on the boat tied to the walkway next to him and told them to get down.

"Rupert, *reveiren,*" Stevens commanded and pointed at the vans ahead of them. Rupert trotted ahead and searched the closest van, sniffing at the doors. He moved on to the second one parked in front of the first. He trotted back to the closest van and sat. "Let's go," Stevens said. "He doesn't detect anyone."

Fruen and Stevens, rifles up, approached the first vehicle. They waved at people walking on the sidewalk to move away. Val could tell Fruen and Stevens had worked together before. They moved in sync without communicating, each covering the vehicle ahead and each other. Fruen moved forward and looked in the windows of the van. He signaled with his left hand, waving palm down, that it was clear. Then he pointed to the second vehicle.

Fruen went left, Stevens right, and they worked their way to the second van. Ross searched it and relaxed, lowering his gun. He waved for Val to join them.

"Let's go, Bruce. There might be something you can help with up there." Val exited the Suburban and walked around to let Bruce out. He grabbed him by the elbow again and guided him up to meet the other agents. People on the boat had their cell phones out and were shooting video and photos of what was happening on the sidewalk. Val thought the captions with FBI agents and a handcuffed Batman would be good.

Using Amazon delivery vans was smart, Val thought, as they walked by the first one. They were everywhere, and nobody paid attention to them now. Stores and restaurants lined the sidewalk on the left and these vans could've been delivering to any of them. On the right, Val noticed an empty boat slip. He didn't feel good about that.

Val and Bruce got to the second van and joined Fruen, Stevens and Rupert. "What've we got?" Val asked.

"The other van is empty," Fruen said. He pulled open the double doors of the second van. "This one's got something in it."

Stepping forward, Val saw a pile of superhero costumes. Bruce was right, they'd taken them off. Now they looking for a group of pirates. On the floor of the van next to the costumes was a larger figurehead laying on its side. "Well, we got the right vans." He looked at the empty slip. "Looks like they unloaded the vans here onto a boat. This was too big, too heavy, or they got interrupted." He eyed the water channel running parallel to the boardwalk and thought about the boat. If it left here, it turned right into another channel protected by a manmade strip of land. Then it turned east past a lighthouse, and they were out in the harbor. Then it was north or south. They weren't going across the Atlantic.

Fruen said, "We'll call the Harbormaster, have them be on the lookout for our boat, see if they have any video."

"Sure," Val said. He pulled out his cell phone and shot a photo of the figurehead. Then he switched it to video and recorded the delivery vans, their location and the boats on either end of the empty boat slip.

"Let's get Salem PD to secure these vans, talk to some of the people docked along here. Once they're here, we'll head back to the museum and check in with Palmer," Ross said.

Val was curious what the thieves ended up taking. "Yep, let's do that."

· · ·

THE ACTIVITY outside the museum was calming down. The firetrucks and bystanders were gone. A few police were still positioned around the outside of the building.

Inside the museum was a little calmer too. Agent Fruen radioed Palmer to let him know they were back.

Val escorted Bruce over to the conference room, rolled a chair outside the room and placed it next to the door. "Sit and stay here until we need you," he said. "If you think of anything else that might help, you let me know." He motioned to a police officer to watch Bruce and joined Agents Fruen and Stevens at the conference table.

"That was a bust," Stevens said. "The art's gone."

"We're not done," Martinson said. "Let's find out what they took, let the techs analyze video and records, see if the police get anything from their interviews."

Palmer walked into the conference room accompanied by Doctor Lewis with his iPad.

"Gentlemen, Doctor Lewis and I have walked the museum, and he's inventoried what's here and made a list of what's missing. Let's sit and talk."

They settled into their seats at the table. Val sat on the left this time, Fruen in the middle and Stevens on the right. Across from them, Palmer was on the left and Doctor Lewis to the right. "Do we know what was taken?" Val asked.

"A lot," Doctor Lewis said. "It's all irreplaceable."

"I understand," Val said. "Have you identified what's missing?"

Doctor Lewis appeared broken. His shoulders sagged, and his voice quavered. "The main items they stole were five maritime paintings by James Buttersworth. There are other works of art that were taken, but these five are the most valuable."

"I'm sorry," Val said. "Do you have descriptions of them and values?"

Doctor Lewis propped his iPad at an angle using the case and turned it so the agents could see the screen. "These are the five." He swiped his finger over the screen to advance from one image to the next. "The Chaquita, the Dauntless, the Dreadnought. He flipped through two more screens. I'm heartbroken. These were in my care, and they're gone. They're irreplaceable."

"What's their value?" Val asked. He thought he knew, but wanted Doctor Lewis to say so Palmer and team would see what they were after.

"Depending on the environment among the collectors and museums, the economy, what else is on the market, five hundred thousand to one million."

"Dollars?" Stevens asked.

"Yes," Doctor Lewis answered.

"For all of them?" Fruen asked.

"No. Each."

"Wow," Fruen responded.

"What makes them so valuable?" Stevens added.

Doctor Lewis turned the iPad back and shared the screen with Palmer. "James Butterworth is among the top American ship portraitists of the nineteenth century. His style and detail showed the ships in motion battling the seas and the wind. He made it appear as if the ships were moving in front of your eyes."

"How big are these paintings?" Fruen asked. "Are they as big as the one out there?" The painting Bruce and Clark had hidden behind and that Val shot leaned against the museum wall by where it had fallen.

"No," Doctor Lewis answered. "These are two feet by three feet at the most. Easy to carry. Easy to transport."

"What else did they take?" Val asked.

"Some other paintings by less renowned artists. Other maritime artifacts. A couple of figureheads. Maybe thirty items. I think they knew what they wanted," Doctor Lewis said.

"I think so too," Val said. "Can you give me a list of all the items? I'll distribute it to all of my contacts and we'll know if anything surfaces. I'll focus on the Buttersworths, but if any of the items show up, it may point us in a direction to pursue the rest of the items."

"Yes, of course."

"We did find a figurehead in a truck down by the wharf," Val said. He pulled his phone out of his pocket, opened the photos app and slid it across the table to Doctor Lewis. "We don't know if they left it behind because they were in a hurry, it was too heavy, or maybe they damaged it and didn't want to waste the effort of moving it."

Doctor Lewis studied the photo on the phone and slid it back to Val. "I hope no other pieces of art get damaged." He directed his gaze at Val.

"I'm sorry about that. I hope it can be repaired."

"The painting's a fake?" Doctor Lewis asked.

"It's a good one. But I believe the real one is somewhere in Europe."

"I always had my doubts about this one. I guess I didn't really want to know if we'd been fooled or not." Doctor Lewis paused in thought and then returned his gaze to Val. "It's a magnificent representation of the battle. Our visitors liked it. We'll have to get it repaired."

Palmer took control of the meeting back. "All right. I'll follow up with Salem PD and the Harbormaster on anything they've found with interviews and video. You two," he pointed at Fruen and Stevens, "see what else Batman can give us and then release him to the police to process. His partner, Superman, seemed to be more of the muscle of the two. And you," he looked at Val, "get the info out on your network, see what else you can come up with for ideas." He turned to

Doctor Lewis, "Are you able to hang around for a while and answer any other questions we may have?"

"I'll give you all the time you need to get the art back for my collection. You can find me in my office or call my cell phone if I'm not there."

"Doctor Lewis, can I accompany you to your office?" Val asked. "I'd like to get the list and ask you some more questions."

"I'm ready to help anyway I can."

Palmer glanced at his watch. "Meet back here in a thirty minutes."

CHAPTER ELEVEN

Val walked with Doctor Lewis up the stairs. Their footsteps echoed in the empty stairwell. Along the way he made small talk, trying to get to know Doctor Lewis better and to calm him down. He talked about his interest in art and offered some more info on the fake painting. He left out the fact that he shot it. He asked Doctor Lewis about Salem and the museum.

Everyone was a suspect at this point, including the director of the museum and all of its employees. Finding out from Bruce that the thieves got access to the museum through information they learned from an employee and they'd killed him raised a lot of questions. Rare art and money drove some people to do some weird things. Val had seen it many times in his work investigating other art crimes.

The clock was ticking, and he had to track down this art before it got too far away and ended up on a collector's wall in their office, villa, or private art gallery, never to be seen by the rest of the world again.

Doctor Lewis led the way into his office. It was a combination of corporate executive and museum gallery. One end held a large, neat modern desk with a couple of chairs facing it. The other end, a couch, chairs and coffee table. Maritime paintings hung on all the walls, illuminated with overhead lighting. Other maritime related objects sat on shelves and end tables.

"Let's sit here," Doctor Lewis said. He led the way to the couch and chairs. Val took one chair and let Doctor Lewis sit on the couch. "Will we get the artwork back?" Doctor Lewis asked. One of his legs shook with nervous energy.

"That's what I want," Val said. "I specialize in art crimes. It's why I'm here. But the longer we take, the harder it will be."

"Anything I can do to help," Doctor Lewis said. "Anything." He faced Val with a look of despair on his face.

"How long have you had the five Buttersworth paintings?"

Doctor Lewis closed his eyes and held a hand up to his mouth. Then he opened his eye. "How to say this? We built the collection over time. Thirty years ago a supporter donated the first. Over the next twenty years we added another painting about every five years. So, we've had the entire collection of five for the last ten years."

"How long have you been here at the museum?"

"Ever since I finished graduate school. Forty years? My team and I have built this museum from a small collection into a major maritime museum."

"Have you had any other thefts in recent years?"

"No. Not of the art." Doctor Lewis said. "We've had things taken from the museum store, purses and phones grabbed. But no art thefts."

"Who on your team besides you would want to take the paintings?"

"What?" Doctor Lewis' eyes widened, and he shook his head. "No, no, no. I'm shocked you'd even think I or anyone on my team would have something to do with this."

"Everyone's a suspect until I can eliminate them from the list," Val said.

"This museum and the collections are my legacy. I want to be remembered for what we've built, not what was taken."

Val held Doctor Lewis' gaze without responding. Neither blinked. Then Doctor Lewis looked down at the floor. Val asked, "Anyone come to mind that's been interested in the Buttersworth collection over the years?"

Doctor Lewis thought for a second, shook his head. "Nobody in particular."

Val checked his watch. He could feel time slipping by and pictured the art getting further away. "Do you have video from the museum from before today? Over the past month? Any from the gallery where the paintings were displayed? I'm thinking this heist was well planned and that the thieves came here to do some reconnaissance to plan it out."

"Yes, we have plenty of video that we can share with you. Security hasn't flagged anything suspicious in the past few months that I know of." Doctor Lewis rocked forward to stand. "I can take you there right now."

Val held up his hand. "Just wait. I have a few more questions and then we'll get someone to work with your security team to review the video."

Doctor Lewis held his iPad in his hand. He seemed as anxious as Val to get going to find the stolen art. Val doubted that this man in front of him had anything to do with this heist. He was quick to offer help. His nervous energy wasn't a trait he'd expect from a criminal mastermind. He'd keep him in mind, but he'd probably be a better source of information steering Val in the direction he needed to go. "Who else has maritime art in the area?"

"There's the Salem Maritime National Historic Site. There's the Pirate Museum. I can get you contact information for those."

"Any galleries or private collections?"

Doctor Lewis shook his head. "There are no private collections of that type here in Salem. Maybe Boston. You'd know more about that." He set the iPad in his lap. "There are a couple smaller galleries." He tilted the screen so Val could see the map of Salem. "The blue pin here on the map is a gallery near the wharf. It's owned and run by Annie Fisher. Her great grandfather helped us acquire our first Buttersworth."

"What?" Val asked.

"He was an artist and collector. He couldn't afford to get the Buttersworth himself, but he helped negotiate with the owner."

"It's a connection," Val said.

"It's just a connection," Doctor Lewis said. "His collection helped Annie get started. She's a talented photographer and has produced a number of books with her photos."

"What's her gallery called?"

"It's The Boathouse. It's housed in an old warehouse, boat building shop, down at the wharf."

Val typed notes into his phone. "And there's another gallery?" he asked.

Doctor Lewis punched another search into the maps app and put the iPad on the table. "The Drydock. It's an old farmstead a few miles outside of town. They have a few large barns, small artist studios, classes and a small permanent collection as well with shows by local artists. It's run by Gerald Pepper."

"No connection to you or the museum?"

"No."

"What do you know about him?"

"He's a talented artist," Doctor Lewis said. "Great supporter of the community."

Val waited. Doctor Lewis knew why they were talking

about this. After an awkward silence, Doctor Lewis started talking.

"I don't think Gerald had anything to do with stealing the paintings. There's less of a connection there than there is with Annie."

"Okay," Val said. "I'll check them out. Anybody else you think I should know about?"

Doctor Lewis shook his head. "No. I'm getting nervous that the paintings are getting farther away while we sit here."

Val checked his watch. He had the same feelings. It was time to check in with Palmer and team to see if they had any new info. He pulled a business card out of his pocket and handed it to Doctor Lewis. "If you think of anything, and I mean anything, call me." He pushed himself up out of the chair. "Can you show me where the security tapes are located? I'll get someone to start reviewing those and I'll go follow up on finding your paintings."

CHAPTER TWELVE

After getting an officer to sit down and review the past few weeks of videos in the museum's security office, Val joined Palmer and the other agents in the conference room.

"You two learn anything?" Palmer nodded towards Fruen and Stevens.

"We checked with some of the stores facing the museum entrance. Watched some videos," Fruen answered. "We didn't learn anything new. Saw two Amazon trucks arrive and leave."

"Did you learn anything from the Doctor?" Palmer asked Val.

"Lewis is genuinely distraught. I don't think he's our guy," Val said. "He gave me a couple of galleries I'd like to check up on. Have we heard anything from the Harbormaster?"

"No," Palmer said. "I'll check in with them again."

Val checked his watch. "We have to get moving and find the trail of these paintings. I'm heading back to the wharf. One gallery is near there and I'd like to see if we can figure out where the boat went with the paintings." He stood up. "Call me if you hear anything?"

"As soon as I hear," Palmer answered.

"I'm out of here," Val said.

"Take them with you," Palmer said. He motioned to Fruen and Stevens to get up. "You can cover more ground with help."

"I got it," Val said. "I don't need them." He headed for the door.

"They're going with you," Palmer said.

Fruen and Stevens got up from their chairs. Rupert crawled out from under the table and followed the agents out of the conference room.

Val didn't need any help. He banged through the exit door and went down the steps on the stairs, two at a time, to the parking lot. Rupert caught up with him and stayed with him on his left.

"Martinson," Fruen called out from behind him. "We're coming."

Val raised his hand to signal he'd heard him. He pushed the button on the key fob, and the rear door popped open. Rupert jumped into the back and settled down. Val hit the button again, and the door swung closed. He got in the driver's seat and started the SUV. Fruen jumped into the passenger seat next to him and Stevens behind him. Val pulled out, spinning the tires before they shut their doors.

"Geez, Martinson. In a hurry?" Fruen pulled his seat belt across and clicked it in place.

"The paintings are slipping away. We don't have a lot of time. I was hoping the Harbormaster would've seen and stopped the boat by now." Val turned the corner, following the route to the wharf they'd taken earlier. "I think I can move faster alone."

"We won't slow you down." Fruen said. "Where are we going?"

"Doctor Lewis told me about a couple of private galleries

in town. These places don't always deal just in legitimate art. They're often on the fringes. Running a profitable gallery is hard and the money to help move or deal stolen art is tempting." Val signaled his turn, hit the horn to warn some pedestrians out of the way and drove on. "Down at the wharf there's a gallery run by a woman. Lewis said she's the great-granddaughter of the man that helped the museum get the first Buttersworth painting for its collection. It's the only connection I have right now to follow."

"Sounds like a place to start," Fruen answered.

Picturing in his mind the map that Doctor Lewis has shown him, Val slowed and turned left onto a street, a wide alley really, that ran between two old brick buildings and stopped. The Boathouse should be in the building on his right. "I'm going in here," Val said.

Fruen unbuckled his seatbelt and opened his door. "I'll go with you."

Stevens exited the back seat. "Rupert and I will stretch our legs and see if we spot anything on the street."

Fruen fell into step next to Val. "Remember," Fruen said. "They've killed somebody. So be alert."

"Right," Val answered. He glanced at the sign over the door. They were at the right place. He pushed open the door. A quiet chime signaled their entry. The gallery walls were brick. The floor was old, worn planks. Track lights hung from the ceiling and illuminated the artwork and photos hanging on the walls. A man and woman pushing a stroller were looking at some photos along the far wall. The man glanced over, a look of concern on his face.

Val held up a hand, smiled, and shook his head to signal everything was fine.

A smiling witch approached Val and Fruen. Her footsteps echoed in the gallery, her boots clicking on the old floorboards. She wore black tattered clothes, a tall black hat, and she had a long crooked nose with a wart on the end. Not her real nose. It was hard to tell how old she was, but her eyes sparkled and she had some dimples when she smiled. "Can I help you gentlemen?" she asked. Her eyes focused on Val's vest and then she looked at Fruen dressed in his tactical gear. Her smile disappeared. "FBI? Looking for someone or something?"

Val responded, "We'd like to talk with Annie Fisher."

"That's me. How can I help you?"

"Ms. Fisher, I'm Special Agent Martinson with the FBI's Art Crimes team. I got your name from Doctor Lewis at the Peabody."

"Call me Annie," she said.

"I'm Special Agent Fruen," Ross said, introducing himself.

"Nice to meet you."

"Mind if I look around while you two talk?" Ross asked.

"That's fine," Annie responded.

Ross excused himself, leaving Val with her. She redirected her attention to Val. "So it's true? They got robbed this morning? I heard it from somebody. Can't remember who. Is everyone okay? What did they get from the museum?" The words spilled out.

"I'm afraid I can't share any details, but yes, they were robbed early this morning in a sophisticated heist. The art world is pretty well connected. Have you seen or heard anything in the past six months that may seem strange or out-of-place now?"

Annie put a hand to her forehead and looked down. Val watched her like a poker player looking for a tell, a tic that would tell him she was lying.

She raised her head and met his gaze. "I'm sorry, but I can't think of anything."

Val dripped another piece of information. "Doctor Lewis said your family is connected to the Buttersworth collection."

"Oh no, did they get those?"

"I'm sorry, I can't say," Val said.

Annie put her hands up to her head and heavily exhaled. Then she reengaged with Val. "Yes, my family has been supporting the Peabody for a long time. My great-grandfather, grandfather and father all helped the Peabody acquire paintings in the Buttersworth collection and other works over the years. Pieces we couldn't get ourselves, but we could take pride in helping the Peabody with their collection." She scanned her gallery walls. "You don't think I'm a target, do you?"

"The thieves appear to have targeted particular pieces. Do you have any works that a collector would be interested in?"

Shaking her head, Annie answered, "I don't have anything at that level. I have customers who follow particular artists or commission a piece. We have some pieces in storage that we rotate for showing. But, I don't think we have anything that a professional thief would want to take."

Agent Fruen rejoined them. "We gotta go," he said to Val. "The Harbormaster called."

Val pulled out a business card and handed it to Annie. "Excuse us. If you think of anything, call me."

CHAPTER THIRTEEN

Tony and Dick didn't have much luck fishing. They weren't trying very hard.

"Do you even have any bait or a lure on your line?" Dick asked Tony.

Tony shook his head. "Just a weight and a bare hook." He didn't want any distractions, like catching a fish, while they carried out the rest of his plan. They were slowly trolling northeast of Misery Island, following a circuitous route along with a couple of other fishing boats out for the day.

"How long we sticking around?" Dick asked. "It's getting hot out here."

Tony glanced at the watch on his wrist. "Can't be much longer." He swung the boat around to head back on the northwest track. "Here they come," he said and nodded south of Misery Island.

A police boat slowed as it passed the anchored La Fiesta.

"Now we wait and watch," Tony said. He steered the fishing boat east to get further out from shore.

∽

VAL AND AGENT Fruen hurried back to the car. "What's up?" Val asked.

"The Harbormaster called Palmer. They've spotted a boat that they think was the one berthed at the dock from the video images and photos from people at the dock."

Val climbed into the driver's seat and Fruen scrambled into the passenger seat. "Where are we going?" Val asked.

Stevens answered from the back seat, "The Harbormaster office. I have it mapped on my phone."

"How far?" Val asked.

"Five minutes."

"Hang on," Val said. He honked the horn and reversed into the street from the alley. "Which way?"

"Left."

Val turned the wheel sharply to the left and accelerated. The tires spun before gripping the street and they rocketed down the street.

"Right at the next intersection."

Val turned on the lights and sirens and turned right.

"It's a straight shot down this street for a while."

"So what do we know?" Val asked.

Fruen answered, "They've spotted a boat anchored about four miles out by an island. It looks quiet. They're waiting for us before they approach."

"I thought they'd be a lot farther away by now," Val said. "Four miles away and anchored doesn't make sense."

"We'll see when we get there," Ross said.

They traveled in silence for a short time. Cars on the road pulled over and Val zoomed past them.

"Turn right up here at Winter Island Road and follow it to the end," Stevens said. "They have a boat at the dock waiting for us."

The road split to the right. Val slowed enough to make

the turn and followed the curving two-lane road until they encountered a line of cars backed up on the road.

"They're waiting to get into the parking lot," Stevens said. "Go around them."

Val steered into the opposite lane. Exiting cars pulled over to give him room. The road led to a parking lot filled with cars.

"Straight ahead there's a boat launch and docks," Stevens said.

Rupert stood in the back end of the Suburban and whined when they slowed.

They parked at the top of the ramp. Fruen and Stevens grabbed their rifles. Val jumped out and headed for the dock. "Rupert and I will be right there," Stevens said. "I need to put him on his lead."

Val spied a uniformed man with a life jacket, sunglasses and a tanned face standing on the dock next to a large white idling boat with Police and Salem Harbormaster on the side. Val approached him and introduced himself. "FBI, Agent Martinson."

"Officer Gregor." He stuck out his hand, and Val shook it.

"I'm Agent Fruen," Ross said and stuck out his hand.

Val continued, "As soon as the others catch up we can head out. Where are we going?"

"About four miles out. There's a boat anchored by Misery Island. We think it's the one you're looking for."

Stevens and Rupert joined them on the dock.

"Climb in," Officer Gregor said. "Grab a life jacket." He studied Val. "You might need two. I'll cast off the lines and we'll be on our way."

Officer Gregor removed the lines holding the boat from the dock cleats in the rear and front. He jumped on board and slowly navigated away from the dock. "Hang on," he said. He moved the throttle, and the boat surged ahead, the nose rising as it sought the speed where it would plane out and shoot over the water.

"We have two boats surveilling it," Officer Gregor said over his shoulder to Val. "And keeping other boat traffic away."

"What kind of boat?" Val asked.

"Kind of like this one," Officer Gregor answered. "A little bigger, a little slower, older. It's named La Fiesta. The owner lives up north and says he doesn't know why it would be here. It's supposed to be in its boat slip there."

"If there's nobody on it, where'd they go?"

"The island is right there. But I'm guessing another boat? It's less than a mile to shore. Or they continued out into the ocean, up or down the coast? Hard to say."

Val swore under his breath. He didn't believe they'd find anything on the anchored boat. "They're still looking for other boats?"

"Roger that," replied Officer Gregor. "But, we don't know what to look for and it's a beautiful day to be on the water. There are lots of boats out and lots of traffic in and out of the harbor with the festival going on today."

"Well, let's see what we find on this boat. Maybe there's a clue that will help us," Val said.

The police boat skimmed across the water. There were all types of boats out on the water: sailboats, fishing boats, pleasure craft. A needle in a haystack if they switched boats.

Stevens sat in the front with Rupert, whose nose was in the air, catching all sorts of scents. Fruen stood behind Val. He scanned the water to their sides and behind them. Val still didn't think he needed them along. He could focus on pursuing the art, analyzing clues. They could cover more ground if they would split up.

The boat slowed and then coasted in the water as Officer

Gregor put the engine in neutral. Val hung on to keep himself from stumbling forward.

"It's up there a few hundred yards," Officer Gregor said.

Val held his hand up to shade his eyes. A dirty white boat with a cockpit sat in the water.

"Use these." Officer Gregor handed him a pair of black binoculars.

Putting the binoculars to his eyes, Val could see the details of the boat. An anchor rope stretched out from the bow, which gently rose and fell with the small waves caused by the boat traffic. He didn't spy any sign of life. No movement.

"Anything?" Fruen asked.

"Nope," Val answered. He held out the binoculars for Fruen to use. He noticed that Stevens was watching the boat through the sight on his rifle.

Fruen lowered the glasses after studying the boat. "Stevens, come here," he said. To Officer Gregor he said, "Nobody has seen anything since they spotted the boat?"

"Nothing," Officer Gregor answered. "I just checked with the other boats. All's quiet."

Stevens and Rupert joined the others in the rear of the boat. Rupert jammed his nose against Val's hand. "Hey, guy," Val said and scratched Rupert around the ears.

"He doesn't do that with me," Fruen said. Then he addressed the group. "All's quiet. I guess we board, see if it's our boat. If it is, see if they left any clues. If it's not, we need a new plan."

Val and Agent Stevens nodded.

CHAPTER FOURTEEN

O fficer Gregor said, "I'll idle up to the boat from the rear. When we get close, I'll get on the speaker and ask that anyone on board make themselves visible. Then I'll announce our intentions to board."

"Rupert and I will go first," Stevens said. "I'll let him clear the deck. When all's clear you two follow," he nodded to Val and Fruen.

"Sounds like a plan," Val said.

"Check your weapons," Fruen said. "When you're ready," he said to Officer Gregor.

The boat glided forward as Office Gregor engaged the throttle. "I'll first announce when we're about fifty yards out." He steered the boat in an arc to approach from the stern.

Val pulled his Glock from his holster, his finger rested on the body of the gun. They were about one hundred yards from the target.

Stevens issued a command to Rupert, "Rupert, *Zit*." He immediately sat, fully alert and ready for the next command. He locked eyes on Stevens.

Officer Gregor picked up the microphone, thumbed the

talk button and announced, "This is the Salem Police. If there's anyone aboard the white boat, La Fiesta, anchored by Misery Island, show us your hands. Prepare to be boarded."

Val watched the boat, looking for movement as they glided closer.

"Prepare to board," Office Gregor said.

Val stood by the left side of the boat. He couldn't remember if it was starboard or what it was called. His eyes were locked on La Fiesta as they guided closer, looking for movement. A flash of light blinded Val, he flinched, there was a roar of noise and a wave of hot air blew him back. He stumbled to his left, lost his balance, and fell over the side of the boat into the water.

WHEN TONY DIALED the number on his cell phone he expected the light, the pieces of boat flying into the air, but he flinched at sound of the explosion when it reached him. Then a gush of air and a wave in the water rocked the boat.

"Holy shit," Dick said.

"That oughta keep 'em busy," Tony said, holding onto the steering wheel to steady himself. "Let's go." He dropped his rod into the water.

Dick started reeling in his line.

"Drop it in," Tony said. "We gotta go."

"Oh, man. This is my good rod," Dick said.

"I'll buy you a new one."

Dick hung his arm over the side of the boat and dropped the rod into the water. Tony pushed the throttle forward, and the boat took off leaning to the left cutting a path south.

"Where're we going?" Dick asked.

"Out of here before they notice us. Back to Salem," Tony said. "They won't be looking for us there."

~

VAL OPENED HIS EYES. He coughed and spit salty water. He kicked his legs to keep his head above the water and paddled with his arms while he gasped for air. The police boat floated about ten yards away.

Burning debris floated down from the sky, and ashes swirled in the wind. A dark cloud of smoke rose from the other side of the police boat. He heard a muffled voice yelling his name. He blinked and focused his eyes on a blurry image above the side of the boat. He blinked again. Agent Fruen leaned on the side of the boat and yelled at him. Val saw his lips move and heard a muffled noise, but couldn't understand him. All he heard was a loud ringing noise. He opened his jaw wide to try to clear his ears.

Agent Fruen pointed at the water. "Grab the ring!"

Val turned his head and spied the white donut floating on the water. He felt like he was sinking. He started kicking harder and stroked towards the ring.

"Grab it!" Fruen yelled.

It felt like he was in an ocean of oil. It was hard to move against the thick liquid. Val rolled onto his stomach, kicked his feet and tried to swim a couple of strokes towards the life ring. He didn't feel like he was getting any closer.

"Come on. Grab it!" Fruen yelled. "You're almost there!"

Val scissor kicked once, twice and grabbed onto the ring. He stuck his right arm through it, bent his elbow to hook the ring.

"You okay?" Fruen asked.

Val nodded, hanging onto the ring. It helped him float. He didn't feel like he'd go under now.

"Hold on!" Fruen yelled. "We're pulling you in. Kick your legs if you can."

Officer Gregor joined Fruen at the side of the boat. The

rope tied to the ring grew taut and Val slid through the water towards the boat. He tried to kick his legs to help. He grabbed his right wrist under the water with his left hand to lock his grip on the ring.

"Don't let go," Fruen yelled. He and Officer Gregor worked to pull the ring to the rear of the boat. There was a ladder next to the motor. "Grab a hold of the ladder and climb up," Fruen said.

Val grabbed the ladder with his left hand and freed his right from the ring buoy. He grabbed the ladder with his right and tried to find a place for his foot. His arms shook as he tried to pull himself up. Shocked, water-logged, he struggled.

Fruen reached forward and grabbed his ballistic vest to help. With the two of them struggling to get him on board, Val pushed up the ladder and tumbled over the transom onto the floor of the boat. He lay on the floor, his head resting on the life jacket around his neck. "Thanks," he gasped. Water dripped off him and puddled on the floor. Rupert walked over and sniffed his hair.

"Hey, buddy," Val said.

Stevens called Rupert back to the front of the boat.

"You sure you're okay?" Fruen asked.

"Yeah. I just need a minute," Val answered. He wriggled into a seated position and leaned against the side of the boat. "What the hell happened?"

"The boat exploded as we approached it. Not much left."

Val heard the flames of the burning boat. The smell of smoke and oil filled the air. He rolled onto his side and got on his hands and knees. Then he pushed himself up and stood. He grabbed onto the edge of the boat cockpit to steady himself. The windshield was shattered, and parts of the boat were scorched.

"Wow," he said. "You guys all okay?"

"We're good," Fruen said. "It was close."

Two other police boats had pulled up to the side of the burning boat. Officers sprayed the boat with fire suppressant.

"Palmer and some other agents are on the way. Stevens called him. They'll be on the road over there," Fruen pointed past the island. "The coast is about a mile away."

Officer Gregor was slowly driving the police boat towards the burning boat. Stevens stood on the bow to assist in fire suppression. Val noticed objects floating on the water. He reached over the side and plucked a soggy painting from the water. The canvas was torn, the wooden frame broken and attached on two sides. He set it in the bottom of the boat. "We should try to recover what we can," he said to Fruen. "Some of it, if there are solid pieces, may have survived." He stepped over to Officer Gregor at the helm. "We need to save what we can from the water."

Like any accident or fire, gawkers started to gather. Boaters out for the day, closed in on the scene and idled a safe distance back to watch. "Maybe we can get some of them to help," Val said. He nodded at the group of boats.

Officer Gregor replied, "We'll have this fire knocked down enough in five or ten minutes. I'll pass the word we're salvaging art pieces from the water and the boat."

"That'd be great," Val said. "If you could get whatever you recover to Doctor Lewis at the Peabody, I know he'd appreciate it. The FBI will secure and analyze whatever you can salvage."

"Roger that," Officer Gregor said.

Val watched the black smoke from the boat rise into the air.

"Palmer's here," Fruen said. "Can you get us over to shore?" he asked Officer Gregor.

"We can head over soon. Be there in fifteen or twenty minutes?"

"I'll let him know," Fruen said.

Val joined Fruen again at the rear of the boat. "This wasn't an accident," Fruen said. "The boat blew right when we got close."

"Right. It was a diversion," Val said. "They sacrificed some art and kept some. We'll never really know what went up in flames. But I bet we won't find any evidence of the Buttersworth paintings."

"Palmer and team will scout the area while they wait for us. See if anything or anyone looks out of place. See if anybody along the shore saw anything."

"If they were on land," Val said. He scanned the water. If they were in a boat, they could be anywhere: south to Boston, north to any number of cities along the coast, maybe Canada, or east, anywhere out on the Atlantic.

CHAPTER FIFTEEN

Officer Gregor maneuvered the police boat until the bow touched the beach. "Lucky it's not very windy today, or I'd be idling offshore and you guys would be swimming in."

"I already took my swim," Val said.

Palmer stood on the beach back from the water, waiting for them. Sun bathers and families dotted the sand in either direction. People stood on the beach watching the smoke rise from the other side of the island. A few watched Palmer and the police boat. Others continued enjoying the sun. Two HRT agents stood guard on the beach, one to the north and the other to the south. Seagulls circled overhead with their calls, waiting for sunbathers to drop some food.

"We'll search the boat when it's safe, if it doesn't sink, to see if we can figure out what caused the explosion," Officer Gregor said. "We have a maritime arson, explosion expert. If it goes down, we'll dive on it."

"Let us know what you find," Fruen said.

Stevens and Rupert jumped off the boat onto the sand. Fruen followed.

"Thanks officer," Val said. "Remember, any art you can recover, get it to the Peabody."

"Will do. You take care of yourself," Officer Gregor said.

"Sorry about your boat."

Val stepped off the bow and dropped onto the wet sand. He followed the other agents across the beach and joined them to talk with Palmer.

"You okay?" Palmer asked him.

"I'm fine now. I was a little shaken up, but I'm good," Val said.

"So, they blew the boat."

"Yep, we lost some art," Val said. "But I'm sure it was a diversion and a sacrifice. We don't know what we lost. We also don't know what they kept. I'm sure they kept the Buttersworths and maybe a few other pieces."

"Strange timing of the explosion," Palmer said.

"Not a coincidence," Fruen said.

"Why did they wait to blow it? Why wait until you were all so close?" Palmer asked. "They could have blown it and taken off a couple of hours ago."

Val answered, "I think they waited to use up time. And with the police around, it keeps them busy investigating the boat, fighting the fire instead of chasing them."

"Well, all they've done is piss me off," Stevens said. "Rupert and I were in the front of the boat, closest to the explosion." He pulled a tennis ball out of a pocket of his vest and threw it down the beach. Rupert chased it. "We're lucky to both be okay."

Palmer said, "I was ready to pack up the team and return to Quantico after we secured the museum. Let Agent Martinson here pursue the art. But with this close call, we're sticking around. Martinson, you pursue the art. We'll pursue the bad guys. If we overlap, so much the better."

"Works for me," Fruen said.

"Me too," Stevens said.

Rupert returned, dropped the ball at Stevens' feet and sat, waiting for another throw. Palmer bent over, picked up the ball and threw it again. Rupert chased after it.

"What's next, Agent Martinson?" Palmer asked.

Val watched Rupert chase down the ball. He felt the same as Rupert, still chasing the art.

"Val," Fruen said.

"Yeah." Val reengaged with the group.

"What's next?" Palmer asked.

"We let the harbormaster continue to try to find a boat they might be using to transport the art. There's another gallery I want to check and I want to spend more time at the gallery by the wharf. We got pulled out of there before we could spend too much time talking with the owner."

"Sounds good. Fruen, Stevens, thoughts?" Palmer asked.

"I think Agent Martinson's ID'd the next steps," Fruen said. "I don't have anything else."

"Let's go find these guys," Stevens said.

"I'll give Bruce another go to see if I can learn anything else from him," Palmer said.

"Can you drop me off at my vehicle at the Harbormaster's station?" Val asked.

"We'll all squeeze in. Let's go." Palmer signaled to the two team members watching the beach and led the way across the sand towards the public parking lot.

CHAPTER SIXTEEN

A fire department boat sped out of the harbor, lights flashing and siren blaring. Tony drove the opposite direction into the harbor. He slowed the boat and glided into a slip at the public dock. After tying the boat in place, he and Dick lifted two large wheeled coolers out of the boat and set them on the dock. They'd set the wooden cases containing the paintings inside the coolers, standing on end, side by side.

"Just act natural," Tony whispered to Dick. "Smile. We're just a couple of guys coming in after a morning on the water."

They climbed out of the boat, stood on the dock and stretched. Tony didn't notice anyone giving them any extra attention. People were all going about their business. "Okay, let's go," he said. He grabbed a collapsible handle attached to one end of the cooler, lifted the end off the ground and pulled it along behind him, the cooler rolling on the two wheels in the trailing end.

Dick followed him on the dock with the other. The dock wasn't that wide, and they needed to make room for people going the opposite direction.

"You guys have any luck?" a guy in a boat tied to the dock asked.

"Nah," Tony said. "But it was a great morning to be on the water."

"That's right," the man answered. "You catch anything on a day like today and it's just a bonus."

"Good luck," Tony said as he continued pulling the cooler across the dock.

The dock ran up to a sidewalk that ran along the public parking lot. Tony pulled the cooler along. He didn't need to act tired, like he'd been out on the water all day. After the early morning robbery, the getaway and now this, he was tired.

Dick caught up and walked next to him. "Now what?" he asked.

"Let's get them in the truck and then we'll talk." Tony looked for the pickup. He'd rented it in Boston for a week. Charged it to a card that wasn't his. He spied it up ahead, one row over. Wheeling the cooler to the pickup, he continued to casually scan the parking lot. Everything seemed fine. Reaching the pickup, he lowered the tailgate. "Help me lift this up here," he said to Dick.

They lifted the cooler into the bed of the pickup. They repeated it with the other. Tony climbed up and used a couple of nylon straps he'd left in the truck to tie the coolers in place so they were secure. Standing in the pickup bed, he used the opportunity to scout the area again to make sure nobody was watching them. He didn't see anything suspicious. He jumped to the ground and said to Dick, "Get in. Let's go."

Tony started the truck and blew out a big breath. Then he smiled and held in a laugh. He turned to Dick and punched him in the shoulder.

Dick flinched.

"We did it." Tony punched Dick in the shoulder again. "We fuckin did it."

"Quit hitting me man," Dick said. He turned in his seat towards Tony and put up his hands to protect himself.

Tony punched Dick in the palm. "We did it."

"Yeah, we did," Dick said. "Now what?"

Tony settled himself behind the steering wheel and tried to calm down. He smiled and quietly said, "We did it." He drummed his fingers on the steering wheel and checked the time on his watch. He turned to Dick. "I'm thirsty. You thirsty?"

"Sure," Dick said.

"We've got time until we need to check in and deliver the goods. Let's go get a drink. I'm buying." Tony shifted the truck into reverse and backed into the driving lane of the parking lot. "I know just the place," he said.

~

TONY CLIMBED into the truck and handed Dick a greasy, brown paper bag.

"What's this?" Dick asked.

"Lunch."

"When you said you knew just the place, I thought you meant something with a brunch buffet or something. Not burgers." Dick opened the bag and reached inside for a french fry.

"These aren't just any burgers, my friend. These are Salem's finest. Eighty-five percent ground beef with a little chopped garlic, fresh tomatoes, crisp lettuce, home made mayo and a special blend of secret spices mixed in. Grilled medium rare and a pretzel roll. You are going to love it." Tony pulled into traffic.

"Where we going?" Dick asked.

"The wharf. We're going to sit outside, blend in with the people, hide in plain site and watch the truck until it's time to make our delivery."

"We have to wait?"

"Yep. Close the bag to keep the burgers warm. We'll be there in a few minutes."

TONY AND DICK sat on a concrete retaining wall where they could watch the truck and see the area around them. They'd picked up a couple of beers after they parked and settled in for their lunch.

"Everything's going as planned," Tony said.

"I'm surprised, but you're right." Dick took a bite of his burger and slowly chewed it. "You're right about this morning's job and this burger. It is fantastic." He grabbed a napkin and wiped the grease that dribbled down his chin.

They ate in silence and watched the people walk by.

Dick crumpled up his burger's paper wrapper. "Tell me something."

"What?" Tony said with a full mouth.

"Tell me why we had to transport the pictures in the frames. Why not just cut them out? They'd take up a lot less room."

Tony swallowed and glanced around to make sure no-one could hear them. "Keep your voice down." He leaned towards Dick and said, "The order was for them in the frames. Full price if they're delivered whole. Discounted if they're cut out." He took a drink of beer. "I'm selfish and wanted all the money. That's why."

Dick thought about it for a second. "Okay. Makes sense. Made the job harder, but makes sense if you can execute the plan. And we did." He held his fist out for a bump from Tony.

Tony gave him a quick bump.

"Now what?" Dick asked.

Tony leaned back and let the sun warm his face. "We relax and we wait."

CHAPTER SEVENTEEN

Palmer drove without emergency lights. "Bruce is talking, but we're not getting any new info. Just the same stuff told a different way. Sounds like Tony, the leader, kept him and Clark in the dark. They only knew what they needed to know for the job," he said.

The Suburban had room for all of them. Val was in the front passenger seat because of his size. Fruen sat in the back seat between the two agents on his team. Stevens was in the back cargo area with Rupert.

"If he's willing to talk, there has to be more," Fruen said. "He was with the gang long enough where he had to hear something. We just need to trigger it."

"Sharing with him that they blew up the boat may kick something in," Palmer said. "You guys feed me any new info you learn and I'll see what Bruce knows that could help."

Stevens added from the back, "You don't think he's stalling to let the team and art get away, do you?"

"I don't think so," Palmer said. "He genuinely seems to want to help. He's mad as hell at Tony for leaving them behind, sacrificing them for the heist. And he's even more upset since his buddy Clark got shot. Just keep feeding me more info and we'll see if it helps Bruce remember anything."

The GPS navigation system said to turn left at the next intersection. Palmer did as told.

Val's wet clothes clung to his skin and pulled taut from his bent knees and elbows. He pulled his cellphone from his vest pocket and tried to check the screen. It remained blank. "I think my phone's shot," he said.

Palmer glanced over. "I think you'll need a new one. They don't like water and they really hate salt water. Putting it in a bag of rice isn't going to save that one."

"You have a radio I can use to keep in touch?"

"You'll have Fruen and Stevens with you. They can call," Palmer said.

Val wanted to work on his own. "I don't think you need to send us all. They might be better served chasing the bad guys."

"That's why they're going with you," Palmer said. "You find the art, you'll find the bad guys. They just tried to blow you up."

Fruen reached over the back seat and grabbed Val's shoulder, "You may need someone to pull you out of the water again, big guy," he said.

"Thanks for that," Val said.

Palmer pulled into the parking lot at the Harbormaster office. "Where's your vehicle?"

Val pointed through the windshield, "It's that one over there."

"The FBI looking black Suburban?" Palmer asked.

"Yeah, that's the one," Val answered.

Palmer stopped behind Val's vehicle and pushed the tailgate release. There was a beep, and it swept open. "Thanks for the ride, Boss," Stevens said. Rupert jumped out and Stevens followed.

"Go find some art," Palmer said to Val. Then he turned to Fruen, "And go catch some bad guys."

"Catch the bad guys, save the art," Fruen said. "Got it."

Val climbed out of the vehicle, wishing he had some dry clothes. The agent sitting behind him got out to let Fruen out and took his place in front next to Palmer. Fruen shut the door and Palmer drove away.

CHAPTER EIGHTEEN

"Shotgun," Fruen said and walked to the front passenger side of Val's truck.

Val pulled the key fob out of his pocket and looked at it.

"Think that's going to work?" Stevens asked.

"All we can do is try it," Val said. He pushed the button and heard a clicking noise came from the car.

Fruen opened his door. "Still worked to unlock it," he said.

Val pushed the button for the rear gate. There was a beep, and it swung open. "Small miracles," he said and climbed into the driver's seat.

Rupert jumped in the back. Stevens closed the gate and climbed in the back seat behind Val. "So where are we going next?" he asked.

Val started the vehicle.

"Something smells worse than a wet dog in here," Fruen said. He lowered his window. Stevens did the same.

"Thanks," Val said. "These wet clothes aren't too comfortable either."

"So, where're we going?" Stevens asked again.

"I want to hit another art gallery, The Drydock, and talk to the owner and then back to the first one we stopped at," Val said.

"Sounds like a plan. Let's go," Fruen said.

VAL TURNED into the dirt drive. Ahead of them was a group of buildings, made up of barns and sheds. The center one had a sign, The Drydock, over the main door. There were a number of cars in the parking lot outside the buildings. A few people walked between the buildings outside. "I'll go in and talk to the owner, Gerald Pepper," Val said.

Stevens said, "Rupert and I will stretch our legs by the road and check any cars that leave."

"I'll keep an eye out front here," Fruen said. "You let us know if you need us," he said to Val.

They exited the car, and each agent headed for their post. Val stepped into the main building. The smell of incense hit him. A quiet soundtrack of musical chords and waves lapping on the shore played from speakers somewhere. He walked to the welcome desk where a gray-haired woman sat wearing a loose colorful dress, hoop earrings and a peace sign hanging from a thin cord around her neck. Val smiled. He'd bet money this had been a hippie commune back in the day.

The woman returned his smile. "Can I help you?" she asked. "Officer, agent," she added.

"Good afternoon. I'm Special Agent Martinson."

"You must be here about the Peabody robbery. It's all the talk around here this morning."

"Yes, ma'am. Word travels fast."

"Especially in the art community. How can I help you?"

"I'd like to speak with Gerald Pepper," Val said. "Is he here?"

"I believe he's in the studio painting. I'll get you there."
The woman pushed back her chair, placed her hands on the
desk for balance and stood. She grabbed a short walking stick
and stepped out from the desk. "Can I take your arm?" she
asked.

"Yes ma'am," Val said. He moved to offer her his arm.

"Call me Audrey." She grabbed onto his arm with her free
hand. "You're a big one, aren't you?"

"Yes ma'am, um, Audrey. I'm bigger than most." Val felt
her feeble grip on his arm and carefully pressed his arm
against his side to help keep her hand there, careful not to
hurt her.

"Your a little wet and..."

"Probably a little smelly," Val finished for her. "I apologize.
I fell into the harbor a little earlier."

"Those things happen," Audrey said. She started forward.
"Don't go too fast. It's not far to the studio."

"So what brings you to The Drydock?" Audrey asked.

Val helped Audrey down a couple of wooden steps onto
the path. Audrey pointed to the left, and they started to walk
before Val answered. "The Director at The Peabody said you
were one of the studios in the area that may have ties to
maritime art. I'm looking for info that may help us." Val felt
the heat of the afternoon sun. Sweat dripped down his back
between his shoulder blades.

"Well, I can tell you I don't have any info," Audrey said.
"Gerald probably doesn't either, but you can ask." They
walked a few more steps along the path and Audrey asked,
"You said one of the studios. Was the other The Boathouse?"

"Yes, yes, it was."

"You may have better spent your time there. They're
more of a gallery. Annie's an ambitious one. She's got a good

eye. You should check out her photographs. We're just more of a community here. All types of artists: painters, graphic, textiles, clay, we cover it all here."

"How about Gerald?" Val asked.

"He's a painter," Audrey said. "Quite good." She directed him to the right down a ten foot long walk to a white shed. The door stood open, and they stepped in. The voice of Mick Jagger filled the air. The music was loud, not too loud, but loud enough to make Val lean down to hear Audrey when she tugged on his arm. "That's Gerald."

Gerald stood about five foot eight inches tall, wore a red bandana, speckled with paint, around his head. Black and silver hair poked out the back of the bandana. He wore a white t-shirt, also speckled with paint, faded green cargo shorts with brushes sticking out of the pockets, and he was barefoot. The painting in front of him was large, four feet high, six foot long and well along to being completed. Two modern sailing ships racing in moderate seas, the wind filling their sales as they listed with the wind, resisting the force trying to push them over and using it to plow forward.

Audrey let go of Val's arm and walked over to the bench with the turntable on it. She lifted the arm, and the music stopped. "Gerald, there's someone here to talk with you." She sat in a chair at the end of the bench.

"Ma, I'm in the zone," Gerald said, continuing to face the painting. "Tell 'em I'll talk to them later."

"He's here now," Audrey said.

Gerald turned around. His eyes got large. "Shit, you could've said it was FBI. A big FBI agent."

His front said artist as much as his back did. He had a peppered, short beard, paint on his arms, chest and face.

"Special Agent Martinson with the Boston office," Val said. "Mind if I look at your painting?"

"Knock yourself out," Gerald said. "I've been stuck, but just got going again."

Val walked to the painting and studied it. He stepped closer and leaned forward to examine the paint and the strokes. "Hmm," he said. "Nice work. Where did you study?"

Gerald joined him at the painting. "Mostly self-taught, a couple of retreats when I was younger."

"I see a couple of different influences here," Val said.

"I try to learn from others. You know art?" Gerald asked. "You paint?"

"Studied it some it college. I dabble. Mostly landscapes. Thought I'd try a maritime scene while I'm here."

"I could give you some tips."

"Maybe after my work is done," Val said. "I'm with the Art Crime Team and we're here since the Peabody got robbed this morning."

"What'd they get? The Buttersworths?"

Val turned to face Gerald, rose to his full height and looked down at him. "Why'd you ask about those?"

Gerald looked up at Val and didn't flinch. "Cuz if I was going to pull off a heist of the Peabody, that's what I'd be after. The best paintings they got, the right size to handle, they'd probably find someone that wants them or ordered them from an underworld dealer."

"You seem to know what you're talking about," Val said.

"I've been around this all my life." Gerald nodded at Audrey. "She's been around it longer." He set down his brush and grabbed a water bottle.

"Have you heard anything?" Val asked.

Gerald shook his head. "Nah, it's been quiet."

Val turned to Audrey. "You?"

Audrey smiled and shook her head.

"Have you talked to Annie at The Boathouse, down at the wharf?" Gerald asked.

"That's what your mother asked."

"She'd know." Gerald answered. "That's where I'd start."

"Thank you both for your time." Val handed Audrey a business card. "You all call me if something comes up or you think of something?" He chuckled and shook his head. "Leave a message at that number. My phone was in my pocket when I fell in the harbor, so it's out of commission right now. But I'll be able to pick up the messages."

Audrey smiled. "You've had quite the day."

"That I have," Val said. "Can I walk you back?"

"No," Audrey said. "I'm going to watch Gerald paint for a while."

"Well, thank you both for your help." Val gave Gerald a little wave and headed for the door. Jagger's voice filled the studio again.

CHAPTER NINETEEN

V al walked out to the Suburban and found Agent Fruen standing in the shade.

"We done?" Ross asked.

"Yep, let's go," Val responded.

Ross put his fingers to his mouth and whistled. Stevens looked over and Ross circled his finger in the air, signaling they were leaving. Val started the car to get the AC running and popped the back door open for Rupert.

Stevens and Rupert trotted over, Rupert hopped in the back. "Let's go, Stevens," Val said. Stevens was sticking his head in the back with Rupert.

"What's this stuff back here?" Stevens asked.

"Come on, Sherlock. Let's go," Val said. "I'll tell you."

Fruen climbed in the front seat next to Val and Stevens jumped in back. Cool air finally started to blow from the vents. Val reversed, turned and exited the parking lot.

"Where're we going?" Fruen asked.

"Back to The Boathouse," Val said.

"Nothing here?" Stevens asked.

"I spoke with Gerald Pepper and his mother. They both

suggested that we go see Annie Fisher at The Boathouse. We had to leave this morning before we even started talking with her earlier," Val said.

Fruen said, "You don't think they were trying to throw you off their scent and onto hers?"

Val thought about it for a second. "No. They're artists. Nothing more. Gerald was painting when I got there and from what I could see of the paint, he'd been working on it all morning. He was busy worrying about his painting, not a heist. They just didn't give off any kind of illegal art dealer vibe. But they were both quick to point me to Annie, separately." Val gave it another thought. "We can always come back. Maybe call Palmer and see if the police can watch them for a while. Just to be safe."

"I'll text him," Fruen said.

Val looked longingly at Fruen's cell phone.

"Feeling a little disconnected?" Stevens asked from the back seat.

"Yeah, I guess. I told Mrs. Pepper to call me and then remembered my phone was out of commission."

"What's the stuff in the back end with Rupert?" Stevens asked.

"When I go out on assignments, I throw my painting supplies in. If I need to think or if I finish a case, I decompress by painting. I try to do something from the locale I'm in."

"Like what?" Stevens asked.

"The last one was a landscape out on the Texas range. This one will be related to Salem. I just don't know what it'll be until it's time to paint."

"That's cool," Stevens said. "Me, I just try to get a few phone numbers from the local girls."

"The key word there is try," Fruen added.

The three of them laughed.

CHAPTER TWENTY

Fruen's mobile phone rang. "It's Palmer."

"Put him on speaker," Stevens said.

Fruen pushed the button, "Hey, Boss. You're on speaker. It's me, Stevens and Martinson."

"A few updates," Palmer said from the phone speaker. "The police will stake out the Pepper's until you say we're done, Agent Martinson." He paused, "I got a call from the Harbormaster. They stopped a stolen boat up north near Gloucester. Two men on board. No art, but a bag full of money. They aren't talking, but they're transporting them back here and we'll see what we can learn."

"That's great news, sir," Val said. "Two down, two to go. And they didn't have the art, so that means we find Tony and the other and we should find the art."

"I'll work Bruce against them and see what I can learn," Palmer said. "What's next for you three?"

Val turned to Fruen, who motioned for him to talk. "We're heading back to The Boathouse to talk to the owner at that gallery. She's the one with the connection to the Buttersworth paintings that were stolen and the Pepper's pointed me towards her as well. We don't have much, but we need to push her."

"Roger that," Palmer said. "Be careful, remember, they blew up a boat."

"Roger that," Val said.

"We'll give you an update when we have more info," Fruen said. He ended the call. "Ideas?" he asked Val.

"Just a feeling right now," Val said. "We'll see how it plays out."

∼

"WEATHER REPORT SAYS a storm's coming in," Stevens said.

"Does it matter?" Fruen asked.

"We might get wet," Stevens said.

"I already got wet today," Val added.

"Yes, yes you did," Fruen laughed. "We're almost there. What's the plan?"

Val answered, "I think we go in like we did before. Talk with the witch, Ms. Fisher. See if we can learn anything. Pick up on anything she might say or do."

Stevens added, "Rupert and I will stay with the truck. Leave it running with the AC on and we'll be ready if somebody runs or shows up outside."

"Sounds like a plan, sort of," Fruen said.

"It's all we have," Val answered. He pulled past the gallery, did a U-turn and parked a few spots back in a spot by a driveway so no one would be parked in front of them. "Let's go see the witch."

∼

VAL LED THE WAY IN. The door chimed again. This time there were more lights on in the space, illuminating the objects on the wall. Walking in a few steps, Val stopped. Fruen joined him. A man and woman, fortyish, held hands and examined some of the pieces on the wall. When the man spied Val and Fruen, he did a double-take and led his companion from the gallery.

A woman approached them. She had long dark hair, tan skin, a sleeveless silky top, white baggy pants and wore gold sandals. "You're back." The woman smiled, white teeth, red lipsticked lips and dimples.

Val thought that her smile had probably sold a few items from this gallery in the past. "You've changed since we last met."

"Just a little," she said. "The parties over, now it's time to get to work." She folded her hands in front of her. "You left in a hurry earlier."

"Pardon us, but we've had a busy day," Val said. "Maybe we should start with introductions again."

"Well, I'm Annie Fisher." She turned to her right and motioned with her arm to the area behind her. "Proprietor, owner, tour guide of this gallery. We have paintings by local artists, sometimes we have exhibits by better known regional or national artists." She turned to her left and swept her left arm in that direction. "This area is dedicated to photographs. Most are mine, but we have others as well."

"I'm Special Agent Martinson and this is Special Agent Fruen." Fruen nodded his head. Val continued, "I'm with the Art Crimes Team out of our Boston office and we're in Salem today because of the heist at the Peabody this morning."

"And how can I help you?" Annie asked.

Val started to answer, but Annie interrupted him. She reached out and touched his forearm ever so slightly and moved a little closer. "Why don't we go find a place where we can sit and talk."

Fruen said, "I'm going to look around the gallery, if that's all right."

"Of course," Annie said. She turned to Val and smiled, "Follow me."

Val walked with Annie across the floor to a rustic table. Annie offered him a seat and sat across the table from him. She immediately started talking. "I heard there was an explosion on a boat filled with art. Is everything gone?"

"We don't know," Val said. "We're operating as if everything wasn't on the boat unless we recover enough pieces from the water and confirm with Director Lewis that we've accounted for most, if not all of the art. The Harbormaster and civilian boats are gathering up what they can from the water and returning it to the Peabody."

"What about the Buttersworths?" Annie asked. "That's why you said you stopped by earlier today."

"We don't know. They're the most valuable pieces taken today and I haven't heard that they've found any sign of any of them yet today."

"I hope they're okay," Annie said. "As we discussed earlier, my family was very involved in acquiring pieces and building the collection." She paused and bowed her head for a second. She raised her head, inhaled and blew out a breath. "I'd just be crushed if the Buttersworths were destroyed. If not, you have a chance to find them and return them."

"That's the goal," Val said. "We're looking for them until we know they're gone or we find them."

Annie reached across the table and touched Val's hand. "What can I do to help?"

Val pulled his hand back. "You haven't heard anything about a collector looking for a Buttersworth or about the Peabody being robbed, anything like that?"

"Nothing," Annie said. "My father and grandfathers were more involved in that collector world than I've ever been. I'm more connected to local, regional customers. People looking for a painting or photo for their home or vacation property. Maybe get a commercial customer once in a while if a new office opens up. Nothing like the Buttersworths or anything from the Peabody."

Val pulled his card from his pocket and pushed it across the table to Annie. "I can't remember if I had time to give you one earlier. But, if you think of anything, feel free to call and leave a message." He pulled his phone from his pocket and smiled. "I can't take any direct calls. Wrecked my phone when I fell in the harbor today."

"Oh, no," Annie said. "You're okay?"

"I'm fine," Ross said. "Just wore wet clothes most of the day and wrecked my phone." He spun in on the table. "But leave me a message and I should be able to retrieve those. If something really urgent comes up, call Director Lewis and ask for Agent Palmer. He'll know how to get a hold of us."

"I'm sorry I can't be of more help," Annie said. "I will call if I think of anything. I just can't think of anything right now."

"Can I get your cell phone number in case I need to reach you?" Val asked.

"Of course," Annie said. "Let me grab a card and a pen." She got up and walked across the gallery to a partitioned cubical in the corner.

Val had a feeling about Annie. Was it because he didn't have anything else? He hoped not. The boat they blew up with the art in it, the Buttersworths themselves, Annie's tie to them. He wasn't ready to give up on the lost art yet.

Annie returned with her card. On the back she pointed at the number "It's my personal cell phone number. "If you hear anything, you'll let me know?"

"Of course," Val said.

Annie walked him back to the entrance where he joined up with Fruen.

"Thanks, Ms. Fisher," Val said.

"Annie, please," she said and reached out and touched his arm.

VAL AND FRUEN walked quickly back to the Suburban. "She was flirting with you," Fruen said.

"Not my type."

"What's that mean? She's gorgeous, the right age, interested."

Val stopped at the truck. "I try not to date criminals." He pulled her card out of his pocket and handed it to Fruen. "See if Palmer can get us a warrant on the number on the back. It's her personal cell phone number."

"How long?" Fruen asked.

"As quick as possible and maybe for a week unless we can break this tonight," Val said. He added, "And call logs from today, yesterday, maybe the past week?"

Stevens lowered the driver's seat window. "I'll drive."

Fruen pulled his cell phone out and called Palmer and relayed Val's request to him. "Just a second," he said into the phone. To Val, "You think it's her?"

Val said, "If it's not, then we got nothing. I'm betting she's the broker. Using daddy's old connections."

"You hear that?" Fruen asked.

Val walked around and jumped in the front passenger seat. Fruen climbed in back.

Val said, "Let's back off a bit. Keep the exit in site. I think it's the only one. We'll see who comes or goes and hopefully, the warrant comes through so we can track her phone."

A couple of rain drops splattered on the windshield.

"Here it comes," Stevens said.

CHAPTER TWENTY-ONE

Raindrops hit the windshield of the pickup.

"The paintings going to stay dry in those coolers?" Dick asked.

"What do you think?" Tony replied. They were parked a couple of blocks up from The Boathouse. They'd watched the agents in their tactical gear enter the gallery and come back out. Now, Tony watched them move their Suburban, but they didn't drive away. They were waiting. For something.

"What we're the Feds doing there?" Dick asked. "You think we're blown?"

"They're doing what I'd do," Tony said. "Following up on other art galleries. We're fine as long as Annie plays it cool. And she will. She's smart."

The change in temperature with the rain started to fog up the windshield. Tony opened his and Dick's windows a crack to try and clear up the glass.

The rain started coming down harder.

"You want to turn on the wipers so we can see what's going on?" Dick asked.

"No," Tony answered. "A little more rain and there'll be

enough water on the glass so we can see better. I don't want the wipers to get their attention and let them know we're in here."

"That's smart," Dick said.

Tony checked his watch. He was supposed to contact Annie in twenty minutes. If all was clear, they'd deliver the coolers, get their money and go. With the Feds sitting there they needed to move to plan B. Tony pulled out his cell phone and called.

"You're early," Annie said.

"The Feds, The Jolly Green Giant and his sidekick, haven't left," Tony said.

"You're watching?" Annie asked. "You have to stay back. What if they see you."

"We're plenty far back from them. They're watching you. We're watching them. And none of us can see a thing because it's starting to rain."

Tony listened. All he heard was Annie's breathing. "It's plan B, Annie."

"Okay. Give me time to close up."

"They're watching the driveway," Tony said. "Is that where you're driving out?"

"My cars in the lot on the side of the building. That's the exit."

"Is there a back way out?" Tony asked. "Someway you can get out of there without them seeing you? A door to a street they aren't watching?"

"I can go out the side and walk out a sidewalk that exits on the parallel street. But, I don't have another car."

Tony thought about it. "It's plan C, Annie."

"There is no plan C."

"There is now. Now listen to me. Don't turn out the lights. Don't lock the front door. I don't want them to see you. You go out the side and we'll meet you on the other street in our pickup. Do it now, Annie. I want you there by the time we drive around the block."

"I'll be there," Annie said.

Tony ended the call and started the pickup. He turned on the wipers and slowly pulled away from the curb. "Don't look in the direction of the Feds, Dick. Look at me." Tony turned left at the corner on this end of the block and continued to the next corner, where he turned right. Annie better be in the middle of the block.

In the middle of the block, Tony pulled over to the curb. Annie stepped out from an open doorway between two buildings. "Let her in," Tony said to Dick.

Dick popped open the door for the back seat of the crew cab. Annie climbed in and slammed the door shut.

"Annie, Dick. Dick, Annie. That's it for introductions." Tony pulled away from the curb.

"Where are we going?" Annie asked.

"I'm not sure yet," Tony answered.

Dick said, "You have all of our money in that little purse?"

Annie had a small clutch purse on a strap hanging around her neck. "No, I'm wiring you the money."

Dick looked at Tony.

"That's right," Tony said. "We get her the paintings and her client wires her and me the money and then I pay you."

"That's not what we talked about, Tony," Dick said.

Tony said, "Well, that's the way it is."

Annie turned and checked out the back window.

"Nobody's following us," Tony said.

Annie leaned forward over the seat. "The paintings are in the back in the coolers?"

Tony nodded.

"How about you give me the truck," Annie said. "I check the paintings. Everything's good and I call my client and he wires us our money?"

"No can do, Annie. We're together until you call your client and until the money gets wired to my account. Then you can have the truck, the coolers, the paintings. Hell, I'd even give you my clothes." Tony caught Annie's eye in the rearview mirror. "We're together until then."

Annie sat back in her seat. "Okay, so where should we go to get this done. Not somewhere out in the rain."

CHAPTER TWENTY-TWO

Stevens hit the button for the windshield wipers and they swiped across, clearing the water from the glass. The Boathouse was ahead of them, lights on. In the rain there weren't many people or cars out and about. The festival was over.

"Where is she?" Val said. "It's been too long. Nothing's moving in the gallery. Did we get the warrant yet?"

"Calm down," Fruen said. "Palmer will let us know when it's done."

"I'm going to check the gallery," Val said.

"Go ahead. She liked you. Tell her you have some more questions," Fruen said.

Val climbed out of the Suburban into the rain. Great. Getting wet again. What a day. He quickly strode to the gallery and looked in through the windows. He didn't see anyone. He opened the door, the bell chimed and stuck his head in. "Hello?" he called out.

There was no answer. He didn't hear a sound except for the rain on the windows. He stepped further into the gallery.

Annie wasn't at her desk. The bathroom or a back room? Val called out again. "Ms. Fisher. It's Agent Martinson."

He tried a door, locked. He knocked on the unisex bathroom door. No answer. He stuck his head in. It was dark. Damn it. She was gone.

Val ran across the gallery. His wet shoes squeaked on the floor. He banged out the door and ran through the rain to the truck. He climbed in and slammed the door shut. "She's gone," he said. "Let's go."

"Where?" Stevens asked.

"I don't have a clue. Drive around. Maybe we'll spot her," Val said.

Fruen pulled out his cell phone and called Palmer.

～

"Where can we go?" Tony asked. "This is your town? A barn, a storage locker, you don't have any other storage for your gallery?"

"We can't go to my apartment," Annie answered. "How about just a parking ramp?"

"That could work," Tony said. "Where are they?"

"There's the Waterfront Garage. It's a couple of blocks from my gallery."

"Too close to the Feds hanging out there. They're probably already checking on you and know you're gone."

"There's a garage a block from the Peabody museum."

Tony thought about it.

"No," Dick said.

"There's no way they'd look for us there," Tony said. "Let's check it out."

Annie said, "It might work."

～

"You want me to keep circling?" Stevens asked.

"No," Val said. "Didn't I tell you she was involved?"

"You were right," Fruen said. "How about we head back towards Palmer? Regroup at the museum. See if something comes through on the warrant."

"Sure," Val said. He couldn't believe they'd lost her.

Fruen's phone buzzed. He checked the screen. "It's Palmer."

Val crossed his fingers.

"Hey," Fruen said when he answered the call. He switched it to speaker. "Anything?"

"The warrant came through and we're starting to get info from the phone company. Ms. Fisher got a call about fifteen minutes ago from a burner phone. A short call."

"That's about when we were sitting in the truck outside the gallery and then she disappeared," Val said. "Anything on her location?"

"A different department is working on that. We should have it soon. What are you three up to?" Palmer asked.

Fruen answered, "We just decided to head back your way."

"Sounds good," Palmer said. "If we get anything on the location, I'll call you. Else we'll see you at the museum."

"Wait," Val yelled out. "Anything out of the two guys the Harbormaster grabbed?"

"No," Palmer said. "They're staying quiet. They're mad at this Tony, just like Bruce is. When the Harbormaster examined the money, they found some of it was real, but most of it was bundled around fake money. See you soon."

Fruen stuck the cell phone back in his vest pocket.

"That's some progress," Val said. "We know she got a call from a burner about when she disappeared. She's working with someone. Could be her client or Tony with the painting."

CHAPTER TWENTY-THREE

The parking ramp appeared clear. "Annie, get down in back there," Tony said. "Dick pull your cap down. These ramps have cameras." Tony pulled his own hat down and put his sunglasses on. Anything to make it harder for the pictures to identify them. He pulled the ticket out of the machine and the arm swung up to allow them to drive into the ramp.

Tony drove up the ramp looking for a quiet, isolated spot to park. He spied a darker corner, no other cars parked there. He pulled past the spot and then backed into it. "Just wait," he said. He watched up and down the ramp for traffic or people. He rolled down his window. It was quiet. "You see any cameras?" he asked Dick.

"I don't see anything."

"Okay, Annie. Let's go examine the paintings and get this done."

~

STEVENS PARKED Val's Suburban in the Peabody staff parking lot. The firetrucks were gone. The staff's cars were gone. They walked up the metal steps and entered the museum. Palmer was set up in the conference room with a couple of other members of their team. He spied them and waved them over.

They entered the conference room and Palmer said, "You won't believe this."

Fruen, Stevens, and all just looked at Palmer. Finally, Val said, "What?"

"We got a location on Ms. Fisher's cell phone."

"Where is it?" Val asked.

"It's in the parking garage the next block over."

"What are we waiting for?" Val asked. "Let's go."

Palmer put up his hand, palm out. "Just wait. I have an agent ready to block any vehicle from exiting. We don't know who's with Ms. Fisher. Or how they're armed. We need a plan."

"Okay, what do we do?" Val said.

"We gear up and wait for everyone from the team to be here. Five minutes."

Fruen joined Martinson along the conference room wall. "I suggest you take a quick bio-break, get a drink of water and check your weapon and ammo."

"Sure, I can do that," Val said.

VAL JOINED the HRT members in the conference room. Palmer stood at one end of the table. "We send a team up the stairs to come down the ramp from above. Fruen and Ramirez, that's you. Lock or jam every stairway door on your way so nobody can sneak out a door.

"Stevens, take Rupert and Martinson and start at the street. Both teams are clearing every car they pass, check for hidey holes, anyone from the general public. Fruen, you two send anyone you find up. Stevens, you send them down. I'll be at the bottom along with Gronowski. You let me know your progress and location floor by floor."

Palmer checked his watch and held his phone to his ear. "The phone's in the same location? Thanks." He set down his phone and reengaged with the team. "Just because her phone is there, does not mean she is. We're assuming it's true, but we may find nothing. Let's go find out what we've got."

The team left the conference room and headed for the parking garage.

"You satisfied?" Tony asked. "All the paintings you wanted. I think it's time to make a call."

Annie stuck out her hand. Tony grabbed it and they shook. "Nice job. I had my doubts we'd actually be at this point. We're all going to be wealthy in an hour." Annie pulled out her cell phone and tried to make a call. "I think this parking garage is blocking my signal. I'm going to move over to the side where it's open to the outside."

"Sure. Hurry up," Tony said. He closed the coolers and tightened the straps to hold them in place for now. He watched Annie as she tried to place her call. She kept glancing at her phone and holding it to her ear. She glanced back at Tony and gave him a thumbs up. She must've finally gotten through.

Tony climbed out of the pickup bed and lit a cigarette. His own little celebration until he could sit on the beach with a drink. He hadn't smoked all day. Saving it until now.

Annie looked like she ended her call and started walking back up the ramp to join him and Dick at the truck. Then she stopped. Her voice echoed in the concrete chamber.

"Well, hello Agent Martinson. What are you doing here?" is what he heard. Annie was looking down the ramp towards the corner where Tony couldn't see.

Tony jumped into the driver's seat.

"What's up?" Dick asked.

"I don't know," Tony said. He reached over and pulled a pistol out of the glove box.

"What's going on?" Dick asked.

Tony lowered the windows and strained to hear. He leaned over to try and see who Annie was talking with. He heard a command and saw Annie put her hands in the air.

It's time for plan D. Tony started the truck and shifted into Drive. "Get down," he said. He pressed hard on the accelerator and the truck's engines roared and the tires squealed.

VAL SAW the pickup rocketing down the ramp towards him. He ran to Annie and tackled her to knock her out of the path of the truck. Tires screamed and echoed in the parking garage as the truck turned the corner to head to the next lower level.

Stevens yelled, "Halt!" and jumped out of the way, pulling Rupert by his collar. Val heard him yell into his radio that the truck was heading down and he shot a couple of short blasts with his assault rifle at the pickup as it headed down the ramp.

Stevens glanced back at Val. "You okay," he asked.

"I'm good," Val answered. "I got her."

Stevens and Rupert took off down the ramp at a sprint.

Val handcuffed Annie and heard gunfire and what sounded like a crash. He helped Annie to her feet and hustled her down the ramp.

"You almost got away with it," Val said to Annie. "Are the Buttersworths in the pickup?"

Annie nodded.

At the bottom of the ramp the pickup had smashed into the side of a Suburban the FBI HRT had parked at the exit. Stevens had his rifle aimed at the pickup. Rupert sat at attention by his side, whining. Palmer and Gronowski pulled two men out of the pickup and handcuffed them.

Val got Annie to sit on the concrete about ten yards in front of Rupert.

"He'll watch her," Stevens said. "Rupert, E*rop*."

Val continued down the ramp to the bed of the pickup and climbed in. He glanced at Palmer, who nodded his approval. He loosened the straps and opened one of the coolers. He found that his hands were shaking, either from the adrenaline or nervousness. He pulled one of the paintings out and examined it. "We got them," he said to Palmer.

Fruen joined Palmer at the side of the pickup. "I'll help you, Martinson."

Val put the painting back in the cooler and closed it. He handed one cooler to Fruen and then the other. Then he jumped out of the pickup bed with a big smile on his face.

Palmer said, "Why don't you two return those to the museum so Doctor Lewis can sleep tonight."

"These things are on wheels so it should be easy to get them back there," Fruen said.

Val grabbed the handle of one of the coolers and started walking. Then he stopped and looked at the smashed Suburban. He hung his head and shook it and then looked up at Palmer. "That's mine, isn't it."

"We didn't have any vehicles," Palmer said. "We came by bus."

Fruen said, "You said you weren't heading back to Boston right away if we recovered the paintings."

CHAPTER TWENTY-FOUR

Ross, Stevens and Rupert ran on the trail through the woods at Quantico. It was back to the daily training grind until they got some time off or another mission spun them up.

When they reached a fork in the trail, Ross stopped and bent over, resting his hands on his knees while he tried to catch his breath. Stevens and Rupert joined him. Rupert lay on the ground, panting, his big pink tongue hanging out of his mouth.

"How's he doing?" Ross asked Stevens. Rupert had been injured when he and Stevens were partners in the army in Afghanistan. It didn't seem to slow him down, but he wasn't able to perform at the level that the army required.

"He's fine. How are you doing?"

"I'm sucking air. This humidity still gets me. Growing up around here you'd think it wouldn't bother me," Ross said.

Stevens paced around in circles. He always kept moving. "It's got to start getting drier out here soon," he said. His phone buzzed.

Ross' phone buzzed next. They both pulled them from

their pockets and looked at the screens. Palmer wanted them back at the base. "Guess we're cutting this run short."

"Yes," Stevens said and pumped a fist. "Back the way we came is shortest. Race?"

Ross shook his head. "No, not today. You guys set the pace. Ready?" Ross stretched his back, twisting from side to side.

Stevens and Rupert headed back on the trail. Ross followed.

WHEN THEY REACHED THE BASE, they stopped and grabbed some water and ice from the concessions area and then headed to Palmer's office. They knocked on his door.

"Enter!"

Ross led the way. Stevens and Rupert followed. They stood in front of Palmer's desk. "You wanted to see us?" Ross asked.

"How was the run?" Palmer asked.

"Great, if you want to run miles through a sauna," Stevens answered.

Palmer pulled a bowl from his desk drawer and placed it on the desk. He pointed at it with his finger. "He needs it more than you two do."

Ross and Stevens both stepped forward and poured some of their ice and water into the bowl.

Palmer set the bowl on the floor next to his desk. "Here you go, Rupert. Have something to drink."

Rupert approached the bowl, plopped onto the floor and lapped up the water.

"Okay, I got something in the mail today. I thought we should open it together." Palmer stood and walked to get a flat box that leaned against the wall. He carried it to his conference table and set it on top. He nodded to Ross and Stevens. "Come on over."

"What is it?" Stevens asked.

"Not sure," said Palmer.

Ross looked at the address on the package. It said to Agents Palmer, Rupert, Fruen and Stevens. The return address was the Boston FBI Field Office. "It's too big to be a bill for the painting Val shot," Ross said.

Palmer said, "I'm almost afraid to open it." He pulled a knife from his pocket, pulled out the blade and cut the tape sealing one end of the box. "Ready to see what it is?"

"The suspense is killing me," Ross said. He reached down and held the end flaps of the box open. "What's in there?"

Stevens reached in with his fingers and pulled out what was inside. He laughed.

"What is it?" Palmer asked.

Stevens set it on top of the box on the table. It was a framed painting. Nobody said anything. Then all three laughed.

"It's really pretty good," Ross said. He pointed at the signature in the lower corner. "He signed it. He must've painted it."

"Rupert has a peg leg," Stevens said.

"You have a patch over your eye, Boss," Fruen said.

"That's me?"

Stevens laughed. "That's you. I think you hang it in your office, Boss."

"I can do that."

The painting was titled *Save The Art* and depicted a pirate ship in the Salem harbor, cannons firing, ripped sails, smoke filling the air with Val, Stevens, Ross, Rupert and Palmer all dressed as pirates in various battle poses on the deck of a pirate ship.

THANKS FOR READING

Lost Art is the third novella in the FBI Hostage Rescue Team, Critical Incident series.

SuperCell is the first in the series
Free Fall is the second in the series.

If you haven't read The Ninth District - the FBI thriller that started it all, check it out.

Join the Dorow Thriller Reader List by visiting www.douglasdorow.com to stay up to date on releases, offers and other writing news. You'll get four FREE short stories when you join.

If you enjoyed this book, one way to show it and support my writing is to leave a review at your favorite online bookstore.

Read for the *THRILL* of it!

AFTERWORD

People ask where I get my ideas.

The idea for Lost Art- Critical Incident #3 came about after I created Special Agent Val Martinson for a short story I wrote. Agent Martinson, with the FBI's Art Crime Team, was a character I wanted to explore some more, so Lost Art was written to do this. I'm sure Agent Martinson will be back again.

Get the short story where I created Val Martinson by signing up for my email at www.douglasdorow.com.

For my family, my readers, and the agents and staff of the FBI.

ABOUT THE AUTHOR

Douglas "Doug" Dorow, lives in Minneapolis, Minnesota with his wife and their two dogs.

For more info on my writing:
www.douglasdorow.com
or email me at
Doug@DouglasDorow.com

Read for the *THRILL* of it!

ALSO BY DOUGLAS DOROW

FBI THRILLERS:

The Ninth District - FBI Thriller #1

SuperCell - spun off of this story. See where Ross Fruen was before joining the HRT.

Twice Removed - FBI Thriller #2

Empire Builder - FBI Thriller #3

CRITICAL INCIDENT SERIES:

SuperCell - Critical Incident #1

Free Fall - Critical Incident #2

Lost Art - Critical Incident #3

Made in the USA
Coppell, TX
10 September 2021

62120564R00196